Looking for You

'McCall Smith's novels are shaped by ideas of
community, tolerance, and civility'
TELEGRAPH

'As always with McCall Smith there are hidden depths, both
psychological and moral, delivered with bubbling
humour and wit'
HERALD

'A wonderfully amusing and heartfelt addition to *The Perfect
Passion Company* series set around a dating agency in Edinburgh'
LOVEREADING, BOOK OF THE MONTH

'The second in a new feel-good series . . . [from] one of the
world's best-loved and most prolific authors. Brimming with joy
and, most important of all, love'
SUNDAY POST

'A beautifully tender novel from the author of *44 Scotland Street*'
SCOTS MAGAZINE

'As ever, McCall Smith writes beautifully and with a dry wit and warmth to create a novel that envelops you like a lovely warm bath'
SCOTTISH FIELD

'A charming new novel from the beloved author'
MY WEEKLY

'I loved the Edinburgh setting, the characters, an old-fashioned love story, warm and comforting as porridge with a dram'
SAGA MAGAZINE

ALEXANDER McCALL SMITH

Looking for You

Polygon

This paperback edition published in Great Britain in 2026 by Polygon,
an imprint of Birlinn Ltd. First published in 2025 in Great Britain
in hardback by Polygon, an imprint of Birlinn Ltd.

Birlinn Ltd
West Newington House
10 Newington Road
Edinburgh
EH9 1QS

9 8 7 6 5 4 3 2 1

www.polygonbooks.co.uk

Copyright © Alexander McCall Smith, 2025

The right of Alexander McCall Smith to be identified
as the author of this work has been asserted in
accordance with the Copyright, Designs
and Patents Act 1988.

All rights reserved. No part of this publication may be
reproduced, stored, or transmitted in any form, or by
any means electronic, mechanical or photocopying,
recording or otherwise, without the express written
permission of the publisher.

ISBN 978 1 84697 728 2
eBook ISBN 978 1 78885 746 8
Audiobook ISBN 978 1 78885 763 5

British Library Cataloguing-in-Publication Data
A catalogue record for this book is available on
request from the British Library.

Book design by Nicholas Alguire
Printed and bound in Great Britain by Clays Ltd, Elcograf S.p.A.

This book is for Mike and Catriona Kennedy.

Looking for You

CHAPTER ONE

Why we marry whom we marry

The lecture was due to begin at six in the evening and already, by five-thirty, the first few rows of the lecture theatre in George Square were filling up with two separate tribes: students—chattering, voluble—and members of the general public—quiet, with that certain sobriety that marked an Edinburgh audience. A few years earlier, Katie would have identified herself with the students; now, at the age of thirty, she accepted that she had become a member of the public, and that the decade or so that separated her from the students in the room was an increasingly significant gap.

Not that she minded too much. We all had to grow up, she reminded herself, and there were plenty of consolations that came with getting a bit older. Not having to share a flat, for instance, was something that only came in your late twenties, if then, and was something that she had particularly welcomed when she returned to Edinburgh. Throughout the years she had spent in London she had been in shared accommodation, often with people whom she might not have chosen as flatmates—had she been given the opportunity to pick and choose.

Helen, for example, with whom she had shared just before she came back to Scotland, had an irritating way of chewing her food to which Katie had never become reconciled. She did not exactly eat with her mouth open, but it was close enough, and Katie had found herself watching with reluctant fascination the mastication of the buttered toast that her flatmate so enjoyed eating. Then there was Julie, who had emerged from a crumbling manor house in an obscure English shire—Northamptonshire, Katie thought, or was it Rutland?—and who had a braying laugh with which Katie had never been able to come to terms. She was markedly vacuous, Katie decided, being principally interested in finding a man who would spirit her back to the countryside and install her in a house with a garden large enough to accommodate a duck pond. "I just love ducks," she had confessed to Katie. "They are such intelligent creatures. I just adore them."

Katie had expressed the view that ducks were not intelligent at all—at least in her experience—and that whilst they made good eating, they were less than stimulating company. This had brought a shocked reaction from Julie, who said that she pitied anybody who could not see the sheer character of ducks, and that eating them showed scant regard for the feelings of sensitive and sympathetic fellow creatures. Katie, in fact, although not formally vegetarian, generally ate little meat, and very rarely, if ever, had duck. Her reaction to Julie's enthusing over ducks was provoked out of impatience with the other young woman's gushing enthusiasm, and the conversation went no further. But she was relieved when a not-very-bright young man called Roland began to visit the flat. His intention was to lure Julie off to a hamlet in Gloucestershire, where he had a converted farmhouse with four acres of land, quite enough, Katie believed, for not one but several duck ponds. Roland was employed in his father's estate agency and spoke in the language of that calling. Views were always *sought-after*, houses always had *character*, and neighbourhoods were always *up-and-coming*. He was a keen member of a clay-pigeon shooting club—clubs were always, in his view, *exclusive*—and was, Katie thought, an ideal partner for Julie. But then she felt guilty: she had been too dismissive, even to the point of lacking charity. Julie had her good points, and no doubt Roland had his too. She should not condescend to them just because she found them dull.

Sharing, though, came to an end when Katie left her job at the London gallery in which she had been employed, and returned to Edinburgh, where she had been born and brought up, to run the business of a relative who had taken an adult gap year in Canada. Her father's cousin, Ness, was a woman in her early fifties, a lively and entertaining devotee of Greek mythology and Jungian psychology, who had decided that time was passing rather quickly and that if she did not travel now, she never would. Her business was an unusual one—an introductions agency, or marriage bureau, as she sometimes described it, called the Perfect Passion Company.

"There are very few of us left," Ness explained to Katie. "There used to be rather a lot of marriage bureaus, but now we are *rarae aves*, as they say—rare birds for the non-Latinate. There are one or two still soldiering on in London, but we are the only one in Edinburgh, indeed all Scotland, I believe. In other words, Katie, we are *it*."

Katie was not sure that she wanted or was qualified to be *it*, but Ness had been sanguine. "You'll cope wonderfully," she assured her. "All you have to do is to introduce the right man to the right woman, and vice versa. Then let nature take its course. Simple."

Katie had absorbed this, but had still been concerned that she might not have the necessary skills to bring about a meeting between compatible and potential soul-mates. Once again, Ness had been breezily confident.

"There's nothing to it, Katie," she said. "You interview the clients. You make notes on their files, recording their preferences and so on. *Can't eat asparagus*, or *Wants somebody musical, but no jazz*, that sort of thing. Then you bring them together—if they seem suited to one another—light the blue touchpaper, and step back. Nature, sooner or later, takes its course either way."

"Either way?" asked Katie.

Ness explained. "Sometimes it works—sometimes it doesn't. You'll get used to assessing the chances. You'll learn that it's not just a question of bringing like together with like: in some cases—not in all, but certainly in some—it's a matter of bringing together people who appear in some ways to be different in their interests. You'll have heard of Jack Spratt and his wife? Jack could eat no fat and his wife could eat no lean. Terribly mismatched, poor dears. But they got on famously. Nursery rhymes may embody very important psychological insights, you know. You have to read their second-degree meaning. Have you heard of second-degree meaning? No?"

Katie shook her head. "I'm afraid not."

Ness could be didactic. "Gérard Genette," she began, "talked about literature in the second degree. He was a French literary critic—frightfully Gallic in all respects. They love their theory, the French." She rolled her eyes. "They adore people like Ferdinand de Saussure and Jacques Derrida. They consider us Anglo-Saxons—and I suppose many Scots are a sort of Anglo-Saxon, although they'd hate to admit it—they think of us as being extremely literal—hardly worth deconstructing. We don't see the meaning behind the meaning, they'd say. Everything can be read in the second degree—including the weather forecast, I suppose."

Katie laughed. "Hardly."

"Perhaps I exaggerate."

You do, thought Katie, because you are unashamedly flamboyant. You love to exaggerate, but perhaps your exaggerations should be read in the second degree, which makes them not exaggerations at all, but understatements.

"But to return to the point," said Ness. "I have complete confidence in you, Katie. The Perfect Passion Company will go from strength to strength under you *senza ombra di dubbio*. There's no doubt at all about that."

Now, sitting in the lecture theatre, Katie remembered snatches of that conversation with Ness as she waited for the rest of the audience to arrive. It looked as if there would be a good turnout, which was not always the case at inaugural lectures. She had been to two of these after she returned to Edinburgh: one had been on the philosophy of economic redistribution, and had gone on for almost two hours, against all the conventions applicable to such events. The other had been on the fashion in the Persian court in the fifteenth century, which had been considerably more entertaining. Having applied for tickets for these lectures, she was now on a list somewhere within the university, and she found herself receiving invitations to every such occasion, which was part of the explanation why she was there that evening. But only part of the explanation: the title of the chair being inaugurated had caught her eye, and she would have come if only for that. This was the inauguration of a personal chair, recently created by the university for a distinguished member of its staff, the title of which was the Chair in Human Matching. For one who ran an introductions bureau, such a title was difficult to ignore.

The newly appointed professor was one Deborah Wilson, a psychologist and author of a book titled *Why We Marry Whom We Marry*. To that was added a subtitle, *And Why We May Come to Regret It*. Professor Wilson, it was explained in the leaflet handed out to those attending, was the author of numerous scientific papers on what was described as *assortative matching*. Katie was not sure what that was, but hoped that the lecture would throw light on that question.

She looked about her. There were a couple of comfortable-looking middle-aged women sitting not far from her—they struck her as being the types, she thought, who went to every inaugural lecture at the university, irrespective of subject. Beyond them was a thin young man wearing round spectacles, who was paging through a photocopied article, annotating it with a propelling pencil. He was a research fellow, Katie decided, one of those wandering scholars who move from post-doc position to post-doc position, until they faded away into the obscurity of low-level academia. She had known one or two such people in London, and she did not envy them their uncertain life-style, surviving on timed research grants, and never being given the tenure for which they yearned above all else.

And then, immediately to her left, was a woman who had slipped in without Katie noticing her. She was attractive, somewhere in her early forties, thought Katie, and was wearing a smart blue pinstripe jacket. Had this been anywhere else, Katie would have put her down as a lawyer, or an accountant perhaps, accustomed to dressing smartly for the office, but opting for a casual smartness that would enable her to move in academic circles without being conspicuous.

As Katie glanced at her, the other woman met her eye and smiled. "It's filling up," she said, looking over her shoulder at the rows of seats behind them.

"Yes," said Katie. "There was an article about her—Professor Wilson—in the paper the other day. Did you see it?"

The woman nodded. "I did. It was rather interesting. They said she was likely to ginger up the Department of Psychology, as I recall. I think it said that."

"It did," agreed Katie. "It described her as being somebody who was capable of making psychology relevant to ordinary people." She paused. "And I suppose that's what she intends to do today. This is going to be about choosing partners. Who isn't interested in that?"

The woman laughed. "I'm Clea," she said. "And yes, I'm fascinated by that sort of thing."

Katie gave her name. She did not reveal what she did for a living—and Clea did not ask, although she did enquire as to whether Katie knew much about psychology.

"I don't," Katie answered. "But sometimes I think I do."

"No harm in that," said Clea, with a smile. "Everybody's an amateur psychologist these days."

Katie asked about assortative matching. What precisely was that?

Clea had looked it up. "It's all about why people choose the partners they choose. The idea is that there are reasons why we choose our partners."

"Of course, there are," said Katie. "Isn't it because we like them? Isn't that the main reason?"

Clea was interested in *why* we liked others. "That's not always obvious," she said. "We may be looking for things that we don't know we're looking for. Such as for somebody who looks like our mother or father. That's very common, I believe."

"Really?"

"Yes," said Clea. "I had a girlfriend who turned down numerous eligible men until she found the one man she wanted to marry. And you know what? He was as dull as ditch-water—seriously dull—but, surprise, surprise, he looked exactly like her father, to whom she had always been very close. Her father was a professor of physics, and this man who looked like him taught physics. Just what she had been looking for."

"She wanted to marry her father?"

"So it would seem."

Katie asked whether the marriage had worked.

"It was brilliant," said Clea. "They're both very happy. And you know what I discovered? I happened to see a photograph of his mother, and she was the image of my friend. Not a coincidence, I think."

Clea now gave Katie a sideways look. "What did you say you do?" she asked.

"I didn't," Katie replied.

"Ah." There was another inquisitive look. "I thought you did."

Katie hesitated. "Actually, I might as well confess. I run an introduction agency. Here in Edinburgh—something called the Perfect Passion Company."

Clea looked at her in astonishment. Then she laughed.

"No, seriously."

"I am being serious," said Katie.

Clea looked embarrassed. "I'm sorry. I didn't mean to . . ."

She did not finish. A door at the back of the stage had

opened, and Professor Deborah Wilson emerged, along with two university officials in academic gowns.

"She's very tall," whispered Clea.

"So I see," Katie whispered back.

"People ask me," said Professor Deborah Wilson, "what is the single most important factor in the choice of a partner. They make it clear that they want me to identify one quality, rather than give them a confusing list. And I can understand that: Who amongst us, when it comes down to it, doesn't want a simple explanation for why things are? Hence our desire for a simple cosmology. If you read the Book of Genesis as literal truth—and there are people who do just that—then everything is clear enough. But for most of us, well, that is perhaps a rather tall order, and we reconcile ourselves to the more complex picture. And the point about complex pictures is that the explanation for anything tends to be multifactorial. My students, by the way, love that expression. 'It's multifactorial,' they say, whenever they can't quite remember the reason for whatever it is they are considering."

This brought laughter. Katie thought: Yes, it *is* multifactorial. She glanced along the row of seats and saw that the thin young man with glasses had written something on a notepad. Multifactorial, she imagined. Her gaze rested on him for a few moments longer. He was unhappy; she could tell that, even without ever having spoken to him. He lived alone in an ill-heated room, perhaps behind the old veterinary school. He had the use of a kitchenette, shared, and there would be a noisy, small fridge in which he kept his bottle of milk, and a wedge of cheese from the Victor Hugo delicatessen. His unhappiness was multifactorial, she decided. He would have had a girlfriend, who played the piano, she thought, but who went off with somebody else to live down in England somewhere.

"However," the professor continued, "I can produce, if pressed to do so, a list of three or four factors that are of particular significance in assortative matching. These, I believe, are the weightier factors operating in many instances, and any one of them may be *the* factor which tips the scales on the process of choice. Mind you, it is very important to understand that choice in these matters is likely to be a subconscious process. Few of us say to ourselves: I am going to choose Susan because of her dimples, or Jim because of his healthy bank balance, or, as I hasten to point out, Susan because of *her* bank balance and Jim because of *his* dimples. Those may be exactly the factors that predispose us to the identification and acceptance of a partner, but in many, if not the majority, of cases we are unaware of the reasons that lie behind our choice. But that, I suspect, is the way that most of us lead our lives, most of the time: we are unaware of the reasons why we do the things we do; unaware of the extent to which our lives are mapped out by events that may have happened even before we were born; unaware of the way in which the habits and preferences of our parents dictate the way we behave. We inherit so much from those who precede us—their sorrows and their defeats may cast a shadow that conceals from us the sun, although we may never work out for ourselves why it seems so dark."

There was almost complete silence in the lecture theatre. The students, normally a restless audience, sat quite still; somebody cleared his throat, suppressing a cough; a paper rustled almost inaudibly.

"Now," said Professor Wilson, "you might be wondering what factors might be on that short list of mine."

The tension eased. One or two heads nodded. A young woman, a student, seated immediately in front of Katie whispered to her friend, "Green eyes." The friend giggled, and responded, "Pecs."

Katie felt a surge of irritation. You silly girl, she thought. Of what possible importance were firm pectoral muscles, or green eyes, for that matter? Of course, eyes could say something about character, about soul, and that was obviously important, but muscles—what did they say? Nothing. But then she reminded herself that these students were barely nineteen and that was . . . eleven years ago. Eleven years would be time enough for them to learn that there were far more important things than physical characteristics. Suddenly she felt her age. If this was what thirty was like, then what would it be like to be forty? Would she then be thinking about the fecklessness of thirty-year-olds?

"Geography," said Professor Wilson. "That, in a sense, is at the top of the list. Yes, geography. Those of you in this audience who are currently single but who imagine that in the future at some time you will have a partner . . ." She looked out into the audience. There was an outbreak of slightly nervous laughter. "That destiny, of course, is increasingly less compulsory in a world of individual self-determination; but for those of you who are in that position, you have no doubt an idea of whom you might like to find. A sympathetic mate? Somebody who makes you feel good? Somebody who shares your interests? Yes, to all of those, but that is likely to happen only—and this is an important qualification—only if such a person turns up in your immediate vicinity. In other words, the fact that such people exist *somewhere*, does not mean that they will occur in *your* life. You, I have to tell you, are likely to marry somebody who lives very close to you. So if you fancy the person a couple of seats away from where you are now sitting—or in the row behind you—then my message to you is this: you're in with a good chance."

Necks were craned. In the front row, a group of students chuckled. Somebody seated directly behind Katie said, "Oh no."

"Let me explain," the professor went on, "*homogamy* is the practice of marrying, or entering into a union with, a partner who is similar to oneself. This means that in a homogamous relationship, the partners share something important, whether it is a cultural outlook, a religious viewpoint, socio-economic status, or a moral position."

Katie listened. She allowed herself to think that she knew all this; academics could spend a lot of time dressing up the most elementary truths in complicated language. Sometimes their conclusions were no different from those we all might reach, if we used our common sense. She remembered the tedious lecture on the philosophy of redistribution and the lecturer's conclusion at the end, after the recital of swathes of data and theoretical verbiage, that people did not like giving up what they had, but had to be made to do so.

"Sharing interests and attributes," continued Professor Deborah Wilson, "appears to be important not only in making the decision to embark upon a union in the first place, but also in terms of the stability and duration of the marriage or partnership. The folk wisdom expresses this in the old adage *Like marries like*. Like many of the things our mothers said, even if we may have been tempted to dismiss them in the past, research keeps finding a scientifically sound underpinning for this. 'You were right after all, Mother,' we say—or think of saying."

Katie perked up. That was her mother. That was her—not that she had admitted it, to her mother, or to herself.

"There are many factors that have been identified as important through the psychological scrutiny of matching. Level of education is one that consistently appears at or near the top of the list. If you are educated to degree level, then you are very likely to marry somebody who has the same level of educational achievement; you are very unlikely to marry somebody who has only a basic high school education. Such a person may be as intelligent as you are, of course, even more so, but statistically you are unlikely to end up together."

"Then there are shared values."

Round the room, a few heads nodded. Katie noticed that a woman sitting a few places to her left briefly closed her eyes, as if what had just been said caused her a momentary pain. She imagined what lay behind that reaction: an ill-starred marriage of a couple who had no common interests. If you read different things, liked different music, enjoyed the company of different types of people, what hope was there of a shared life? Her gaze remained on the woman, who suddenly turned towards her. Their eyes met, and an unspoken message of understanding and sympathy passed between them. *She knows that I know*, thought Katie, and she reflected on how often that realisation came to people who happened to connect with one another unexpectedly, as strangers.

"Without shared values," the professor said, "a union has a higher chance of being unstable. There will be room for disagreements, sometimes quite serious ones, if partners take a fundamentally different view of politics, for instance. How many couples do you know, may I ask, who are on opposite sides of the political spectrum? A few, perhaps, but not many. Well, there is hard evidence in the literature that on really core issues, such as which party they would choose to be in government, couples tend to agree.

"But quite apart from these issues of shared interests, pure physical propinquity emerges as a major consideration in its own right." She paused before continuing, "There are various studies that have reached this conclusion. Haandrikman and van Wissen, for instance, published an important paper on this precise issue in the *European Journal of Population* in 2012. Their title is quite striking: 'Explaining the Flight of Cupid's Arrow: A Spatial Random Utility Model of Partner Choice.' At the beginning of their paper, they quote a general law of geography, proposed back in 1970, to the effect that everything is related to everything else, but things that are close to one another are more related than things that are far apart." She looked out over the audience, and smiled. "In other words, girls—many of you are going to marry the boy next door."

A female voice shouted out, "No, anything but that!" There was laughter, shared by Professor Wilson, who, when the hubbub of reaction died down, looked at the audience and said, "I did."

"Do you think he was tall?" Clea whispered to Katie.

"Boys next door are *always* average height," Katie replied. And she thought: *But not always interesting:* boys next door were almost always *safe*.

"True," said Clea.

Katie was thinking. She wondered whether shared political views emerged before or after marriage. She thought it possible that people of differing views might marry and then, as they spent more time with one another, might find a natural process of convergence taking place. This suggested that there was another factor that was important for the stability of a union: willingness to moderate views to take account of how a partner felt. Rigidity was anathema in any relationship; flexibility and compromise were vital.

"I did just that. I married the boy next door, and I'm extremely happy," announced the professor. "And he tells me he is too."

There was a cheer from the front row. The dean, seated on the platform in her academic robes, looked at her watch—pointedly, thought Katie—which was a pity, as she thought that the audience was having a good time, which had not been the case during the lecture on the philosophy of taxation. Several members of the audience had left that lecture early, sneaking out bent-double to avoid creating a disturbance, although in one case a woman in high heels had suffered heel failure in one shoe, and had stumbled noisily as a result.

At the end of the lecture, Clea, the woman next to Katie, turned to her and said, "Interesting."

"Yes," said Katie, rising to her feet.

Clea seemed to be about to say something, and Katie waited.

"I hope that we meet again," said Clea.

Katie nodded. "Perhaps at one of these lectures. I seem to come to quite a few of them."

"I do so too," Clea said.

They said goodbye, and Katie made her way towards the exit, where a group of students was milling around. Some of them were laughing; one young woman was hugging a young man, who seemed embarrassed; another had dropped a folder of lecture notes on the floor and was being helped by friends to pick them up. Katie glanced back over her shoulder to where she had been sitting. Clea was still in her seat, but was looking across the room, directly at her. Katie thought that she raised her hand slightly, in a gesture of farewell, but could not be sure. She waved anyway.

CHAPTER TWO

The weaker brethren

Katie had inherited William from Ness, in the way in which those moving into the shoes of others sometimes acquire their friends and neighbours—not to say their problems. William, of course, was both friend and neighbour—his studio was next door to the office of the Perfect Passion Company—but she would never describe him as a problem. From Katie's point of view, William was an unexpected bonus, who had quickly become a sympathetic ear and support in the management of a business that, as she had to remind herself, she was completely unqualified to run.

On the morning after the lecture, as she made her way to the office on Mouse Lane, she reflected on what she might tell William about Professor Deborah Wilson's talk. It had been packed with detail and anecdotage, and Katie thought that William would appreciate some of the more offbeat observations with which the audience had been entertained. She had made notes, but they were not very full, and she thought that there was much that she might have missed. If she missed too much, though, there was always the book *Why We Marry Whom We Marry*, which would presumably cover much the same ground as the lecture. She would order that book, she thought, and would be able, quite properly, to claim it as an expense on her tax return. She might also get a copy for William, but no sooner had she thought of that than she put the thought out of her mind—giving him a book like that could be misinterpreted. The thought made her blush, as she imagined him looking at the title and then giving her a guarded, sideways look. If you were somebody like William, with his easy charm and his beguiling good looks, you must be accustomed to unwanted attentions—and there was no indication that he thought of her in that way.

She sighed. Professor Deborah Wilson had talked about a whole raft of factors that played a part in people's finding of one another, but she had not mentioned time. And timing was important: both people had to be ready for an attachment, and if they were at different stages of what one might call the romantic cycle, then it was simply not going to work. In particular, people who had recently finished a relationship might not be in the mood to start another too quickly. They might want a period of detachment—a time to lick their wounds, if a relationship had ended messily. And then there was the whole issue of rebound affairs, which people always recommended should be entered into with great caution. Katie had never been involved in one of those, but she knew from the experience of friends that such romances could come to an end rather quickly. The best cure for the loss of a lover was not the taking of another lover—Katie was fairly convinced of that. A lover acquired in such circumstances might be a distraction, but no more than that—unless one were to be lucky, which, of course, some people were.

As she made her way along the street that led to Mouse Lane, just around the corner, she allowed her mind to dwell on William. She remembered her first meeting with William, when Ness was yet to go off to Canada. She remembered how she had warmed to him immediately, and how they had exchanged glances, each appraising the other shyly, without wanting to be seen to be doing so. And she had known right from the beginning that they were going to be able to talk to one another and that they would enjoy each other's company. These are the things that could sometimes be picked up at a first meeting, before anything very much was said. The eyes came into it, she thought, although she was not sure precisely how that happened.

Ness had been quick to tell her that William was engaged. In spite of herself, she had felt a stab of disappointment, even though he was a few years younger than her; even though she had only just met him; even though she had told herself that she did not want another emotional involvement just yet. William, Ness explained, had a fiancée in Melbourne—a medical student named Alice. They had been engaged, she said, for over a year and, as far as she knew, were planning to get married when Alice completed her course. Katie had wondered why William had chosen to come and live in Edinburgh, at the other end of the world from Alice; Ness had suggested it was to do with his career. "He needs the exposure," she said. "He's the next Kaffe Fassett."

"But Australia's not a backwater—not these days."

Ness agreed. "No. Far from it. But their artists still seem to want to prove themselves overseas. They want to show that they can make it abroad."

Katie thought about this. Had William chosen his career above his relationship with Alice? Or did they think that the requirements of both could be satisfied? As she got to know William better, she had come to realise that he was serious about both, and that he was uncompromisingly loyal. A long-distance relationship might involve unforeseen temptations, but not in this case, she felt. William was clearly attractive to women, but it was equally obvious that he would be loyal. People with William's looks could know it—and be flirtatious. He was not.

William was out of bounds, and Katie felt that there was never any sense in going after the unattainable. He became a friend, and she decided that this is what he would remain. Friends and lovers occupied very different territory in one's life, whatever temptation arose to blur the divide. It was, she thought, rather like being on a strict diet: temptation was obvious—it was to hand—and yet you knew that you had to say no to yourself. If you were strong-willed, you could face down the chocolate or the buttered croissant; but not all of us were strong-willed. Some of us were what they used to call the weaker brethren. *The weaker brethren*: she could just picture them—a ragged, rather miserable assembly of people who had given in. And yet that may give quite the wrong impression of the weaker brethren; they might just as easily be content in their sybaritic life-style, delighted to have put the struggle behind them, ready to tell others of the fun they had with the fallen angels.

Now she sat at her desk, watching the hands of the clock move slowly towards the time when she knew William would emerge from his studio next door and offer to make coffee. It had become something of a ritual: he would let himself into the office and ask her whether she felt it was time for coffee. She never said no, but he asked the question anyway, and waited for her to reply. Then he would go into her office kitchenette and talk to her over his shoulder while he ground the beans and prepared the coffee machine.

"You said you were going to a lecture," he began. "Did you go?"

"I did," she replied. "And it was all about what we do."

He sounded puzzled. "About what we do?"

"What we do here—in the Perfect Passion Company." She had taken to treating him as a colleague, although he had no formal connection with the agency. And he had slipped willingly into that role, discussing the affairs of the company and making suggestions as to the matching of clients.

"About introducing people?"

She explained the gist of Professor Wilson's conclusions. "We don't choose at random," she said. "We end up with people who satisfy certain criteria. We go for people of a certain background."

He laughed. "You sound like my mother," he said. "She always said that you should marry people from the same background. That's the way she put it 'from the same background.' What she meant was from the same social class. She did not like to say that, but it was pretty obvious."

The coffee grinder buzzed loudly, and for a few moments their conversation was suspended. But in the silence that followed Katie said, "I thought that Australia was a classless society. I thought you prided yourself on your egalitarianism."

She heard William laugh. "We like to tell ourselves that," he said. "But it's not really like that. It's quite a stratified society—like everywhere else. Like America, which also thinks that it's classless, but isn't at all. It's money in the States, and which college you went to, and which golf club you belong to, and so on. Australia's a bit different, but don't tell me there's no difference between the ordinary suburbs and the expensive ones. We're not so snobbish about it, I suppose, and there's greater fluidity, but the divisions are there all right." He paused. "And we do a good line in intellectual superiority. If you're interested in the arts and have travelled a bit, you like to distance yourself from the beer-drinking types in the local pub. I don't think like that, but I know plenty of people who do."

He emerged from the kitchenette with the coffee. He placed a steaming mug on Katie's desk.

"So you learned something useful," he said, as he perched himself on the edge of the desk.

"One or two things. Such as: people tend to choose people from the same background. Just as your mother said."

He sighed. "So much for the fairy tales?"

"Fairy tales?"

"Fairy tales love it when the prince marries down—the kitchen maid's an ideal choice if you're a prince."

"That's because people think that love overcomes all obstacles," Katie said. "It's an old trope, that one, but people lap it up. Remember *Love Story*? Ivy League boy meets girl from a bakery, wasn't it? It's a great theme. And it happens, doesn't it . . ." She stopped herself, as she realised that there had been a disparity between the financial position of William and Alice. William came from a well-off family; Alice could not afford her medical school fees.

He picked up her hesitation. "You aren't thinking of me, are you?" he asked with a wry smile.

She was about to say no, but thought better of it. "I wasn't, but now that you mention it, I suppose you could see it that way."

He looked thoughtful. "I didn't care," he said quietly. "I never have. It makes no difference to me whether people have money or not. I don't judge them by something like that."

"Of course not," Katie reassured him. "I never thought you would." She paused. "I was wondering: Did your mother approve of Alice?"

She asked the question tentatively, and was ready to change the subject if it seemed that he thought she was being intrusive. And one had to be careful about criticising, even indirectly, another's mother . . .

But he did not seem to mind. "No," he said. "She couldn't stand her. She tried not to show it, but you can always tell whether somebody likes or dislikes somebody."

"Body language?"

He smiled. "Sometimes. Also tone of voice. In my mother's case, it was her voice. You could tell. It became really cold—absolutely no warmth—not a scrap. Whenever Alice said something, my mother would say 'Really?' as if she very much doubted whatever it was that Alice said. Ice formed on the word. *Really*. Like that."

Katie asked whether Alice had noticed it. "I thought at first that she hadn't," William replied, "but then she said something that made me realise she had been aware of it right from the start."

Katie waited.

"We had a party in Melbourne to celebrate our engagement." William swallowed before he continued.

He feels guilty, Katie thought.

"We had some of Alice's uni friends and some of my friends from school—the ones I'd kept in touch with. A lot of them had left Melbourne—gone to other places in Australia, but there were still some there. We had a party in an Italian restaurant in North Fitzroy. They had a room at the back that they let out for parties. We had a band that stopped playing halfway through because the cops came to arrest their bass guitarist. I'm not making this up. They came in, and he tried to get out the back, but they got him. The singer was his girlfriend, and she started to cry. The music stopped."

"That was a bit inconsiderate of the cops," said Katie.

"They're like that sometimes," said William. "They can be quite tough. Your cops over here are all softly-softly. Not ours—or at least not some of them. Anyway, the party got going again, and then Alice said something to me that I hadn't expected. I was a bit taken aback, actually."

"She said something about your mother's attitude?"

"You could put it that way. She said, 'Your mother's a cow, William.' Those were her exact words. She said it out of the blue. We hadn't been talking about my mother. She just said it."

Katie tried not to laugh. "That was a bit . . ."

"A bit extreme? Yes, it was, I thought. It was meant to be our engagement party. But there we are. So I asked her why she thought that, and she said it was because she could tell that my mother thought she wasn't good enough for me."

How right she was, thought Katie.

"But then don't most mothers think that about their sons?" William asked.

Katie knew what he meant. Mothers frequently entertained high hopes for their sons' partners, and these hopes were not always met. "Some of them do," she replied. "Then they come to accept their son's choice, and everything can end up fine."

"She never accepted her," said William. "If anything, it got worse."

"And you think it was because she felt that you were going to marry beneath you—socially?"

William shrugged. "Possibly."

"She might have seen something in Alice that you didn't."

"That's possible too. It doesn't matter anymore. When Alice came here for a visit, we ended our engagement."

Katie asked him whether his mother had said anything about the breaking off of the engagement.

"Oh, she phoned me," he said. "She said she wanted to console me. But she couldn't help getting in a bit of advice. She said that next time I should be careful to choose somebody I had a lot in common with. That was her usual line. Same background." He paused. "But I think I made it clear to her that I have no intention of getting involved with anybody for a long time. I'm taking a break from all that."

Katie wondered whether he was serious. "But surely if somebody came along . . ."

"Somebody from the same background?"

She laughed. "I didn't say that. Somebody you get on well with. If somebody like that came along, wouldn't you like it?"

He shook his head. "Maybe in a few years' time. Maybe then. For the moment I'm going to be a monk."

She took a sip of her coffee. "Surely not."

"No. Absolutely. I'm not going to get involved in any rebound affairs. Those are always disastrous."

"But after a while," Katie pressed. "After a few months, it wouldn't be on the rebound."

"It would," said William. "I just don't want it. I'm happy as I am. Single. Unattached. It's a great state to be in."

"I hope you find somebody," she said quietly, adding, "in the fullness of time."

He looked at her fondly. She looked back at him.

Katie took a final sip of her coffee. For some reason she felt restless and disinclined to stay at her desk. She stood up.

"Going out?" William asked.

She made up her mind. "I'm going to go to the deli. I feel like cooking something. I think I'll ask somebody to dinner tonight."

"Lucky person," said William, adding, "a man?"

"Yes," said Katie.

"Who?"

Katie hesitated—but only briefly. "I thought you might be free."

William grinned. "Me? But of course. What can I bring?"

"A bottle of . . . let me think. A bottle of Brunello di Montalcino, 2009."

William shook his head. "A very good year, I imagine, but . . ." He held his hands out in a gesture of failure. "I can't do it, I'm afraid. South Australian Cabernet Sauvignon, last year—any good?"

"Perfect," said Katie.

Suddenly she felt more cheerful. She would have William's company this evening to look forward to. It did not matter that he had committed himself to monasticism. It did not matter that he had forsworn a rebound affair. At least they could have dinner together.

CHAPTER THREE

I met a wonderful man

The gastronomic cavern of Valvona & Crolla opened up behind a modest, green-painted façade on Elm Row. On one side of the shop, stretching up to the ceiling, were towering shelves stacked with Italian provisions, both day-to-day and exotic: tins of sardines and anchovies, colourful boxes of panforte, dried pastas in all their geometric forms, and arborio rice, which was what, in particular, Katie had come to buy. Not that she would leave with anything so modest: she needed the rice for the risotto she was planning, but she also wanted a block of parmesan cheese, pitted olives, and sun-dried tomatoes. She knew that William liked Italian food and that risotto was one of his favourites. He had made her dinner a few weeks ago and had served mushroom risotto, but he had made it with the wrong sort of rice—and the wrong sort of mushrooms too. She had said nothing, but this evening she would tactfully stress the importance of using arborio rice and of heating it in oil or butter before cooking. She had expected William to be a good cook—a man who could knit was, after all, highly likely to be at home in the kitchen, but perhaps he had never been encouraged in that direction. She found herself imagining William in her kitchen, not tonight, but at some time in the future. She saw herself sitting at the scrubbed pine table, a glass of wine before her, and the smell of garlic in the air. She saw him slide something from the frying pan onto a plate, and then hand it to her before joining her at the table. And she saw him smile at her as a candle guttered and . . . She stopped herself. It was a nice thought, but it was not going to happen.

Her purchases paid for, she made her way to the café at the back of the shop. At mid-morning there were still empty tables to be had—it would be a different story at lunchtime—and she soon found herself seated under a skylight, allowing her gaze to wander over the pictures lining the walls. She felt vaguely guilty about having left the office, but she was up to date with work, and there was no reason to be in the office at slack times. The concept of rigid office hours, anyway, was an outdated one, she felt, and in many offices it did not matter where you did your work, as long as you did it. And she was, after all, not only the boss but also the only employee of the Perfect Passion Company.

She looked about her. At a neighbouring table, two young men were engaged in earnest conversation. Katie noticed that they were well-dressed: one in a double-breasted navy blazer and the other in a rough linen jacket of the sort worn as working clothing in the nineteenth century but now fashionable and expensive. By a trick of the acoustic—the ceiling on both sides of the room was combed—their conversation was audible at her table as well as at theirs.

"My father doesn't like you," said the young man in the blazer. "He says . . . well, he says that you're not a good influence."

The other young man smiled. "But he's right. I'm a terrible influence."

"You shouldn't joke about it. It's serious."

"But I am being serious. You *need* a bad influence."

The young man in the blazer looked away. "And my brother thinks the same. He says he can't stand the sight of you."

This brought a shrug. "No? I'm not surprised."

"He says that you're typically English."

"But I *am* English. And he's typically Scottish, now that I come to think of it."

"I wish I didn't feel the way I do about you. Life would be simpler . . ."

The waitress arrived to take Katie's order. As she did so, the young man in the linen jacket spilled his coffee over his trousers. He rose to his feet; the waitress turned to pass him a paper napkin. The other young man caught Katie's eye, and smiled.

Katie looked away, embarrassed. She had not intended to eavesdrop. Now the waitress turned back. "I'm sorry about that," she said.

Katie ordered. The two young men had decided to leave. She looked around. A few tables away, a woman was staring at her. As the two young men walked past her table, the one in the blazer stopped. He hesitated, and it seemed that he was about to say something to the woman. But then she looked up at him, and Katie saw the slightest shake of the head—a signal, she thought. The young man looked away, and walked off with his friend, who had stopped to wait for him. Katie looked at the woman again, and their eyes met. It came back to her now: it was Clea, the woman who had sat next to her at the lecture.

Clea picked up the coffee cup in front of her and made her way over to Katie's table. "Do you remember me?" she asked. "The other day, at that lecture. Clea Long."

Katie indicated the vacant chair on the other side of her table. "Please . . ."

Clea sat down. "I wasn't sure that you'd recognise me. You know how we depend on context."

"Of course. We remember seeing people in one place and then . . . well, they take us by surprise when they pop up elsewhere." She paused. "Did you know those two young men—the ones who have just left?"

Clea frowned. "Just a moment ago?"

"Yes. One of them spilled his coffee."

Clea was staring at her coffee cup. Katie sensed that her question had been unwelcome. She had been right when she thought that there was something odd going on.

"I know one very slightly," said Clea.

Katie waited, but nothing was added. And now Clea wanted to move the conversation on. "I found that lecture extremely interesting," she said. "I thought about it a lot—afterwards."

Katie agreed.

"And you," Clea went on. "You told me that you're a professional matchmaker. You did say that, didn't you? We didn't have time to talk about it."

"I run an introduction agency," said Katie evenly. "The business belonged to my father's first cousin. She went off to Canada and left me in charge. I'm keeping it going for her."

Clea was looking at her intently. "Fascinating," she said, when Katie finished. "I didn't think anybody did that any more. I thought it was all done online."

Katie said that although most people met online, there were still some who did not like the idea. "We act as a sort of filter," she said. "We check up on people. We do what we say we're going to do—we match them." She paused. "And that's not such an unusual thing. There are plenty of communities that like to bring people together in that way. There are always going to be people who find it difficult for one reason or another. Along comes the matchmaker."

Clea was listening with interest. Now she said, "I can see that. And why not?"

"Absolutely," said Katie. "Why not?"

A smile flickered about Clea's face. "Are you successful?"

Katie did not hesitate. "I think we are."

"Always?"

"Not always, but probably in the majority of the cases we handle. There are some people, of course, who are hard to place."

Clea's smile broadened. "You mean, you have some hopeless cases?"

"A few. Not many." Katie paused. "We have more women on our books than men. And that reflects the way it is out there. After a certain age, there are more women looking for men than the other way round. There's a demographic reason for that."

Clea asked for an explanation.

"Men die younger," Katie said. "That means that there is an imbalance in the population. The men die, and the women are left."

"But only in the older age groups?"

Katie looked thoughtful. "Even in the younger age groups there seem to be more women looking for partners," she said. "That's the impression I get, anyway."

Clea nodded. "I think that too." She thought for a moment. "I've always believed that women tend to look for husbands when they're at university or college. But now the women in these places outnumber the men, and so the women can't find anybody."

Katie doubted whether that was still the case. "Women are far more interested in their careers now," she pointed out. "But there may be other reasons for the scarcity of men interested in long-term relationships. A lot of men don't want to be pinned down."

"They've tasted freedom," said Clea, with a smile. "And why commit when you can play the field?"

"Which has been a problem that women have had to deal with for a long time." She paused. "I'm not anti-man, by the way. I actually like men—or most of them."

Clea laughed. "I do too. Poor men."

"Poor men? It's not easy for them. It's a bit more complicated now."

"It's considerably more complicated," Clea agreed. "It used to be simpler, but now—"

"You could say that it *always* was difficult," Katie interjected. "The only difference is that now we're prepared to look at things that in the past we didn't want to acknowledge. We were in denial of so much."

Katie took a sip of coffee before saying, "Do you mind my asking, Clea: What do you do?"

"I'm a psychotherapist," Clea answered. "I did a general clinical psychology training. But then I did an analytical training, although I tend not to undertake full psychoanalysis. That goes on forever, as you probably know. I'm not sure that I have the patience."

"And costs a lot?"

"Yes. People can have five sessions a week. That mounts up. It could be the cost of a mortgage. I usually see people for five or six sessions—sometimes more, but I don't encourage dependence."

Suddenly it became clear to Katie what had happened with

the young man in the blazer. He was one of Clea's clients, but she had, quite properly, not wanted anybody to know that. She thought for a moment: the young man in the linen jacket probably did not know that his boyfriend was seeing a therapist. And there might be an obvious reason for that: he, the linen jacket, was the reason why the blazer needed therapy in the first place. That was it—that must have been it.

Clea was looking at her as if she was trying to make sense of something. Now she asked, "Do you get invested in the cases you handle?"

Katie was not sure how to answer this. "I try to do my best for the people who come to us. If that's what you mean by getting invested, then the answer is yes."

"I didn't really mean that," said Clea. "What I meant, I suppose, was whether you tried to steer people in a particular direction. Let's say that somebody has been taking up with the wrong sort of person—for them, that is—and you think they should go for somebody different, then will you act on that?"

Katie had thought about this. There had been times when she had wanted to tell people they were making the wrong choices, but she never had. "It's not really my job," she said at last. "I can take a view as to suitability—and that affects the introductions I suggest—but I don't tell people they're getting it all wrong."

"And do many people get it all wrong?" asked Clea.

Katie said that she thought there were some who did that time and time again. Clea agreed, and said, "We repeat our mistakes, don't we?"

The waitress brought Katie's order and Katie sipped at her coffee. She was enjoying this conversation with Clea. She liked intelligent company—people who were not afraid to bring up challenging subjects and to spend time discussing them. Now she took a moment or two to assess her new friend—if that is what Clea would turn out to be. What age was she? Late thirties, thought Katie—possibly even early forties. Smart in appearance; perceptive; interested in the world. She realised that she was using the headings on her client profile forms—she should watch that. The world was not just one large dating forum.

Clea seemed to sense she was being appraised. "I think you're wondering about me," she said. It was not an unfriendly comment; it was not a rebuke; but Katie found herself blushing. "I do that, I suppose," she said. "And I suspect you do too. Maybe our jobs are more similar than we imagine."

Clea laughed. "You may be right. But should I tell you a bit about myself?"

Katie nodded. "If you don't mind."

"I won't go into all the details. I'm not sure if my life has been all that interesting."

Katie said that in her view every life had its high points, its issues. "I've never been bored by anyone," she said. "Once you get them talking. The most ordinary life is full of drama."

"That must be because of the way you look at it," said Clea. "If you have the right attitude—which I suspect you do—then everything is interesting. Even a pebble on a beach—an ordinary pebble. How did it get there? How old is the rock? And so on."

"Go on then," said Katie. "Tell me about yourself. Where you come from. Your friends. Your ambitions. Your . . ."

"Emotional entanglements? If any . . ."

Katie looked away. "I didn't want to pry."

"But it's what interests you, isn't it?" pressed Clea. "It's because of what you do, I suppose."

Katie shrugged. "If you want to talk about that, then do."

Clea sat back in her chair. From a speaker somewhere in the background, there drifted a jaunty Neapolitan song, *Comme facette mammeta*.

"I love that song," said Katie. "Do you know it?"

Clea shook her head. "I'm bad at remembering songs."

"The words are lovely," said Katie. "*When your mother made you, she took all the colours of the flowers in the garden* . . . Something like that."

"Lovely."

There was a silence. Then Clea said, "I'm single." She paused, and for a moment her voice faltered. Katie felt a surge of sympathy for her. She thought of all the suffering that loneliness caused, a giant sea of it. "I'm single," Clea continued, "and I don't want to be."

Instinctively, Katie reached across the table. She placed a hand on Clea's forearm in a gesture of fellow feeling. The waitress, walking past their table, plates balanced, noticed, but it was nothing unusual: so many lunches were confessional; so many were a consolation. "I see," said Katie, and then added, "I might say the same about myself."

Clea looked apologetic. "Do you mind if I tell you about it?"

She had not expected this. It would be a request. She should have seen it coming, she thought; but she did not mind. If she could be of any help, she would be. And there was always a possibility that there was a man on her books who would like an introduction to this lively, attractive woman. And yet a question niggled at her: lively and attractive people often did not need any help. Was there something here that made it difficult for Clea to find somebody? She wondered if being a psychotherapist was a hindrance. People, she told herself, could be put off by the thought that somebody understood them. Was that an issue for Clea?

"I might as well admit it," Clea began. "I'm telling you this for a reason. I'll be upfront about it."

Katie smiled. "As a last resort, be upfront."

Clea returned the smile. "Yes. One might add that to the list of last resorts. As a last resort, read the instruction manual . . . That sort of thing."

"I was wondering if you might help me to find somebody," Clea said, adding, quickly, "I feel very embarrassed about this."

Katie assured her that there was no need for embarrassment. "It's nothing to be ashamed of."

"It feels like a bit of an admission of failure. One's putting oneself . . . well, up for sale. Bargain basement. No reasonable offer refused."

Katie dismissed this. "Nonsense," she said. "It's nothing like that. Outfits like mine are simply doing what, in a more intimate society, would be done by the woman round the corner—bringing people together. That's as old as the hills."

The reassurance seemed to work, and Clea, who had been tense when she first made her request, relaxed visibly. "You make it all sound so normal," she said.

"It *is* normal," said Katie.

They looked at one another. "You wanted to know about me," said Clea.

Katie nodded. "Just to know where we are."

"It's a bit of a cheek on my part," mused Clea. "You come in here for a cup of coffee, and you get this person coming up to you and asking you to introduce them to somebody. It's as if somebody came up to me and asked me to sort out their emotional problems before they go back through there and buy the salami and the cheese. It's a bit like that."

Katie laughed. "Don't speak too soon. I might ask *you* to sort me out. Just tell me a bit about where you are with . . . with relationships."

The waitress had topped up their coffee. Clea lifted her cup to her lips. "I can take two cups of this a day. This is my third."

"It'll help with the story."

"All right. A quick recap. When I was at university, I had my first serious boyfriend. He was called Tim, and we went out for two and a half years after we graduated. He did engineering. I was madly in love with him, and I thought that was going to be it, until he said something that stopped me in my tracks. I don't want to tell you what it was, but I thought, *I can't stay with somebody who thinks that way*. All I'll say is that it was a heartless comment, and it broke the spell. And when I brought our relationship to an end, he said something even worse. I was well out of it.

"I was then doing my clinical psychology training. That went on for some time, but I got the qualification and worked in the health service for a while. I was doing a lot of work with children, and I met a paediatrician called Rob. He was a New Zealander who had been working here in Scotland for five or six years. He was a bit older than I was. We were together for three years, and then he suddenly announced that he wanted to go and work back in Christchurch. I offered to go with him, but I think that my offer threw him, and he came up with all sorts of reasons why that was a bad idea. I realised then that he wanted to get away from me and that I wasn't making it any easier. He's still single. He's in touch occasionally—he sends photographs now and then, but it's over. I think he's one of these people who's content with his own company. He just is. There are people like that, I believe—perhaps rather more than one might imagine." She paused, and said with a grin, "I'm not one of them."

"Nor me," said Katie. "I can manage a day or two by myself, but that's it."

"He was mad about rugby," Clea went on. "Have you noticed that with New Zealanders? They're never happier than when they're watching a group of men running about with an odd-shaped ball, pushing one another over. Look at those scrums they have. All those beefy men grunting and shoving. It's bizarre."

"It's very physical."

"You can say that again. I suppose we don't understand it, not being men. Anyway, Rob loved it. One of his rugby friends from New Zealand came to visit him once. He was built like a tree. He was a Pacific Islander, and they can be very large. He said very little—Rob said that was because he had some sort of head injury and hadn't recovered from it. That's a risk with rugby.

"After Rob, I was by myself. I'm forty next year, by the way. When Rob went back to New Zealand, I had just had my thirtieth birthday. Forty sounds . . . well, it sounds so old, doesn't it."

"Call it grown-up," said Katie.

"You're younger, aren't you?"

Katie nodded. "I'm thirty." She paused. "You've been by yourself for ten years?"

"Yes, apart from two years of marriage."

Katie raised an eyebrow. "Not a success?"

"He died. A very aggressive brain tumour."

Katie was apologetic. "I'm very sorry."

"Graham was a lovely man. He was an actuary with a big insurance company. I loved him so much. He said that he had worked out the odds of the two of us meeting, and he said that they were very small. He said that was why he felt so lucky. That's what comes of being married to an actuary."

Katie said nothing. Was it worse to be widowed or deserted? Did the two states feel, as people sometimes said, very similar?

"It took me some time to get over Graham's death," Clea continued. "I did, though. It's seven years ago."

"You're all right now?"

"Yes, as far as that's concerned, yes. I did my grieving, and came out the other end—exactly as people say you do. After a while I said to myself that I should meet somebody else. I was ready."

"But you didn't?"

Clea hesitated. It seemed to Katie as if she was weighing up whether to continue.

"You don't have to tell me," Katie said. "I didn't mean to pry."

Clea shook her head. "No, I really don't mind. I feel that . . ." She looked at Katie. "I feel that we're pretty much on the same wavelength."

Katie was pleased. "That's good to hear. A nice phrase—the same wavelength. It expresses something that would otherwise be difficult to convey. I suppose one could say, we feel the same way about things, or we look at things from the same angle. But wavelength gets it very neatly, I think."

Clea agreed. "I have to stop myself using it in a professional context, though. Psychologists don't like these terms. They want something more scientific. They talk about *shared beliefs*, or *similar outlooks*, but I don't think these do quite the same thing."

"No," said Katie. "They don't. Wavelength issues can occur even before you work out what the other person thinks about things. Wavelength is all about getting through. There are some people you just can't get through to—and you sense it, don't you? They're . . ."

"Unfocused?" suggested Clea.

"Or tuned differently," said Katie.

They both laughed.

"Anyway, you can ask me anything," said Clea. "I don't mind. Remember that I've been through psychoanalysis—I had to, to get my credentials as an analyst. Every candidate has to go through analysis before he or she can sit at the head of the couch, so to speak. And if you've experienced that, you're not going to mind talking about yourself."

"So, you never met anybody else?"

Clea's answer came quickly. "I did. I met a wonderful man."

Katie waited. She sensed, from Clea's expression, that this story was not going to end well.

"Tell me about him," she said.

"It was in a supermarket."

Katie made a gesture that said, *I'm not surprised*. Supermarkets . . . Why did anybody bother to come to the Perfect Passion Company when they had supermarkets? For a moment she allowed herself to wonder whether there were particular sections of the supermarket that were best for romantic encounters. Not frozen foods, presumably, as it could be a bit chilly standing there waiting for the right sort of men to come along . . . Herbs and spices?

"It was about two years ago," Clea said. "I had been in that supermarket on Morningside Road, on the other side of town. You know it? The one on the left as you head out of town."

"Yes," said Katie, "I have friends who go there," and added, quickly, "for shopping."

They exchanged an amused glance.

"Most people do," said Clea. "And that was why I was there, as it happens. I had been visiting a friend on that side of town, and I needed to buy various things. They have a rooftop car park, and it's convenient. So I went in.

"I remember very clearly what I was after. I needed some Romano peppers, which I knew they had, and some pasta flour, and various other things that the local store never has. So I spent about half an hour getting all that, and then went to pay at the check-out. There's a very nice man who works there—I'd met him before. He's Swedish. I don't quite know how he ended up at the till of an Edinburgh supermarket— there must be an interesting history, but he's terrific with customers and everybody likes to have a word with him. He was there, and after I had paid, he said the store was doing a survey. Anybody who did a quick questionnaire would get a free cup of coffee. They have a coffee bar up against one of the windows, just before you leave the shop or take the stairs up to the car park. You get a token if you spend above a certain level, or if you answer their questionnaire, or whatever, and you put this in a coffee machine there and get your cup of coffee. There are often newspapers lying around that you can read while you drink it.

"I was given my token after I had ticked three or four boxes on their form, and off I went for my coffee. There weren't any newspapers, but there were a couple of copies of the food magazine that the supermarket chain publishes itself. I started to page through one of these while my coffee, which had come out of the machine dangerously hot, cooled down.

"A man went up to the machine. I did not pay much attention to him, but there was only one seat left at the bar, and that was the one next to me. He came up and very politely asked whether I minded if he took the seat next to mine. I replied that this was fine.

"I won't bother you with a detailed description, but the main points were that he was about my age, a bit taller than me, and was good-looking in what I'd describe as a non-threatening way. You know how some good-looking people are sometimes a bit off-putting? They're too perfect, and they know it. They know this makes other people feel inadequate, but they don't care. There *are* people like that."

Katie did not disagree. "Oh, there definitely are."

"Well, he wasn't," Clea continued. "He had a kind face, I thought. And he had a really lovely voice—like those voices that some classical actors have. You know the sort. But his was friendlier than that, I thought."

Katie asked, "You got talking straightaway?"

"Yes. He said something about the magazine I was reading. Then that led somehow to something about books. He told me that he was reading a book that everyone else had read ages ago, but that he had only just discovered. Then he asked what I liked to read, and this led on to films. We talked about a film that both of us happened to have seen. We both did not enjoy it—for the same reasons. And so the conversation went on—for almost an hour. It was so easy. And I liked him so much.

"I suddenly looked at my watch. I remembered that I had to see a client that afternoon and that if I did not leave more or less straightaway, I could miss the appointment. I told him this as I stood up, and he looked disappointed. He said that we had only just begun to talk and that he was sure we had a whole lot more to say. He reached into his pocket and took out a pen. He said that we should exchange email addresses or mobile numbers. He said that he could text me, if I liked.

"And that was the point at which I took fright. Suddenly I wanted to get away. I did not want to give him my number. I don't know exactly why—I wasn't afraid of him in any way, but I held back from further involvement. It crossed my mind that he could be married, although I noticed that he was not wearing a ring. Perhaps it was out of fear of involvement—that could be the underlying reason—but the effect of it was that I made a quick excuse and left. I hardly said goodbye. Maybe I panicked—it felt a bit like that."

Katie frowned. "A pity."

"Yes," said Clea. "And do you know something? Not a day has gone past since then but that I've regretted it—not a day."

"Did you go back?"

"Yes, I went back," answered Clea. "I went back five or six times over the following couple of weeks. I deliberately took ages over my shopping. I read more labels on more tins than I would ever have dreamed possible—all to prolong the time I was in the supermarket. Nothing. I never saw him again." She paused. "I don't know why I did it, but then I suppose we can say that about so many of the things we regret. Not knowing why you did something is probably not much of an excuse, is it?"

Katie thought about this. It was an explanation, perhaps; if you didn't know why you did something, it suggested that you did not really *mean* it. And that, surely, was an excuse of a sort. But she wanted to think about Clea, and this rather sad story she had just told her. She had thought that Clea wanted her help in finding a partner, not to find a particular person—that was not exactly matchmaking, she thought.

She expressed her reservations to Clea. "I don't know whether I'd be able to do anything to help you," she said. "It's a rather sad story, but . . ." She remembered that there were *Missed Connections* columns in newspapers, and she mentioned these. "People advertise with something like this: 'To the person I spoke to on the train . . . You got off at the stop before mine . . . There was so much I wanted to say . . .' That sort of thing."

"We haven't got one here—not in Edinburgh. I've read about those in New York, and places like that." She made a gesture of helplessness. "And it's too late now, anyway. It's almost two years."

"I suppose so."

"And anyway," Clea went on, "I wasn't going to ask you to find him. I'm over that."

Katie stopped her. "But are you? You said to me that not a day went past without your regretting it. That doesn't sound like getting over something."

Clea looked away. "No, you're right, I suppose. It doesn't, does it? But I really am trying to come to terms with it. I want to meet somebody—and I know it's not going to be him. I've come to terms with that."

Katie suggested that Clea should come to the office some time the following week. "We have a sort of profile form we fill in for everybody," she said. "And a contract. I know that sounds a bit formal, but we have to do it. Our lawyer insisted on it."

Clea understood. "I do the same," she said. "I have an agreement with my clients. It's best for people to know where they stand." She paused. "Do you think there's any point in my registering with you? Do you think there's somebody . . ."

Katie was encouraging. "I think there's a very good chance there's somebody who's right for you. I wouldn't be in this job if I didn't think that people could be brought together with people who are right for them."

"No," said Clea. "I don't suppose you would be."

"You're positive in your outlook," Katie went on. "You're attractive . . ."

Clea looked embarrassed. "I think you're thinking of somebody else . . ."

"No, you are. You're the sort who catches men's eyes. That's an advantage, you know . . ."

Clea laughed. "I'm not sure. Not always."

"Anyway, there are no obvious reasons why we should find it impossible, but you never know. Sometimes people seem to find it difficult to get a relationship going, and it's hard to tell why. I don't imagine you'll be one of those, though."

"I hope not."

Katie looked thoughtful. "I'm really sorry about him . . . the one that got away. That was bad luck."

Clea sighed. "Yes, but let's not talk about it any more. It's past business. I tell my clients often enough not to let past business clutter their lives—I need to take my own advice, I think."

Katie said that she thought our own advice was often the last advice we wanted to heed. "We know what's good for us, don't we? And yet do we do it?"

"Sometimes," said Clea.

"Yes, sometimes, but not always."

"No," said Clea. "Not always. In fact, hardly ever."

"Although we all think of ourselves as being sensible—and

therefore our own advice is likely to be good advice. That's a bit odd, isn't it?"

"Yes," said Clea. And then, she said, "I'm thrilled you can take me on—I hardly dared hope."

Katie did not want Clea's expectations to be too high. "You must remember what I said. We can't guarantee anything."

"Oh, I understand that," said Clea hurriedly. "But still . . ." She hesitated. Katie could see that there was a question she was keen to ask, but that she was not quite sure about.

"You can ask me," she said.

"Can you give me any idea of the sort of man I might meet," Clea said. "Just in general terms."

Katie sat back. She thought for a moment, and then named a well-known actor known for his looks and quick intelligence. Clea's face lit up.

"Sorry, nobody like him, I'm afraid," she said.

Clea smiled. "Who would want somebody that perfect, anyway?"

"Any number of women," Katie said ruefully.

"Yes," said Clea. "What a pity. People go for the wrong thing, don't they?"

"Sometimes," agreed Katie. "But that's why we exist—organisations like the Perfect Passion Company. We exist to help people not make mistakes."

"That's as good a mission statement as any," said Clea.

CHAPTER FOUR

Mushroom risotto

William approved of the kitchen in Katie's flat.

"If this were my flat," he said, "I'd live in this kitchen all the time—which is what most people do, anyway. We're kitchen-dwellers at heart."

Katie was chopping mushrooms. She had been thinking. She felt extraordinarily happy, and was wondering whether this was because she was with William, with the prospect ahead of her of an evening in his company, or whether it was because she was with him *and* doing something that she had always enjoyed doing? She had always liked making risotto, which was an undemanding dish that very rarely went wrong—unless you used the wrong rice or the wrong mushrooms. Sometimes, people made both mistakes, and wondered, as a result, how anybody could enthuse about the stodgy mess they produced.

"Do most people live in their kitchens?"

From behind her, seated at the plain pine table dominating the room, William said, "Yes, they do. If you plotted out people's lives, you'd find that it's kitchen and bed. If they're not in the kitchen, they're in bed—only when they're at home, of course. People do go out—some of the time."

There was a brief silence.

William cleared his throat. "I mean, sleeping in bed. We spend a third of our time asleep, don't we? That mounts up. Years and years, eventually, when you total it all up."

She turned round and smiled at him. She noticed that he was blushing. "I knew you meant that," she said.

She had poured him a glass of wine, and now he took a sip. "When I was at uni in Melbourne—"

She interrupted him. "This wine is lovely."

The bottle was on the table, and he reached for it to read it. "Oh yes, this is just fine. Margaret River. I've been there. Western Australia—we used to go there as a family when I was young. I had an aunt—my mum's sister—who was married to somebody who had a farm there. He was called Uncle Henry, and he disappeared suddenly."

"Just like that?" asked Katie.

"I was about thirteen, I think. We went there for Christmas, and a few days before we went, my father said to me, 'There's going to be no Uncle Henry this time. It's a pity, but there we are. You won't be seeing him again.' That was all he said—to begin with, anyway."

"Gone? *Disparu?*"

William nodded. "We have an expression in Australia. Gone walkabout. I think that my dad realised he would have to say a bit more, and so that's what he said. 'Uncle Henry's gone walkabout. That happens sometimes.' I asked him if he was ever going to come back, and he shook his head. He said sometimes people came back from walkabout, but often they didn't."

"And your uncle didn't?"

"No."

Katie said that she liked the expression. "It sums it up, doesn't it? Sometimes people just . . . well, walk off."

"It has a particular meaning though," said William. "Among Aboriginal people it had spiritual connotations. You went walkabout to get back in touch with your spiritual roots. To see the land—that sort of thing. Land and soul are closely linked if you're Aboriginal. It's something really special."

Katie nodded. "Songlines . . ."

"Yes," said William. "That's part of it. But going walkabout's now used in a more general sense. It often means that somebody has given up on something—abandoned it. You go walkabout if you don't like your job, for instance." He paused. "Actually, now that I come to think of it, your cousin Ness—she's gone walkabout, hasn't she? She just went off to Canada. That sounds a bit like going walkabout."

Katie laughed. "I don't think she'd see it that way."

"People who go walkabout don't," said William. "They usually have a reason."

"And your Uncle Henry? Did they ever tell you?"

"I found out—and once I knew, my mother talked to me about it."

"You found out from somebody else?"

William shrugged. "Everybody seemed to know—except me. I heard from this boy who lived on the next-door property—it was a vineyard. He was called Johnny, and he was about my age. I had met him the previous time we were there—a couple of years before—and I didn't particularly take to him. He was really competitive—as boys of that age often are. You know how it is? They want to prove they're tougher than other boys—that they can run faster, play footie better—all of that."

"Insecurity," said Katie, returning to her mushrooms.

"Of course. But that's what it's like being thirteen. You're insecure. Anyway, Johnny said, 'So where's your uncle, then?'

I told him that I didn't know, and he laughed. He said that everybody knew that he'd changed his name and gone off with some woman he'd met at a wine tasting in Perth. He told me that my uncle now called himself Cosimo Moonflower—his real name was Porter—and was living in Sydney with an Argentinian dancer. Johnny said that he'd been told that this was the one thing you should never do—go off to Sydney like that with somebody you've just met. He said that it was no wonder I hadn't been told."

The mushrooms chopped, Katie had moved on to onions. "Oh," she said. "That can't have been easy. Was it true?"

"I told my mother what Johnny had said, and she was really angry with him. She said that people should mind their own business, and that Uncle Henry had been unhappy, but was now really happy. She said that my aunt was upset, and I wasn't to talk about it. So, I didn't—and this is the first time I've spoken to anybody about it for, well, since I was thirteen."

Katie asked about the change of name. "Moonflower?"

William laughed. "It expresses it rather well, I think. Porter? Boring. Anybody can be called Porter—plenty of people are, I imagine. But Moonflower—that's really something. And maybe that's what he was *inside*, if you see what I mean. You're Porter outside—ordinary old Porter, vanilla Porter, but inside you're Moonflower, which is something quite different.

"I suppose they danced the tango together," William mused. "She would have taught him. Although he was a bit overweight. You have to be thin to dance the tango, I think. Or to dance it with credibility."

Katie grinned. "Poor Cosimo Moonflower. What can one say? It can't be easy being one thing and desperately wanting to be something else."

William looked thoughtful. "I'd like to see him one day. I

might track him down in Sydney. He's still my uncle, as far as I'm concerned. And it was never a brilliant marriage, I think. As a child you don't always pick up what's going on, but I remember how he used to be ordered about by my aunt. He had an oppressed look about him, I suppose. And then eventually he made his break for freedom."

Katie started to soften the onions. "Are you all right sitting there while I do this?" she asked.

"I'm fine," he said. "I like watching you cook."

Just me? she wondered. Or watching *others* cook?

"You must let *me* cook *you* dinner," William went on.

Tomorrow, thought Katie.

"I'd like that," she said, adding, "some time."

"Yes," said William, and with a grin, "we could compare diaries."

She left the onions while she topped up William's glass. He looked up at her, and smiled. "I could sit here forever talking to you," he said.

"I'd be happy to listen." Katie's response was uttered without thinking, but she realised that what she said was true. She could listen to William as long as he wished to go on talking.

"It's a pity we have to work," William remarked. "Life would be so much easier."

"Do you *have* to work?" Katie asked. He had told her about his family circumstances when they had discussed Alice still being supported by his trust. It seemed to Katie that William might not have to work—not if he really did not want to.

"You've got money," Katie continued. She hesitated. She had sounded almost accusing, which was not what she intended. People were envious of those who had money, and they could be dismissive and mean-spirited about it. They lost sight of the fact, she thought, that it was rarely the *fault* of those with money that they had it . . . It was like having a talent you were naturally endowed with: you were not to *blame* for being an Olympic-class sprinter.

"I'm sorry," she went on. "I'm not accusing you of anything. I shouldn't have mentioned it."

He made a face. He did not seem comfortable talking about his position. "I'd never just sit around," he said. "If you can work, you should. It's a matter of self-respect. And my family isn't all that well-off. We were big farmers, yes, and in Australia that can mean really big, but that doesn't mean we have shedloads of money. We don't. There's that trust I told you about, but that's not rolling in it. Not at all. We're not exactly poor, but we're not really rich. We just aren't."

"But there's more than enough?" She asked that without thinking—and saw immediately that it sounded like prying. It was like asking somebody what they earned. It was an intrusive question that should not be asked, even if at times we were really keen to find out. And the financial position of others *was* a matter of interest, at least in some cases—just as were other aspects of their private lives.

He did not answer. It now occurred to Katie that this could be a sensitive matter for him. Perhaps he had been brought up to be wary of people who might be interested in him for his money: that was a real problem for people in his position. They had to be on their guard against gold-diggers. Gold-diggers . . . Gold-diggers . . . She tried not to think of Alice, William's ex-fiancée, but there was no doubt in her mind that this is what Alice had been. She looked at William. Had he ever come to see Alice's motives for what they were? And, had he been upset? She realised that William was even-tempered, and she knew, too, that he did not like to complain. But surely the Alice affair must have left some scars somewhere, or, at the very least, made him think.

She had not intended to discuss Alice, but now she found it hard to contain herself. "Are you over what happened?" she asked, adding, "With Alice?"

He looked away, and she wondered whether she had crossed some invisible boundary. "If you'd prefer not to talk about it," she said hurriedly, "I don't want to pry."

He shrugged. "It's not prying. I'd ask you the same sort of thing if I knew you'd broken up with somebody."

She waited.

"And to answer your question," he continued, "I'm okay with all that. These things happen. People drift apart. I suppose you could say that we fell out of love."

She nodded. "Has she . . ." She hesitated; this was dangerous territory. But she continued nonetheless, "Has she found somebody else, do you think?"

He did not answer immediately. "I'm not sure. She may have."

Katie was silent. He had not found out, or, possibly, was in denial. She felt sure, though, that he was blissfully unaware of what she knew, which was that Alice had not travelled over from Australia alone, but had been accompanied by a lover. The ticket that William's trustees had bought for her—a business class fare—had been exchanged by Alice for two economy class returns, and this had given her the chance to have a holiday in Scotland—and subsequently in Paris—all at William's expense. Alice's lover had stayed in a hotel while he was in Edinburgh, kept well away from William, and it was only by the sheerest chance that Katie had happened upon him in a wine bar.

That meeting, when recalled in the light of what William had revealed about their arrangements, had enabled Katie to work out what was happening. William was the meal ticket for as long as Alice was studying—after that, she would go off with this other man.

She looked at William to see if she could elicit the slightest sign of his having been suspicious.

"You were very good to her," she said evenly. "Your family trust paid her medical school fees, didn't it?"

William nodded. "They did. The lawyers said that it was within the purposes of the trust. They love that expression, by the way: *the purposes of the trust*."

"That seems reasonable enough," said Katie. "After all, you were going to get married. It was a family trust, and she was going to become family."

William said that this was the way he looked at it, and the trustees had agreed. "They're pretty generous," he said, adding, with a smile, "most of the time."

"She must have been very pleased," Katie continued.

William inclined his head. "I think she was relieved when she heard that they'd continue to honour their commitment."

Katie felt that he was being too modest. "But it was *you*," she said. "You were the generous one. You persuaded them to continue to fund her."

"It wasn't her fault. I broke up with her. She had done nothing."

It was only through a supreme effort of will that Katie stopped herself from blurting out that Alice had *not* done nothing—that she had only become engaged to William in order to get her university education paid for by his trustees, and that in doing so, she had used him appallingly. For her, William's decision to come to Scotland was an absolute godsend. What mouse can resist the chance of playing while the cat's ten thousand miles away?

She wondered whether she could allude to this without spelling it out.

"Do you think she might have been having second thoughts?" she asked. "Do you think she might even have met somebody? After all, she and you were on different continents."

William frowned. "I don't think so," he said.

"Of course, if she had met somebody that would have been difficult for her. Her university fees—her living expenses—your trustees might have felt these should be forfeited."

William did not seem interested in exploring this possibility. "Maybe," he said. "But that's not what happened, is it?"

He had asked her a direct question, and she felt that she would have been entitled—perhaps even morally obliged—to answer it. And yet, what was the point? Even if William were to come to the realisation that Alice had been exploiting him, she did not think that it would make much difference to the outcome. She knew William well enough to realise that he would not go back on any promise that had been made to Alice—by him or by his trustees. She would continue to be on the payroll until the end of her university course.

"But *you're* all right," she said. "You often seem to think a bit more about everybody else, and not pay too much attention to yourself."

He smiled. "Me?" he said. "I've got nothing to complain about. I'm here in Scotland doing what I really like doing—and being paid to do it. What's not to like about that?"

She had to agree. William's situation was an enviable one.

He shifted in his seat. "But let's not talk about me."

She laughed. "For most people, that's the most interesting subject there is—themselves." She paused. "Some people haven't got anything else to talk about, it seems."

William smiled. "True. I have a cousin like that. She works in Canberra, and sees all these important people all the time—the minister of this and the minister of that; the ambassador from . . . heaven knows where, San Marino? Is that a place, or . . ."

"A postage stamp?" Katie suggested. "There's a parallel universe, you know, of tiny little states that sell postage stamps to philatelists. It's their principal industry."

William nodded. "I had a stamp album when I was a boy. It had pages for all these countries that have ceased to exist. Nyasaland, for example. I always wondered about Nyasaland—I wanted to go there. They issued a stamp with a picture of a crocodile on it. Or the Gilbert and Ellice Islands. What happened to them? Did they run out of stamps and decide it was just too much trouble to continue to be the Gilbert and Ellice Islands?"

"They changed their names, I suspect," Katie replied.

William said that he thought she was right. "I should know about these things. But I don't." He looked to Katie for support. "You can't know everything, can you?"

"Of course not. And even some of the things you think you know, you may not actually know . . ."

"Then I know even less than I think I know," said William. "God, that's depressing."

They were silent for a few moments. Then William said, "But what about you? That's what I want to know? Are *you* all right?"

Katie hesitated. She was not sure what he meant. "In general, yes, I'm, all right."

"Have you got over that guy in London? The one you told me about?"

She answered quickly. "I think so." She was not entirely sure—there were pangs of regret, but these were rare.

"So, he's history?"

She wondered whether there was an ulterior point to this question. Was William trying to find out whether she was available?

"Yes, he is," she answered. "You talked about falling out of love. That's what happened with me. I fell out of love with him when I realised that I didn't like his values. I don't think you can stay with somebody whose views are diametrically opposed to your own."

William was sure that this was true. "I couldn't do that," he said. "If I thought that somebody didn't like the things I like—even a bit—then I'd find it just too difficult."

"So if somebody said, *I think Kaffe Fassett's rubbish*, you'd show her the door?"

William grinned. "Show her the door? She wouldn't even get in the door in the first place."

He was watching her. "Do you hide your feelings?" he asked. The question was sudden, and unexpected. She felt flustered, although she was not quite sure why.

"I mean," he went on, "do you try to stop things getting on top of you? I think you might, you know. I think you might be one of those people who just gets on with things and doesn't allow herself to feel regret. So even if you did miss that guy in London, you wouldn't allow yourself to think about him too much. You're . . . you're stoic, I suppose." He smiled. "Which is not a bad thing to be, I think. If you're stoic, you're unlikely to be hurt too much by things that happen in the world. Am I right?"

She gave a simple answer. "Yes. Probably."

He seemed pleased. "And I'm glad about that," he continued. "I wouldn't want you to be unhappy, Katie. You don't deserve unhappiness."

"Does anybody?" she asked. "Does anybody *deserve* to suffer?"

He thought about this. "Some do. People who have made others suffer should feel a bit of what it's like to be on the receiving end. That's one of the reasons to believe in God, I think. If you believe in him, then you have the consolation of thinking that somebody is going to call really cruel people to account. We like the thought of that—or most of us do. It makes it possible for us to bear things in this life."

He appeared to be warming to the subject. "Imagine you're Stalin or Hitler, or somebody like that. And you've just died, and you realise, to your horror, that you still exist in some other dimension. And the first person who comes up to you over there is somebody you've murdered. And this person says, *Let me introduce myself.* And you try to run away, but you can't move. Imagine that."

He took a sip of wine. "You know something?"

"Yes?"

"It's got nothing to do with what we've been talking about, but I want to show you something."

She had been at the stove. Now she turned round and sat down opposite him. She watched as he reached for a bag on the floor beside his chair. From this he extracted a piece of folded linen.

"Close your eyes," he said.

She obeyed.

"Now open them."

He was holding a small piece of linen, about twelve inches

square. On it was a sewn image of a red flower, lily-like in shape.

"Crewel work," said William. "I decided to experiment with it. It's a form of stitching, you see. Think Bayeux Tapestry—that's crewel work."

He held the fabric out to her, and she took it gingerly. "It's lovely, William."

He seemed pleased. "The flower is alstroemeria. It's a South American flower that symbolises friendship. And look down at the bottom right-hand corner."

The linen was crumpled. She straightened it out and saw the names *Katie* and *William* worked in blue wool.

"That's us," he said. "It's for you, by the way. A little present. I hope you don't mind that it was my apprentice piece."

She frowned. "Apprentice piece."

He explained that an apprentice piece was a bit of work done by an apprentice craftsman in the past. It allowed them to hone and demonstrate the skills they were picking up.

"That's lovely," she said, and added, "And you're so kind, William."

"It's nothing much," he said. "But when I'm back in Australia, you'll be able to look at it and remember me—perhaps."

She turned away. She did not want him to see the tears that she felt were about to appear in her eyes. She made an effort to stop them. She could always blame the onions, of course, but you could not use that excuse too often.

William now said, "Those books . . ."

Katie looked over her shoulder, following his gaze to the kitchen bookshelf, stacked with books belonging to Ness. Most of these were cookery books—as one might expect—but there were others.

"These books belong to Ness, don't they?" said William.

"Yes."

William craned his neck to make out a title. "*Chiron, the Centaur*," he read out. "Of course, she was into Greek mythology. She talked about Chiron as if he really existed. She liked him."

Katie did not share her cousin's passion for Greek myth. "I don't really see its attraction," she said. "All that . . . that changing into laurel bushes and magic. I'm a bit keener on realism."

William said that he liked some of the stories. "Jason and the Argonauts, for instance—I quite liked that. And the Minotaur. I heard that one when I was about ten, I think. It scared me stiff—the idea of the labyrinth and the annual sacrifice of those teenagers." He shuddered. "And babies being left to die on mountains—"

"To be rescued by shepherds," interjected Katie.

"Yes. Shepherds were the social workers of the day, I suppose." He looked thoughtful. "At least Chiron was unambiguously good. Centaurs were generally badly behaved, but he wasn't. He had a school on Mount Pelion. He taught medicine there."

"I think so," said Katie. "I'm a bit hazy on the details."

"Well, he did," said William. "Ness told me about it. She said that was where Achilles met his friend Patroclus. They were in the same class at Chiron's, so to speak. Then Achilles had to go off to the Trojan War, and Patroclus went along with him. Patroclus was his boyfriend."

"I see."

"They were soul-mates. And then Patroclus was killed, and Achilles was heartbroken."

William took a sip of his wine. "I've sometimes wondered whether women understand that sort of thing."

Katie frowned. "What sort of thing?"

"A relationship like that between two guys."

He fixed Katie with an enquiring look. She did not hold his gaze. "I think I do," she said. "I don't mind."

"I wasn't asking you whether you *minded*," he said. "I was wondering whether you . . . empathised. In other words, do women get it?" He paused. "Just as I might ask whether men get a relationship between two women."

Katie was not sure how to answer. She decided to respond with a question of her own. "All right, do you?" she asked. "Do you understand how it feels to be a woman in love with another woman?"

He thought for a moment. "I think so. I think I can imagine how anyone can feel about anyone else—irrespective of what sex they are." He sighed. "These are difficult questions. I suppose that anything to do with love and sex is never simple." He sighed again, and then smiled. "I'm relieved I'm out of it."

She caught her breath. "Meaning?"

"Meaning it's hypothetical now for me. I'm not going there. Chastity. That's it. No more getting involved. Finito. Or, shall I say, finito for the time being."

She busied herself with the risotto. "Are you sure?" she asked.

"I'm sure," he answered. "Romantic entanglements complicate life. And I may as well admit it; I made a bad mistake with Alice. I've learned my lesson."

Katie found herself leaping to refute his conclusion. "But that was just one bit of bad luck. That happens to all of us from time to time. We get it wrong, but that doesn't mean that it's never going to work out. We try again, and, with any luck—"

He interrupted her. "I know that. All that I'm saying is that I—and I mean I, personally—don't want to go through all the ups and downs again, not for a long time. I just want to be me, by myself. I don't want to claim anybody else, and I don't want anybody else to claim me. That's reasonable enough, surely."

He gave her a challenging look, as if he felt that no argument would dissuade him from the position he was defending.

"But what if you're smitten by somebody?"

He smiled. "You sound so old-fashioned. Do people still get smitten?"

"The choice of word doesn't matter," she said. "*Fall for, smitten, fancy* . . . you can take your pick—the experience is the same, however you describe it."

He looked stubborn. "I'm not going to be smitten. You're only smitten if you're open to being smitten. If you decide that you're not going to fall for anybody, then you won't fall. You decide that it's not on the agenda, and it never will be." He smiled at her. "It's like saying to yourself: *I won't eat chocolate*. And that can work. There are some people who can resist chocolate."

She decided that she could not let this pass. "You're wrong," she said. "You're just plain wrong."

He gave her a mischievous look. "Really? About chocolate?"

She shook her head. She was not enjoying this exchange.

"What you do, or don't do," she said, "is your affair. It's just that I think that nobody can ever say that they are not going to be smitten—that word again, but it really does describe it. You just can't say that. Cupid's arrows and so on—you're struck, and you didn't think you would be."

He listened to her, and once she had finished, he inclined his head slightly, as if to signify agreement. "You're probably right," he said. "People fall in love whether or not they want to. You're right about that . . . All I'm saying is that I don't want to go through it again if I can possibly help it."

They looked at one another, each willing the other to find reasons to conclude that there had been no disagreement.

"Well," she said, "I think we should have dinner."

She served the risotto. He had two helpings. "If I moved in," he said, "would you cook this for me every night?" He added quickly, "I'd do the washing up, of course."

She made light of this. "You'd get fed up with risotto after a few days."

He shrugged. "Maybe. But it would be fun, wouldn't it?"

He was like a teenager suggesting a sleepover.

She drew in her breath. "I'm sure we'd get on well enough."

He laughed. "Until we started to argue about the things that flatmates argue about. Who's used all the milk? That sort of thing."

She shook her head. "We wouldn't."

He looked at her, and she wondered whether he had picked up a note of yearning in her voice. But he simply smiled, and started to talk about a new design he had been working on: a combination of Fair Isle patterns and Celtic devices. He explained it to her, and she nodded from time to time, although her mind was somewhere else. She knew what would happen. He would keep aloof for a couple of months, and then somebody would come along, and that would be that. And that somebody was unlikely to be her, because she was just his neighbour from work, his colleague, a best female friend, nothing more than that. That was the lot of some women—to be a best female friend, when what they really wanted to be was a lover, passionate, fiery, all-consuming. She would never be that to him; she would be a maker of mushroom risotto, a good friend and confidante, but nothing more.

CHAPTER FIVE

A proud man

"I doubt if you will have heard of him," said William.

He spoke almost playfully, and Katie responded in kind. "Of course I've heard of him," adding, "Who?"

William laughed. "I just know people haven't," he said. "Even people who read poetry. Nobody pays any attention to Australian poets—nobody over here, I mean."

"You mean, we're insular," said Katie.

This brought a shrug. "Well, you are an island." He paused. "It's different in Australia, of course."

They were sitting in Katie's office on Mouse Lane. It was morning—one of those crisp spring mornings that occur in northern latitudes, when the sky is filled with light even though the air remains chilly. It took Scotland a long time to warm up, and when it eventually did, summer would almost be over. There were two seasons in Scotland, some said: winter and June. That was not true, of course: summer could be protracted and beguiling, as only a gentle, light-filled northern summer could be. It was just that it could come so tantalizingly slowly.

She heard a voice outside in the street—a man's voice muttering something she could not quite make out, and then a woman disagreeing volubly, saying, *That's what you think . . . You always snatch at anything that supports your view, don't you?* Quite, thought Katie: people believed the things they wanted to believe—we all did, to an extent—but the unseen man below might be particularly prone to that, and now somebody was standing up to him. She felt tempted to open the window and join in—to throw in some remark about confirmation bias into their argument.

Through an acoustic trick, sounds from the street below drifted up to Katie's window with an extraordinary clarity. It was not unusual to hear confidences being exchanged on the pavement below by passers-by who were unaware how their voices carried. Like any snatches of overheard dialogue, the exchanges could be intriguing in their incompleteness—little excerpts from life's drama, left forever unresolved for those who accidentally became party to the script. *Of course, everyone knows that he drinks . . . I told him that I wasn't going to pay another penny until he did something about the roof . . . The new pills had very unpleasant side-effects, you know . . . He's not really her father: he thinks he is, but I happen to know . . .*

The two voices in the street had drifted off, and Katie was once again back in the office, listening to William on the subject of his Australian poet. "So, who is he?"

"He was called Les Murray," William said. "He produced tons of poetry—on all sorts of subjects."

"And he was *the* twentieth-century Australian poet?"

William nodded. "One of the best. I studied some of his work at school. I had an English teacher who thought highly of him. He said that he would ask him to come and speak to us at school, but he never got round to it, or Les Murray couldn't come—perhaps he did invite him. He's dead now."

William had come in for morning coffee, as he always did, and, once again, as he always did, he had launched the discussion with a random observation—this time on poetry. He had been reading Scottish poets—"I need to educate myself," he had said—and had started with MacDiarmid. That had led to the mention of Les Murray.

"I'm not saying that we had a lot of good poets," William continued. "We had some—but not a vast number. There was Murray and a man called Lawson, who was much earlier—and somebody called A. D. Hope. He wrote a devastating poem called 'Australia.' My toes curl when I read it."

"Why?"

"Because it goes straight for the things that we'd prefer to ignore," said William. "The dryness. The emptiness. Our detachment from the country's roots. He called Australians—some of them, at least—*second hand Europeans.*"

Katie winced. "Cruel," she said.

"Yes." William sighed. He seemed resigned. He had always spoken fondly of Australia, Katie thought—this was something new. Would she sigh like that when she thought of Scotland? There were things to sigh about, but then there always were, wherever one looked, and she would defend the country if disparaging remarks were made; of course she would.

William continued, "Australia used to be a bit of a backwater. And everybody knew it. There was something called the cultural cringe—the idea that what was happening abroad was automatically more . . . well, more important. So people left so that they could make their mark back in London or wherever. There were plenty of Australians who did that. Clive James, for instance. Remember him? There were plenty of others."

"You?" said Katie.

William gave her a look of mock disapproval. "I'm not here forever. And I'm nobody, anyway."

She looked away. He was not nobody—his work was beginning to be recognised; his work was beautiful. But *I'm not here forever* . . . The words hung in the air, as a reminder of the fact that this was all temporary, and she did not want that. She did not want William to go back to Melbourne because she had become used to his presence. She would miss him.

"Anyway," William continued, "Australia has changed. That's all in the past. We don't define ourselves by our relationship with anywhere else any longer. We're what we are. It's different." He paused. "A. D. Hope can say what he likes. He referred to our cities as *sores*, by the way."

Katie raised an eyebrow. "That sounds like a good dose of self-hatred." She added, "Or dyspepsia."

"He found his own country dull."

"Every country has its dull side."

William nodded. "We've looked at ourselves in the mirror now. We've looked at our past. There are things to be ashamed of in our history. But we ourselves—I mean, people alive today, didn't do those things. I can't help what happened in the past. I can't undo what people did in those days." He paused. "I suppose it's a question of whether it's anything to do with *us*."

Katie looked thoughtful. "Yet people are still prepared to say sorry."

"Some of them," said William.

Katie nodded. "Coming to terms with one's history can be a painful process. At least in Scotland, we can blame somebody else—which we do all the time. The British Empire? Nothing to do with us." She waved a hand carelessly. "Except that Scots were enthusiastic participants in the whole thing—from top to bottom."

William had made them coffee. Now they both reached for their mugs and took a first sip of the piping-hot milky liquid that William prepared. Their dinner the previous evening had gone well. They had both felt tired, and so William had left Katie's flat well before ten. But they had time enough to talk about all sorts of things—which is one of the reasons why Katie liked William's company. One topic led seamlessly to another, and there were few, if any, disagreements. "I feel that we think the same way," William had observed. "Are we the same star sign, do you think?"

She had laughed. "Astrology is mumbo-jumbo."

William agreed. "Of course, it is. And yet enough people seem to believe in it."

She frowned. "Are you defending it?"

He shook his head. "No—just commenting."

"People will believe almost anything," said Katie. "Ghosts. Telepathy. Crystal energy. Tarot readings . . ."

"My grandmother read tea leaves," William remembered. "We used to go to her place when we were kids. She was famous for her tea-leaf reading. She read our cups every day. We loved it."

"Accurately?"

William smiled. "Oh, yes. She was amazingly accurate. She used to say things like, *You will get a letter through the post in the next month, or maybe a little later. I can't see what's in it, but I can see the envelope.* We lapped that up—and of course, the odds were that we would get something through the post in the space of a month or six weeks, or whatever."

"Of course."

"And then she'd say something like, *Be careful of your bicycle. I can see something—yes, I can see a flat tyre. Be careful, and you'll avoid it.* Of course, that was further proof of how she could see things. If you did not get a flat tyre, then that was because you'd been careful. If you did, then that was her prediction coming true."

Katie laughed. "That was harmless enough."

"Yes. She never said she saw anything threatening, although she always claimed to have predicted major events. There was a light plane that went into a hill nearby, and she said, *I saw that coming days ago. I saw it.* And after an election, she'd always say, *I knew that would be the result—I could have told them.*"

"Did she teach you how to do it?" asked Katie. "It could be a useful skill, don't you think?"

William grinned as he put down his cup. "She showed me once," he said. "She said that a lot depended on how fey you were. That was the word she used—*fey*. I was not sure that I wanted to be fey, of course."

"I can understand that. How old were you?"

"Thirteen or fourteen."

"Not a stage in life when one necessarily wants to be fey," said Katie.

"No, but she did try to teach me a bit. She said that it was usually a woman's skill, but that occasionally men could do it." He stopped, and pointed at Katie's cup. "I'll read your grounds, if you like. It's not tea leaves, but it's the same principle. Leave a little liquid in and swirl it round a bit."

Katie laughed. "Serious?"

"Yes. Go ahead."

She did as he suggested, and then passed the cup over to him. William peered into it. He drew in his breath. "Very interesting," he said. "Yes, very interesting."

"Well, go ahead and tell me."

A smile played about his lips as he spoke. "You're going to get a letter within the next few days."

Katie waved a hand in the direction of the in-tray on her desk. "Surprise, surprise," she said.

"And you have an admirer," William went on. "Yes, I can see that very clearly. There is somebody who admires you very much."

Katie held her breath. This had started as a joke, and she had entered into the spirit of it. But this was something different. *Was William trying to tell her something about himself?*

"Does it tell me who it is?" Katie asked. "I don't suppose it does."

William examined the grounds again. "It is not somebody far away," he said quietly. "It is somebody closer by. I cannot say exactly where—the grounds do not tell us everything, but this person is not too far away. And he's very keen on you."

Katie decided to make light of it. "That's good to know," she said. "Having an admirer is better than having an enemy. At least you didn't see an enemy lurking in my coffee cup."

"Yes," agreed William. "You wouldn't want any enemies staring up at you from the bottom of the cup."

He burst out laughing. Now he looked at his watch and reminded Katie that she had a client coming in five minutes. It was a man who had called in briefly the previous week, to make an appointment, and was now returning for the interview that Katie gave all her new clients.

"Horatio Maclean," he said. "That man who was in last Wednesday. Remember?"

Katie looked at her diary, open on the desk in front of her. "Got him," she said.

"Do you mind if I sit in?" asked William. "I've just finished a bit of work in the studio, and I'd like a break. And I've never met anybody called Horatio."

Katie liked William to be there—she had no objection.

"I didn't take to him, though," said William. "When he was in that first time, I didn't like him."

Katie pointed out that he had seen Horatio for no more than a few minutes. "Isn't that a bit of a rush to judgement?"

William did not think so. "You can tell," he said. "With some people, you can tell immediately. They don't even have to open their mouths."

Katie was unwilling to let that pass. "Oh, come on," she said. "That's a bit extreme, don't you think? How can you form an impression of somebody if they've said nothing? On the way they look?"

William looked thoughtful. "Maybe. It depends."

She waited.

"I know that you'll probably shoot this down," William continued. "But a person's expression shows what's going on inside. Right? You accept that people can look, say, sad or cross or whatever? You accept that?"

Katie thought about this.

"You're looking thoughtful," said William. "See?"

She smiled.

"Now you're amused. And it simply underlines my point. Our faces give everything away."

"Except if you're a good poker player."

William admitted that was an exception. "True, but for most of us, it's all there. If we're holding a royal flush in life, so to speak, then it's going to show on our faces." He gave her an intense look. "So that's the point I'm making. A person's face will tell you just about everything you need to know."

She snatched a glance at William. She would not want him to think she was summing him up, and she would not want him to read her thoughts about him. She was thinking, *I love the way you look*. She tried to stop herself, but the moment you imagined that somebody else could read your thoughts, you thought of all the things you know you would not want them to know you thought.

"You don't like the look of Horatio Maclean?"

He shook his head. "I don't want to sound harsh, but . . . Well, I think he may be a bit arrogant." He looked at Katie, trying to assess her reaction to this. "We all have our shortcomings, of course—his might just be a touch of pride, of arrogance. *Might* be."

Katie realised that she had thought that too. She should admit that to William, but she did not want to concede the general point—that one could judge a person on first meeting—and a brief meeting at that.

"You think he's pleased with himself?"

"Yes. That says it rather well. I think he's probably the sort who looks down on fellow mortals."

"Such as us?"

William shrugged. "Maybe not you. But me—yes. I'm just . . . some Australian guy who makes the coffee."

Katie grinned. "Oh, come on now. I don't see how you can reach that conclusion."

William defended his position. "He would have been thinking something pretty much like that. I could sense it, even if I can't explain to you exactly why I think that was in his mind."

Katie changed tack. "Professionalism, William," she admonished him.

He waited for her to explain.

"There are times when you have to put your personal views to one side. Your client is your client first and foremost."

He looked doubtful. "Even if . . ."

"Even if you can't stand him," she said, adding, "Or her, of course. You have to do your best for your client—whatever you think. It's that way for every profession, really. If you're a lawyer, you may think your client is guilty, but you still have to do your best. You probably have to do the same in your job."

He looked doubtful. "I don't see that."

"You take on commissions, don't you? These people who commission a piece of knitwear—you do your best for them, don't you?"

"Of course."

"Well," she said, "there you are. You'd do that even if you couldn't stand a particular client. You wouldn't want to make her look bad."

William looked thoughtful.

"So," Katie continued, "you're simply being professional."

William grinned. "I've just thought of something that happened back in Melbourne. It caused a big stir a few years ago. There was a dentist, you see. He was from Darwin, but he'd been living in Melbourne for a long time. He was quite a well-known character about the place—he was a bit alternative. He drove a vintage Citroën and was married to a dancer in the Australian Ballet."

Katie said that she could picture him. "Not like my dentist," she said, and thought of poor Dr. Drummond, who looked so defeated by life.

"This dentist was called Shuttlie. I'm not sure whether that was a nickname—I think it was—but everybody called him that. He was involved in local left-wing politics. He was often in the newspapers, talking about how hard it was for people on a tight budget to get by. And he was right about that, I think. He did a lot to prevent the closing of a local school—I remember that—and he made a big fuss when the local council wanted to make job cuts. He had a lot of friends as a result."

"That sort of person makes a difference," said Katie.

"Yes, they do," agreed William. "But Shuttlie got into deep trouble. There was a politician—a real loudmouth, a rabble-rouser—who was in Melbourne for a big political rally. He needed emergency dental treatment on the morning of the meeting, and because Shuttlie's clinic was providing emergency cover that day, he ended up in his dental chair, mouth wide open—as was usual for him.

"Shuttlie knew exactly who he was—and couldn't stand him; they were on the opposite ends of the political spectrum. He fixed the filling or whatever it was, but he managed to inject the politician's tongue with a whacking dose of dental anaesthetic. He couldn't speak as a result, and sounded pretty odd at the big meeting. People tried not to laugh, but apparently it was like listening to somebody whose mouth was full of toffee.

"The politician complained to his own dentist, and the thing blew up in Shuttlie's face. They couldn't prove that he had done it deliberately, but the dental board, or whatever, was obviously pretty suspicious. Shuttlie was lucky to get away with it."

Katie laughed, and immediately said, "I suppose one shouldn't laugh."

"Except, it's pretty funny," said William. "And I suppose it underlines your point about professional detachment."

"It does," said Katie. And then she laughed again. "It must have been such a temptation for him."

"Irresistible," agreed William. "And that's the point about irresistible temptation—you don't resist it."

She looked at him, and then immediately looked away. *You do*, she thought.

CHAPTER SIX

You have to watch shivers

It seemed to Ness that she had always lived there, in that small town in Eastern Ontario, although it was no more than a few months since she had entrusted the running of her business to Katie, installed her in the flat, and left Scotland behind her. This was unsurprising—Ness had always prided herself on her adaptability—and her tendency to approve of her current circumstances, whatever they happened to be. The part of Canada into which she had chosen to sequester herself for a year may have been nothing exceptional in that part of Ontario—it was a landscape of low saliences, of seemingly endless forests, and of wide skies—but it had all the charm that goes with being a real place—not somewhere on show for the visitor. And like any real, working place, it was inhabited by people who did ordinary jobs, had no particular conceit of themselves, and did not expect the attention of others. For Ness, it was just what she wanted: a spot in which she could lead a life quite different from the one she had left behind.

She liked Edinburgh, of course—how could one not?—but the pace of life in any city could become a bit wearying. In her mind, Edinburgh meant architectural beauty and intellectual stimulation—but no city, however habitable, could provide something she found in this small Canadian town. That was an intimacy that comes from knowing that during the average day you are unlikely to see anybody whom you do not already know, or the security of knowing that you could leave your front door unlocked, your gate wide open, and your washing on the drying line without there being the remotest chance of anything going missing.

That was a general rule, of course, and any general rule would always admit of occasional exceptions. Ness's neighbour, Herb la Fouche, had told her that a few years back the climate of trust that prevailed in the town had been marred by the presence over a summer of a man from Winnipeg, who had come to stay with his cousin, a mechanic in the local garage. This man was known to be slightly odd, and was apologised for in advance by the mechanic's wife. "Eddie," she said, "is not entirely all there—not one hundred per cent, if you get my meaning. But he's harmless enough." The oddness manifested itself in his habit of occasionally removing items of clothing from people's washing-lines—and wearing the purloined garments himself. There was nothing sinister in this habit—underclothes were never touched—but men's shirts were definitely at risk, and local men became accustomed to seeing their red tartan working shirts—popular in the area—being worn with complete impunity by Eddie. These would be returned in due course, neatly laundered, by the mechanic's wife, along with a thank-you present for the tolerance shown by the true owners. "Eddie's not like other men," she apologised. "It could have been worse, of course." Eddie returned to Winnipeg, taking only one shirt to which he was not entitled, an old one, that the owner said he would not miss and Eddie was welcome to it if it made him happy. Such were the good-natured attitudes that Ness had detected even after only a few days of living in it.

She slipped into a routine—and gradually discovered that everyone else in the town was in a routine as well. So, when she made her way to the general store, the cavernous emporium in which foodstuffs and hardware were all jumbled up together, she would see the same people, whose regular shopping hours must have coincided with hers. And in the coffee shop over the road, where customers might sit for hours with out-of-date copies of *National Geographic* or *Maclean's* magazine, she quickly got to know the names, and to an extent, the life stories of the regulars.

She was content. If the purpose of an adult gap year is to get away from the pressures of one's normal existence, then her time here was well-spent. Edinburgh, and the cares of running a business, seemed very distant and completely different from this isolated and contented small community of farmers and those who served their needs.

She had made friends in her early days in the town, including her near neighbour Herb la Fouche, and his frequent companion, Jacques, a one-armed French Canadian who lived on the outskirts of the town. They had undertaken various outings together. Amongst these were a number of fishing trips on Otter Lake; she had gone on these without demur until she had managed to convey to them the idea that, by and large, she would prefer to leave fish where they were, rather than catching them from Herb's small fishing boat.

The friendship she had with the two men might have been irredeemably compromised had it not been for Ness's tactful conveying to her new friends—each of whom seemed to be thinking of her as a potential partner—the fact that she was definitely not interested in anything like that. She had been concerned that they might not take the hint, but was relieved to find that they seemed to grasp immediately that they had no chance—a realisation, she felt, that might have been assisted by a history on the part of rebuffs at the hands of women. Neither Herb nor Jacques could be described as good-looking, and yet there was a *comfortable* attractiveness about them. And Herb, even if not handsome, had a kind, trustworthy face.

Ness liked these newly discovered friends, but feared that between them there existed a chasm that would not be easy to cross. Their worlds, she had to admit, were just too far apart. Herb had once said something about school, and about how he had had difficulties with learning French, in spite of his Quebecois antecedents. "They gave up on French," he said, "when they moved to Ontario, and you know how hard it is to get a language back once you give it up." He had also alluded to his shaky grasp of mathematics, that was due, he claimed, to having had ill-fitting spectacles when he was a young boy. Jacques, if anything, was even more ill-informed about the world than his friend, Herb, who frequently had to correct him over some geographical solecism, such as placing Turkey next to Japan. Some such errors are understandable, Herb said— who amongst us could place any of those -*stan*s that seemed to proliferate around the shores of the Black Sea?—but when it came to Turkey and Japan . . . well, Jacques should buy himself an atlas next time he was in Kingston, and seek to remedy the most striking of his geographical misapprehensions.

Ness realised that Herb was the more sophisticated of the two, but even then . . . The truth of the matter was that you had to share at least some common ground if you were to be able to make a relationship work. She knew that from the experience of her mother, who had had much broader intellectual interests than her father. She had sensed that her mother had been bored in her marriage, even if nothing was ever said about it. Or nothing direct: so much could be communicated in a look, an expression of regret, or in an allusive remark. "Your father doesn't read much," she had once said, adding, "Such a pity." No children like to think too much about the marriage of their parents, and Ness was no exception, but she could tell that it was a sterile relationship—one to which they both probably felt themselves sentenced. And like so many sentences imposed in this life, it was borne in silence.

People repeat not only their own mistakes—they often repeat those made by their parents too. Ness was determined to avoid that, and so she had decided that however neighbourly might be her relationship with Herb, it would never progress to anything more than that. And yet, there had been moments when she found herself questioning this determination, especially when she found herself surprised by some unexpected indication that there was more to Herb than she had previously imagined.

That happened one morning when, at her request, he came over to deal with a misbehaving washing machine. It was a plumbing task, and Herb quickly identified the problem. After he had fixed it, she poured him a cup of tea as they sat in her kitchen. Behind them, the now-contented washing machine churned and gurgled uncomplainingly.

"I've been reading a book," Herb said. "More than one, come to think of it."

She passed him his tea. "That's good, Herb. You said you were going to read . . . what was it? *To Kill a Mockingbird*— have you started that?"

He shook his head. "That's still on the list. No, this is

something different. You mentioned that guy, Homer. You remember?"

She did. She had talked about her interest in Greek mythology, but had not expected Herb to be interested. "Yes, the other day. I mentioned him—sure."

"I was in Kingston the day before yesterday," Herb said. "There's a used bookstore near that street market they have down there. They've got a ton of books."

"At least," said Ness. "Probably several tons."

Herb nodded. "There's a guy there with glasses. He knows a lot about books. I asked him about Homer. He said he had a whole shelf of Homer. He showed it to me."

Ness said, "I'm not surprised. They'll read it in college down there."

"He wrote two books," said Herb. "Did you know that, Ness?"

"I did, Herb. The first one was called *The Iliad*, and then there's *The Odyssey*."

Herb gave her an enquiring look. "Have you read both of them?"

"Oh yes," said Ness. "For somebody like me, who's interested in Greek mythology, these are pretty fundamental. I first read *The Odyssey* when I was sixteen. It's stayed with me ever since then." She paused. "I go back to it all the time."

He looked at her in wonderment. "Although you know the way it ends?"

"Yes, although I know the way it ends. When something is as great as *The Odyssey* you don't read it for the plot."

"No? So it doesn't spoil it for you that you know he's going to get home?"

"It certainly doesn't," said Ness. "And I know how a lot of

books are going to end, and yet I can go back to them and start all over again."

Herb absorbed this. "Did you feel sorry for the Cyclops?"

She looked at him with sudden interest. "I did, actually. I've never been comfortable with him having a stake driven into his eye."

"Of course, a lot of people would say he deserved it," said Herb. "He showed no pity for all those people he trapped in his cave. What could he expect? Just like that creep with the bed—the one that stretched folks out."

"Procrustes."

"Yes, I found another book down in Kingston. Robert . . ."

"Graves?"

"Yes. Its cover was torn, but otherwise it was all there. The guy running the bookstore gave it to me for nothing. He said, 'This book ain't going to sell with a torn cover. They won't buy books with torn covers. Not any more.' It's all there. And it is. Procrustes and that wife of his. They deserved what happened to them."

Ness was enjoying this. "Yes, they weren't particularly charming company. I can't say I was upset when he found himself bound to his own bed."

"He asked for that," said Herb. "Theseus did what he had to do."

"Yes, but I still find it surprising how we feel sorry for some of these mythological characters," she said.

Herb considered this. "The Minotaur," he said. "I feel sorry for him."

She struggled to conceal her surprise. "Most people don't."

He nodded. "Sure, most people are vindictive. The Minotaur had a pretty bad life down in that cellar. I'm not saying that we can excuse him for eating those kids from Athens, but . . ." He spread his hands in a gesture of acceptance. "The point is that people do what they do because of the way they're brought up. Not everyone has a good start—and if you don't have a good start, you can end up all bitter and twisted."

"That's true."

"People don't ask to be what they are," Herb went on. "They're made by what happens to them. You kick a dog, and the dog ends up snappy. Everybody knows that."

Ness agreed.

"That's why I feel sorry for the Minotaur," Herb said. "He was a bad mixture. Neither one thing nor the other." He gave her a searching look. "Perhaps that story's all about loneliness. If you belong, then you don't have to be lonely; but if there's only one of you—because you're unlike everyone else—then loneliness is pretty much unavoidable, I'd have guessed."

"You're probably right," said Ness. She reflected on what Herb had said. She had not expected any of this.

Herb was looking out of the window up at the sky. "Nice weather for fishing," he said. "They say that bright skies are no good for catching anything, but I'm pretty sure that's wrong. You can catch fish in any conditions—any conditions at all—especially pike. Old pike sits down in the depths and doesn't care what's happening up above. Then he sees your lure and, bang, he takes it. You've got yourself a pike at the end of the line."

"I see," said Ness, adding, "Oh well, these things happen." There were limits to the extent that she wanted to talk about fish.

"The Germans like to eat pike," Herb said. "Did you know that, Ness? The Germans are mad for pike. They've got a different word for it, of course, but it's the same fish. They can't get enough of it. They like their food, the Germans."

"Who doesn't?" asked Ness.

"Good point," said Herb.

Ness looked at Herb, and found herself smiling. *And I like you*, she thought. He returned her smile. "Oh, gee," he muttered.

She looked puzzled. "Gee what?"

"I don't know," said Herb. "Sometimes you just want to say, 'Oh, gee,' and you do. I'm not sure why."

On that particular morning, Ness had woken early and had made her breakfast and washed up afterwards before eight o'clock. It was a Wednesday—a day on which she had become used to treating herself to lunch at the Lost Lake Diner on the town's main street. She would go for a walk, that would take her the best part of an hour, pick up the mail from the post office in the main street, punctuate the morning with a protracted cup of coffee mid-morning, and then make her way to the Lost Lake. Her lunch rarely varied—mushroom soup, followed by a coleslaw salad and a small piece of grilled chicken. Afterwards, she would return home on foot, tidy up the house—if it needed it—and then read until it was time for afternoon tea at four-thirty.

With time on her hands in Canada, Ness had become a regular correspondent. She had started a letter to Katie, from whom she had heard by email a few days before. Katie kept her up to date on the affairs of the business, and had been able to report a slight rise in profits over the previous month. This, she feared, was temporary, but was at least good news at a time when the news, in general, seemed to be in a permanent downward spiral.

Dearest cousin,

If you don't mind such a formal-sounding term of address—but you *are* my cousin, even if we are, technically, different generations, and you are, without any doubt at all, *dearest* to me. Here am I in Canada, and there you are—I can just see you—in Scotland, putting up with everything that we have to put up with in Scotland (weather, history, politicians eager to goad the poor electorate, and midges, of course). Would I trade places with you—right now, if I were to be granted an unconditional wish? Probably not: much as I love Scotland—and the midges and the politicians are not *all* that bad—I am happy to tell you that I am very much enjoying my new life. At which, I imagine you're turning pale and thinking, *What if she never actually comes back? What if I'm left in the office for all eternity?* Well, I shall return, I think, although I don't imagine that will be for some time yet. So if you can continue to run the business in my absence, I would be most grateful.

My life here is uneventful—at least in that nothing of any real significance happens. That is not to say that nothing at all happens—it's just that such incidents as do occur are small, local, and probably of little interest to anybody beyond the town boundaries. Yet they are, in their way, big things for those of us involved in them. A barn went on fire last week, which kept people talking for days. Was the fire deliberate? The town is split, in much the same way as the Dreyfus case split France. A water main burst. Was it the same water main as the one that burst last year? A car hit a tree. Is the car a wreck? What about the tree? These are the things that keep us diverted.

I have taken a job in the local bakery. I work three hours a day, and get free bread and pastries. I have a white apron and a white cap. I am basking in the self-respect that goes with doing something practical, and useful. For the first time in my life, I am making something—and being paid for it. I am going to be shown how to make doughnuts next week.

Please tell William I think of him often. I am wearing the sweater he gave me for my last birthday, and the whole town has admired it. A passer-by said the other day that she had never seen anything so beautiful. Tell William that. Artists need encouragement, because that is sometimes the only thing that the world gives them. Is that true? I'm not sure that it is, but the temptation to coin aphorisms is always there, and sometimes they embody a truth of sorts.

À propos of William, thank you for telling me about Alice. I would like to say that I was surprised, but I was not—not in the slightest. There was something about her, as he described her to me, that set alarm bells ringing. You say that William has said that he is not envisaging getting involved with anybody for a while. What a waste! I doubt, though, that it will prove possible—not when you look—and act—like William, even if *il n'est qu'un joli visage*. William is such a vision of perfection that women will be fighting over one another to get their hands on him. Will you defend him against the hordes that will be besieging his camp? Protect him, Katie. Don't let him be taken from us by some scheming successor to the dreadful Alice. William deserves more than that. Actually, he deserves you, now I come to think of it, and I believe you deserve him, but it's not for me to interfere . . .

Katie did not reply to this letter immediately, but thought about it for a day or so before replying. In the reply that Katie was writing that morning, she decided that she would not address the rather too direct reference that Ness had made to her suitability for William—and his for her. That was a private matter, she felt, and if she was struggling to keep it off her agenda, how much more important was it for her not to engage with Ness on the subject. So she confined herself to bringing her cousin up to date with the affairs of the agency. That included telling her about her recent meeting with Dan, the company's accountant, in which he had raised issues about cash flow. The business was solvent, he said, but was not as solvent as she had imagined it to be, and something must be done either to increase income or shave a certain amount off operating expenses. Since there did not appear to be many operating expenses, as there were no employees—apart from herself—then her only option was to raise the fees she charged for introductions or, if she kept charges the same, to increase the number of clients. But increasing the number of clients would be difficult, she thought, without spending money on advertising, and that cost money—money that she did not think they had.

She did not go into the details of all that with Ness: a gap year—particularly an adult one—should be carefree, and she did not want Ness to fret about balancing the books of a business that she was trying to leave behind her for a while. So the mention of Dan, the accountant, was restricted to a comment on how he had arrived at the office in his biker's leathers.

Dan was that comparative rarity—a chartered accountant who was also an enthusiast of a small group of bikers called the William Wallace Riders. Why they had chosen that name was a mystery to Ness, when she first heard of it; she assumed that the members were admirers of that early Scottish patriot, and that naming the club in his honour was an act of homage. But there were further unexpected contrasts: Dan was a member of an Indian family that had come to Scotland in the late nineteen-seventies. He was now fifty-four years old, which Ness learned was not old for a biker, but which seemed to be surprising for her. Were there many bikers in Scotland of Indian extraction? She did not think so: people of that background seemed, by and large, to be too serious about life to spend their time shattering the peace with their roaring engines, or sitting in cafés discussing the niceties of motorcycle performance. Yet there was Dan in his biker's gear, with his slender, almost boy-like figure, peeling off gloves and unbuttoning the expensive black leather jacket in which he had cocooned himself.

There were one or two successful matches to be reported, and Katie knew that Ness liked to hear of those. But she knew, too, that Ness did not bury her head in the sand when it came to unsuccessful matches, and there were several of those to be mentioned as well. These were duly reported, and Ness then went to fetch her coat and the keys to the old Chrysler she had bought from Jacques when she first arrived. She stood up, and began to walk towards the door of the kitchen. She stopped. She suddenly felt cold. She sat down and briefly held her head between her hands. It was a strange feeling—not quite nausea, but the beginnings of something struggling to overcome her body's defences—the first intimations of a viral infection—flu, perhaps, or even just a heavy cold.

When she stood up again, she felt sufficiently unwell to decide to go back to her bedroom to lie down for a while. A couple of painkillers and a half hour on the top of her bed would probably be enough, she imagined, to put her back on her feet. Colds could usually be kept at bay with a glass or two of orange juice by which she had always sworn in such circumstances. Orange juice was refreshing in itself, but was also a good source of the vitamin C that Ness had long believed was a powerful booster of the immune system.

She lay on her bed and waited for the effect of the painkillers to be felt. She felt tired, and realised that the fact that her sleep the night before had been disturbed might have something to do with the infection she was brewing. She closed her eyes, hoping to doze off, but was more or less immediately affected by a bout of intense shivering. This was so marked, that she found her arms shaking by her sides, as if she were exposed to a blast of icy air. She pulled a blanket up over her and nestled into the woollen cave she created for herself. The sensation of cold, though, remained, and although her shivering subsided, it soon returned.

During the hour that followed, she drifted in and out of sleep. She could tell that she had a temperature, as her brow was hot to the touch. If it was flu, she wondered where she might have caught it. There had been a woman in the café the day before who had sneezed several times and cleared her throat too. She remembered thinking at the time that the woman must be harbouring something, and she had turned away instinctively to protect herself from droplets that she imagined were released with each sneeze. The woman had looked apologetic, and, after a prolonged bout of coughing, had picked up her things and left. She was the source, Ness decided—not that you could ever blame anybody for passing on an infection. We had to take our chances with these things, as it would simply not be feasible for anybody who was developing an infection to shut themselves away from the world. Colds and flu were the background noise of life in society, and we could not realistically expect to be protected from them.

She called the bakery, to tell them that she was too unwell to come in for her shift. The woman who ran it was concerned: Did Ness need to see somebody? Had she taken her temperature? Was she drinking enough fluids? Ness told her that she was sure she would feel better the next day. These things come quickly, she said, and were shrugged off quickly too, in most cases.

Two hours later, Ness heard knocking. She got out of bed, wrapped herself in a housecoat, and made her way to the front door. Before she opened it, she saw through the frosted glass panel the figure of her neighbour.

Herb sounded anxious. "I was in the bakery," he said. "They said you weren't well."

"It's nothing serious," said Ness. "Probably just a heavy cold."

Herb looked doubtful. "You don't look too good." He shook his head ominously. "You look pretty bad to me."

Ness was about to assure him that she did not feel too unwell, but was overcome at that moment by one of her bouts of shivering. Herb looked on with growing concern.

"That's no cold," he said. "You're real sick, Ness."

She looked about her. Her legs felt weak beneath her, and she decided that if she did not sit down, she would collapse. She lowered herself into a chair and looked up at Herb. "It's better if I'm off my feet. A heavy cold, that's all it is."

Herb hesitated. "I think I should take you to see the doc."

Ness protested, but he insisted. "See those shivers? You can die of shivers. I've seen it myself—up north. There was a guy up there died of shivers. Two days of shivering, then he went. You have to watch shivers."

Ness did not have the energy to resist. A few minutes later, she was in Herb's truck, heading for the medical office she had noticed a few miles down the road towards Kingston. Herb assured her that Dr. Timmins was the best doctor for miles around, had seen everything, and would get her shivering under control. "He's your man for the sort of thing people get round here," he assured her. "And other things too. But he knows about fevers. You pick up malaria somewhere overseas, and you come back here. Your temperature goes through the roof. Dr. Timmins will diagnose it immediately. He knows fevers inside out—and other stuff too. He's your man."

She looked out of the window. It was a warm summer day, and yet she felt chilled to the bone. "Oh, Herb," she said. "I don't feel well. I don't like to complain, but I don't feel well."

Herb slowed down. "You heard of Lyme, Ness?" He nodded towards the thick undergrowth by the side of the road. "Ticks, Ness. Ticks, you see."

CHAPTER SEVEN

Neanderthal genes

William answered the door to see the tall, rather haughty-looking figure of Horatio Maclean. Behind her desk in the inner office, Katie stood up and adjusted her light linen shirt. She dressed comfortably for the office, but with a certain degree of formality. "You want to look a little bit like a bank manager," Ness had advised her. "Not too formal, but smart. Casual smart might be the right look, if you know what casual smart is—not that I'm completely sure myself. People trust those who take care with their appearance, you know. I wouldn't care to take advice from somebody with large rents in their jeans."

"Distressed jeans?"

"Compromised jeans," suggested Ness.

Katie did not argue. She knew what Ness meant, and she thought she was right. She had dressed for her role when she worked in that London gallery, and she understood. So when Horatio Maclean was shown into the office by William, he saw a smartly turned-out young woman clearly confident in herself and in the service that she was to provide. And had he been concerned about the size of the fee he would have to pay, his concern might have been mitigated by the professionalism a person dressed as Katie was presumed to show.

Katie greeted him warmly, gesturing for him to sit down in the client's chair on the opposite side of her desk. As she did so, she gave him a quick appraising glance. Horatio Maclean was tall—slightly taller than William, she thought. He was a man in his forties somewhere, no longer young, but not somebody who was yet firmly in middle age. He had a full head of light hair, neatly groomed, with an evident parting running down one side. There was a well-cared-for look to him, not only in the personal grooming to which he had clearly paid attention, but also in his clothing—in the crisply ironed shirt and the sharp crease of his trousers. This was a man who looked after himself, she decided, and who would be very clear about what he wanted out of life.

She reached that conclusion in the brief moment during which she waited for him to settle himself in the client's chair. Then she entertained another, potentially unsettling thought: Why does this organised, self-confident man need the assistance of the Perfect Passion Company? Most of her clients, she accepted, had some sort of issue that brought them to her doorstep. They had failed, perhaps, in previous attempts to find a partner and had concluded that they needed help. Or they were inadequate in some way that would only become apparent after she had got to know them a bit better. Few of them were like Horatio, who seemed to exude self-confidence and appeared completely comfortable about consulting somebody like her.

She noticed that as he sat down Horatio looked over his shoulder at William, who was hovering in the background.

"My colleague, William," she said. "You've met."

"Briefly," said Horatio. His expression showed a lack of interest.

"I take it that you don't mind his sitting in on our consultation. He works with me part-time."

Horatio glanced again in William's direction. He shook his head. "I've no problem with that," he said. He managed a smile, but it faded as soon as it appeared.

He turned back to Katie, but then seemed to think better of it, and directed his gaze back at William. "Australian?" he asked.

William looked at Katie, who lowered her eyes. "Yes," he replied. "I'm Australian." He paused. "Do you know Australia?"

Horatio did not answer immediately. Then, looking at Katie rather than at William, he said, "I know where it is."

Katie drew in her breath. She did not imagine that William would miss the casual rudeness of this response. And he did not. She saw his face fall.

She forced a laugh. If William thought this was a joke on Horatio's part, then he might feel less rebuffed. But she could tell that the insult—for that was what it seemed to be—had gone home. William looked away.

"I've been to Australia twice," she said, fixing Horatio with her gaze. "You should visit it. It's a marvellous country." She paused. "You don't know what you're missing."

Horatio shrugged. "I'm sure you're right." It was a weak attempt to make redress, Katie thought—very weak.

But he persisted. "No, I must get there some day. I know somebody in Sydney . . . or is it Melbourne? Somewhere, anyway."

"Australia's a big place," said William.

If there was irony in his remark, Horatio missed it. "Yes, very wide, isn't it." He paused. "Are you over here for long?"

William had by now seated himself in the other client's chair. He crossed his legs and seemed to relax as he gave Katie a bemused look. Katie wondered whether he was enjoying this encounter with—she searched in her mind for the right description—this *proud* man. Pride was one of the most ridiculous of the vices, she thought: it was so easily pricked, so easily defeated, and was usually made up of so little. People who could be justifiably proud were usually anything but.

"I'm not sure," said William in answer to Horatio's question. "I don't have any firm plans."

"William's a designer," Katie interjected. "His studio is next door."

This information seemed to interest Horatio, whose condescension towards William appeared to lift slightly. "A designer? And what do you design?"

"Knitwear," William replied.

Horatio absorbed this. "Knitwear? Jerseys? That sort of thing?"

"Have you ever heard of Kaffe Fassett?"

Horatio frowned. "Kaffe Fassett?" He looked at William. "Is that you?"

William laughed. "I wish."

Horatio turned to Katie for an explanation.

"William's work is a bit like his," she said. "He's a very well-known designer. You'd probably recognise his patterns if you saw them."

Horatio nodded. "Perhaps. I don't really know much about that sort of thing. I like Shetland sweaters, though. Nice colours."

Katie was trying to be polite. "I like those too. And some of William's work is influenced by Shetland work. Isn't that so, William?"

He smiled. "We're all influenced by one another. All designers are copycats at heart."

Horatio took a handkerchief out of his pocket and wiped at the side of his mouth. Katie noticed the expensive watch—she wondered if it was one of those you never actually owned, but looked after for the next generation. The handkerchief was off-white silk. Her eyes moved to Horatio's shoes. They were highly polished monk shoes, with the characteristic strap and buckle. They were expensive too. Six hundred pounds, she thought. Watch: ten thousand? Perhaps more. Silk handkerchief: forty pounds, if you bought that down in London, in Jermyn Street.

She stopped herself. There was something demeaning about speculating on another's wealth. If you did that sort of thing, you were effectively conniving in the whole superficial, materialist game. These things, these external signs of wealth, were nothing really. And more than that, they were sometimes lipstick on a pig, as the expression had it. Mutton dressed up as lamb. There were plenty of metaphors to describe the folly of human vanity.

Suddenly Horatio asked a question. "Why Scotland?"

It was addressed to William, who was not expecting it. "Scotland?"

"Yes, why did you choose to come to Scotland?"

William made a gesture that suggested that he was not sure how to answer.

Katie took over. She looked at Horatio. "What did Mallory say about Everest?"

Horatio looked puzzled.

"He was asked why he climbed Everest," she said. "And he answered: because it was there."

William grinned.

"So, I suspect that William might give the same answer," Katie continued. "Because it was there."

Horatio seemed to find this amusing. "A good-enough answer," he said. "Captain Cook might have said the same thing about Australia when he discovered it."

William shook his head. "Captain Cook didn't discover Australia," he said. "Australia was already there." He paused. "And there were people."

Horatio looked doubtful. "Not very many, surely."

"Oh no, there were quite a few," William countered. "People. Languages. Cultures."

Horatio shrugged. "Okay. Point taken." He replaced the silk handkerchief in his pocket. "Are your people Scottish?" he asked. "Was that it?"

"My people . . ." William began, but trailed off.

It occurred to Katie that this might be an uncomfortable point. Some Australians were presumably the descendants of people transported there for minor crimes; others were already there, of course, or were more recent immigrants. She looked anxiously at William, and was relieved to see that he did not seem at all put out.

"My people? Some of them were Scottish. My grandfather on my father's side was from Dundee. And some were Irish, but then everybody's partly Irish, aren't they."

"Of course they are," Katie said quickly. "And an Irish grandmother can be very useful if you want a passport. Or if you're an American politician."

Horatio smiled. "I don't have that advantage," he said.

William raised an eyebrow. "You're one hundred per cent Scottish?"

The reply came quickly, and was unequivocal. "I believe so."

"You should do one of these genetic tests," William said. "They tell you roughly where you came from. You might find that there's a bit of Irish there. And Neanderthal. The one I did will tell you what percentage of Neanderthal genes you have in you. We all have between two and four per cent Neanderthal in us."

Katie held up her hands in mock horror. "Speak for yourself," she said.

"There's nothing to be ashamed of in being part-Neanderthal," William said quickly. "The Neanderthals were not nearly as primitive as they're made out to be. And having more than the normal proportion of Neanderthal genes gives you some advantages in terms of resistance to some diseases. It's not a bad inheritance."

Horatio appeared to take this seriously. "I spend a lot of my time on genealogical research," he said. "It happens to be an interest of mine."

William looked doubtful. "I don't know if I'm all that interested in finding lists of names going back to heaven knows when. I don't see the point, frankly."

Katie shot him a discouraging look. Horatio was their client, and whatever William might think of him, she did not want an argument to develop. She did not take to Horatio, but she reminded herself that she had barely exchanged more than a few words with him, and she should not rush to judgement. Initial impressions could be wrong; it was perfectly possible that as she got to know Horatio Maclean better, she would see another side to him. She decided to take control of the conversation.

"I think we need to get down to the nitty-gritty," she said. "We have a questionnaire, but some people prefer just to talk about things and give us the necessary information that way. It's up to you."

Horatio had no difficulty making a decision. "I'll tell you," he said. "I take it that you want to know about my interests—my preferences, and so on?"

"Exactly," said Katie. "And a bit about . . . well, about your relationship history. Sorry to put it that way, but that's what it amounts to, really. We need to know where you're coming from, so to speak, so that we can—"

"So that you know where I want to go?" interjected Horatio.

"Precisely," said Katie, with a smile. Perhaps this man has a sense of humour, after all, she said to herself.

She reached for her pen. "I'll need to take notes. I hope that's all right." Then she added, "You'll appreciate that this is entirely confidential. We don't disclose anything."

Horatio hesitated. "Not even to anybody you introduce me to? Not even to her?"

Katie explained that they would give the minimum amount of information necessary to make the introduction. "We might say a little bit about your interests," she said. "If you were to be particularly interested in opera, then I would probably mention it to her—particularly if I knew that she had a similar interest. But we wouldn't disclose anything private."

"Such as a divorce?" asked Horatio.

Katie shook her head. "That's not really private. And it's pretty important information for somebody wanting a partner. They'd expect to know that."

"Or an illness?" asked Horatio.

Katie hesitated. "That depends . . ."

"On whether it's communicable," interjected William.

Horatio stared straight ahead. Then, slowly, he turned to look at William, but said nothing.

"William's not being entirely serious," Katie said hurriedly. "We assume that people will reveal anything that's really important in that respect. We assume the normal level of consideration for others."

"There's nothing like that," muttered Horatio, adding, "not that it's really anybody else's business."

"Of course not," said Katie, trying to sound as emollient as possible. "So perhaps you could start by telling us a little bit about yourself. Don't bother about too much detail—just the general picture."

"The general picture," Horatio began, "is that I am forty-four years old. I'm in good-enough shape, I think." He glanced at William. "No communicable diseases. No warrants for my arrest. No history of bankruptcy, unpaid parking fines, or unacknowledged offspring."

Katie laughed. "That's a relief." She gestured towards the piece of paper in front of her. "Shall I write *no skeletons*?"

"You could. Although, like everybody, I've things in my past that aren't exactly skeletons, but . . ."

"All of us do," said Katie. "To a greater or lesser extent. And you don't have to say anything about any of that."

"All right," said Horatio. "I won't. I'll give you the bare bones. I was born in Crieff. I went to a small prep school there—Ardvreck—you may have heard of it. Then we moved to Glasgow, and I was at school there. Hutchesons'. And Glasgow University after that. I studied history."

He paused, and gave Katie an enquiring look. "Is that enough detail?"

"It doesn't tell me a great deal about you," said Katie. "But then I'm not so interested in the early years—it's what's happened more recently that interests me."

Horatio smiled. "You'd think it would be the other way round. Don't they say that it's what happened in childhood that determines what happens later on?"

William had been silent during this exchange between Katie and Horatio; now he intervened. "I think that's absolutely true. Ask any unhappy person why they're unhappy, and pretty soon they'll start talking about what happened a long time ago, when they were kids. Your father was a bully; your mother preferred your brother; there are variations, but it's a familiar story."

Katie said, "People can get over things. They're robust."

Horatio looked sceptical. "They used to be. But now it's all about victimhood." He threw a glance at William, as if to reproach him for the mention of unhappiness.

"My father had a property company," he went on. "We had a portfolio of commercial property—we never did residential stuff. Residential involves too many . . . well, people, if you see what I mean."

Katie caught William's eye. She could see that William was bemused by this extraordinary display of outdated attitudes, but for her part she was prepared to give Horatio Maclean the benefit of any available doubt. Perhaps he was just not choosing his words very well. But *people* . . . People are *us*, she thought: you and me in all our human ordinariness; and Horatio should be reminded of the fact. And yet . . . was it unreasonable to find one's patience tested by having to deal with the members of the public? People could be trying, with their tendency to complain about little things and make demands at every turn. Perhaps Horatio was merely expressing the irritation that anybody might feel in having to deal with fussy and troublesome tenants.

Horatio continued his autobiography. "I went into the firm and ended up running it when my father retired. We've done very well. We have our main branch in Glasgow, but we also have offices here in Edinburgh, and in Aberdeen and Inverness. I actually work in the Edinburgh office, although our Glasgow office is bigger. I've got nothing against Glasgow, of course, but Edinburgh's handier for my interests."

And what are those, wondered Katie. Presumably they would soon learn . . . But then she heard William. He spoke sotto voce, but he was still audible. She froze.

"The *people*," William muttered.

The inference could not have been clearer. There was a long history of Edinburgh looking down its nose at Glasgow, the sprawling, lively city on the other side of Scotland. In that view, Edinburgh was refined while Glasgow was rough and ready. It was an old division—the subject of countless jokes. Nobody took it seriously—except some, Katie thought—and it seemed that Horatio might be one: that was what lay behind William's unguarded comment.

For a moment it seemed to Katie that Horatio had heard, and she inwardly winced at the likelihood that he would take offence. You did not offend the client: that was the uncontested rule number one of any business that depended on individual customers. She felt a momentary irritation at William's presumption, and thought of what she might say to him once Horatio had left. But then she realised that Horatio might not have heard the muttered comment, as he did not turn to look at William, but continued imperturbably with his account of himself. She felt relieved, but made a mental note to talk to William about the importance of self-restraint when it came to dealing with clients one did not necessarily like.

Yet Horatio had heard. Half-turning to William, he said, "The point about Glasgow, of course, is that it's really an Irish city."

William looked puzzled.

"Yes," continued Horatio, in even tones, "much of Glasgow's population arrived in the nineteenth century. Some of it came down from the Highlands, but the influx was mostly Irish. They dug canals and so on."

Katie picked up the dismissive note. *They dug canals . . .* "Important work," she said.

"Of course," said Horatio. "I wouldn't argue to the contrary."

"My maternal grandfather was one of them," said William.

Horatio raised a hand. "I'm not anti-Irish—heaven forbid. All that I'd say is that Glasgow became fairly Irish in its outlook. And the Catholic Church took root as a result." He looked at Katie. "The Irish national temperament is a bit fiery, I've always thought."

William thought of something. "Weren't Scotland and Ireland pretty much the same place, way back? Wasn't St. Columba Irish?"

"You're thinking of the Kingdom of Dalriada," Horatio replied. "That was over in the west, and it included the northern part of Ireland as well as a big part of the Scottish mainland."

"Which makes a lot of people in Scotland Irish—in a sense," said William.

Horatio shook his head. "No, I don't think so. You might say that of a lot of people in Glasgow and thereabouts, but not the rest of the country. Certainly not where I come from."

"Does it matter?" asked Katie. She felt uncomfortable with conversations of this sort. There were enough divisions between people as it was without dredging up ancient ethnic issues.

She did not expect Horatio's answer. "It matters a great deal," he said. "Where you come from defines you. It can explain everything about a person—everything."

"Except what they're like," muttered William.

Katie realised she would have to move the conversation on, or there was a real possibility of a flare-up that would lose them a client. And they could not afford that.

"Let's get back to you," she said to Horatio. "Where were we? Perhaps you might say something about past relationships—if you don't mind talking about them."

"I don't mind," said Horatio. "I've been married before—but only once. We divorced two years ago. We had no children."

"It's easier that way," said Katie.

"Yes. We met when we were both in our late twenties. She was working for a wine dealer in Edinburgh, and I first saw her at a wine tasting they organised. She was called Cecilia, and her father . . ." He hesitated, lowering his voice as if imparting a confidence. "Her father, actually, was an earl. They had a place just outside Edinburgh. It was not an ancient title, I'm afraid—nothing like the Earldom of Elgin, I'm afraid. It was conferred on the first earl back in the eighteen-seventies. He was a prominent wool merchant—a close friend of Gladstone's, as it happened." He turned to address William over his shoulder. "You heard of Gladstone?"

William looked at Katie as he answered. "William Ewart Gladstone, prime minister four times, starting in 1868."

Horatio seemed unembarrassed by the put-down. "Well

done. I'm not sure I could name many Australian prime ministers—if any. Wasn't one of them eaten by a shark?"

"He drowned," said William. "Harold Holt. He was a strong swimmer, but he went in where there was a strong undertow. They never found him."

"But it could have been a shark?"

"Possibly. Nobody knows." William paused. "There were lots of conspiracy theories. Some people said that he had been a spy for China, and they picked him up in a submarine."

"There are easier ways of spiriting people away," said Horatio.

Katie cleared her throat. "Your marriage," she said. "I take it that you and Cecilia went your separate ways."

Horatio confirmed that they did. "It was her decision," he said. "I didn't want us to separate, but she said that . . ." He looked away.

"You don't need to go into that," Katie reassured him.

"I don't mind. She told me that she felt trapped in our marriage. I'm not quite sure what she meant by that, but that was how she put it. She sprung that on me, and was gone a few days later. I thought that there might be somebody else, but one of her friends told me that she had not been seeing anybody."

"So, you were single again," said Katie.

"Yes. That was two years ago. It's taken me that amount of time to decide to meet somebody." He paused. "That's why I'm here. Can you help me?"

Katie replied that they would do their best. "There's usually somebody for everybody. We can certainly introduce you to people whom you might take to. It's hard to tell, though: some introductions work, others don't."

Horatio seemed to think about this. After a while, he

nodded and asked, "May I tell you what I'm looking for in a partner?"

"Of course."

He hesitated. "I know that some people would consider me old-fashioned."

"Being old-fashioned can be a plus point," said Katie. "No need to apologise for that."

He seemed encouraged. "I think that breeding's important."

Katie was taken aback. "You mean children? Do you mean that you want to have children with somebody?"

Horatio laughed. "No, I mean good breeding—how you've been brought up to behave."

Katie was not sure what to say. William smiled.

Horatio fixed Katie with an earnest stare. "I really mean it."

"Perhaps you can tell me what you mean by good breeding," said Katie. She looked at him: Who spoke about breeding today? Horatio *was* old-fashioned.

"You can't just take somebody from any-old-where and expect them to be something they patently aren't," Horatio said. "If you've been badly brought up, it shows."

"Let me get this correct," Katie said. "You want somebody with a particular background?"

Horatio nodded. "Yes. Absolutely."

"Are we talking about class?" William asked. He looked bemused.

"No," said Katie.

"Yes," said Horatio. "If that's how you want to put it. I don't want somebody who doesn't share my outlook on life. That's not too big an ask, is it?"

Katie said that she did not think that it was. But at the same time she did not think that an outlook on life was entirely determined by whatever class one had been born into. She tried now to put this point across.

"People can have very good qualities," she said, "and still come from very ordinary backgrounds." She took a deep breath. Horatio had a point—a shared background helped in any relationship—she remembered the lecture on matching—but what worried her here was his dismissiveness. She would try to see things from his point of view, but he was certainly not making it easy. "In fact, they may come from really hopeless backgrounds, and still make something of themselves."

"Moral qualities have nothing to do with what sort of home you come from," said William.

Horatio closed his eyes briefly as William spoke. It was confirmation, thought Katie, if confirmation were to be needed, that not only he and Horatio had nothing at all in common, but that they felt a mutual antipathy.

"It's important to me," said Horatio, adding, "These things really do count, you know."

Katie looked down at the sheet of paper on which she had been writing notes. One word stood out: *snob*. She shifted the paper, partly obscuring it with her diary, that was also lying on the desk. Ness used a paper diary—"I'm old-fashioned that way," she had explained. "A paper diary can't be erased by a keyboard mistake." Katie had found a spare in a cupboard and had begun to use that. It gave her pleasure to see the day before her on the page—tangible in a way that an electronic diary could never be.

Horatio had more to say on the subject. "I don't know whether you've ever done any genealogical work."

He waited for her response. Katie shook her head.

"It's fascinating," Horatio went on. "I'm a Maclean of Carna," he said. "We're an offshoot of Macleans who came over from Coll in the sixteenth century. We married Campbells along the line, particularly a younger son of one of the early dukes of Argyll in the seventeenth century. They controlled Morvern, you see, and Carna is just off the coast there. There was an earlier connection, too, with Somerled, back in Viking times. You know about him, of course."

"Well . . ."

"He drove the Vikings out, although his mother was probably Viking herself."

"But perhaps a non-combatant," William interjected.

Horatio hesitated. "Interesting point. The Vikings married women from the territories they occupied. They took a lot of Scottish women to Iceland with them, you know. Carted them off. Scots and Icelanders are sort of cousins as a result. Distant, of course." He paused. "I have nothing against the Vikings. They get a bad press, but they weren't as bad as they are portrayed. They brought a significant culture with them."

William had become interested. "So you have Viking blood?"

"No, I wouldn't claim that—not explicitly," said Horatio. "But it's certainly possible—likely, even. I'd put it in genetic terms, actually. Blood sounds a bit . . . well, a bit pre-scientific. It's genes that count."

"But you do have some?" William persisted. "You have Viking genes in you?"

Horatio made a gesture that suggested that this was too complicated a point to admit of a simple answer. "It's likely. But you can't be certain—nobody can."

"Of course, Vikings didn't need introduction agencies. If they fancied somebody, they just carried her off. You wouldn't do that, I assume."

It was meant as a humorous remark, but it made Katie freeze.

Horatio drew in his breath.

We have just lost a client, Katie thought.

Horatio laughed. "I hadn't thought of that," he said, and added, "That's very funny. But Scotland has changed, hasn't it?"

"Just as well," said William. He had realised he had overstepped the mark, and was relieved that Horatio had found his remark amusing. He saw Katie's warning glance, though, and he made an attempt to look apologetic.

CHAPTER EIGHT

On being simpatico

The next day was a Saturday, a day that Katie enjoyed for four reasons, in ascending order of importance: breakfast, which, on a Saturday was always more leisurely and self-indulgent—scrambled eggs, fried Portobello mushrooms, and smoked salmon; coffee at Valvona & Crolla; a visit to the bookshop at the top of Leith Walk; and then lunch with Ell, her friend from school days in Edinburgh, who would often ask somebody interesting to join them but who was also quite happy to exchange news about their contemporaries. As was often the case with old friends, Ell and Katie had a tendency to go over the same ground time and time again, extracting from schooldays memories the last drop of nuance. Was Miss Wardrop quite as dry and old-maidish as she seemed? Was it true she had a lover in Düsseldorf, whom she went off to see immediately after the school term ended? Was it true that this lover played in a jazz band and drove a red Mercedes coupé? Or did Miss Wardrop in reality live with her mother and an ill-tempered Siamese cat in Newington, just next to Eddie's fish shop? Were teachers destined to lead rather desperate lives like that, living with their mothers and a cat, and never going off to Düsseldorf, or anywhere for that matter?

And what about Marjorie Shaw, who made such a fool of herself over that boy who used to win the half marathon every year? She pursued him relentlessly, when anybody could tell that he was too obsessed with mathematics to have the slightest interest in girls. And when he eventually went off to university in London, she spent an entire week in a state of extravagant tearfulness, while people tried to tell her that it was all for the best because it would never have worked out. It was futile, they told her, to imagine that she could change him, because people like that could not be changed. "If somebody's a mathematician," Ell had said to Marjorie, "then they're a mathematician, Marjorie."

"How could she be so naive?" Ell now asked Katie, years later. "Mind you, we were all naive, weren't we? About almost everything."

And Katie replied, "Yes, and sometimes we simply don't see things we don't *want* to see. We convince ourselves that the world is what we'd like it to be."

That was Marjorie Shaw, whom neither of them had seen for years.

"Somebody told me, though," said Ell, "that she ended up marrying a man from New York, and that they moved to Connecticut, where she had a large family. I was told, too, that she never got over that boy—the one who lived in a private world of numbers. That's a bit sad, I think. Her American husband is very nice, everybody says, and their marriage is fine, but she told somebody she's always going to love that boy. Talk about wasting your life . . . Imagine pining for years for somebody who's never going to be available. What a waste of . . . of everything."

At breakfast that morning, while the Portobello mushrooms sizzled in the frying pan, and the carefully prepared scrambled eggs—no milk, and cooked gently, half-on and half-off the ring—she thought about Horatio Maclean, and their unsatisfactory meeting the previous day. It had achieved its main objective—she had found out what she needed to know about a new client—but in that she had hoped to end up more favourably disposed towards him, which would help her do her job with greater conviction, it had been a failure. She had ended up being dismayed by much of what he had said, a feeling clearly shared by William, who had simply grimaced after Horatio's eventual departure. "Not much to say," he had said, and then, with a prolonged sigh, had returned to his studio next door.

Katie did not blame him. Horatio had been condescending, and had she been William she would have felt exactly as he did. Should she have stood up against him and simply declined to represent him? Ness had told her that there might be the occasional client the agency simply could not recommend—"You'll recognise the sort, Katie," she had said. And then, with a dark look, had added, "There are some people you just can't land on some poor woman. You have to be firm."

Was Horatio Maclean such a man? She wondered whether she should write to Ness, and ask for advice. But then she reminded herself that Ness was on her gap year and should not be burdened with such questions. And with that, she made a conscious effort to put Horatio out of her mind, for the time being at least. It was probably too late to get rid of him, anyway, as she had told him at the end of the interview that she was sure she would be able to arrange a suitable introduction. If she were to say the opposite now, then he might reasonably ask why she had not said so at an earlier stage. No, Horatio would at least be given a chance.

She decided to stop thinking about Horatio: the decision had been taken to accept him as a client and there was no going back. She looked at the mushrooms, and thought about them instead. She could not remember when she first started buying them, and how they became a part of her special breakfast ritual. It had been in London that she had first come across them. That was when she had started to take an interest in cooking, and had sought out unusual ingredients. A friend had bought her a cookbook written by the combination of an Israeli author and a Palestinian author, who were renowned for their elaborate recipes with their long lists of out-of-the-ordinary ingredients. Not that Portobello mushrooms were exotic or hard to find: they were stocked by most supermarkets. But they provided a welcome alternative to the standard field mushrooms that most people used, without being one of those misshapen and slightly sinister funguses that should call, she thought, for a mycologist rather than a chef.

Deliberately trying to think about mushrooms, of course, is an invitation to think about something else altogether, and Katie's thoughts obstinately returned to Horatio Maclean. How did he spend his Saturday mornings? she wondered. He lived not far away, but on a markedly more expensive street, India Street, that ran down from Heriot Row, one of the most sought-after addresses in the city. *Sought-after* . . . those words had come into her mind when she thought about Heriot Row, but she realised that they were a cliché implanted by the gushing prose of estate agents. They were always talking about streets or suburbs being *sought-after*. And what about houses that were *not* sought after? There must be such places—parts of the city where nobody wanted to live, or where people were prepared to live only because they had no alternative. Such places, in the language of estate agents, were *up and coming*, and sometimes described as *being in a lively area*, while the houses and flats within them would *benefit from some attention* or were *attractively priced, bearing in mind the growing interest being shown in the area*. The language of deception, or of optimism, perhaps, was creative, even if it promoted obfuscation.

A call from Ell interrupted her train of thought. Was she on for lunch, as usual, because Ell had forgotten to book a table, as she normally did on Friday? She was, said Katie, and looked forward to it. Then there had come a brief silence at Ell's end of the line.

"I've actually got something to ask you," said Ell. "And I don't want you to say yes unless you really want to. I mean, I won't mind—I really won't."

"Ask me," said Katie. "I might say yes. You never know."

She waited, but Ell said nothing.

"Go on," said Katie. "Just ask."

"My lease is coming up for renewal," Ell ventured hesitantly. "The lease of my flat in Stockbridge. I really like it, but . . ."

"The rent's going up?"

Ell sounded surprised. "Yes. How did you guess?"

"Because that's what landlords do," said Katie. "The lease I had in London—the one I shared with those Irish girls I told you about—that was how he did it. He put the rent up every year because that's what the renewal clause said he could do. Do landlords put up rent? Do dogs bark?"

"They're asking too much," Ell complained. "There's a lot wrong with this flat, and he never gets it fixed until the last minute. I had no hot water for ten days last year. Ten days! He claimed it was because he found it difficult to get a plumber. But Edinburgh's full of plumbers. There are places you can't *move* for plumbers. They positively throng the streets—plumbers as far as the eye can see."

Katie laughed. "You can't get by without hot water."

"No. And then there's the kitchen cupboard. The door won't close, and he said that it was because I was putting too much stuff in it—but I wasn't . . ." She trailed off, and then, "The point is this, Katie, do you think I could stay with you for a while—a month or two maybe—while I find somewhere else? I've given him notice here, and I think he's quite pleased to be getting rid of me. Horrible man. Extreme dandruff, not that you can blame him for that, but there is that shampoo you can use, and there's a version of it specially for men—possibly one specially for landlords too. You can see the dandruff on the top of his glasses, by the way."

Katie remembered that that was the sort of detail that Ell tended to notice: small, revealing facts that showed the quiddities of others. Ell should be more charitable, Katie thought, but the charitable were not infrequently less entertaining than those who saw others' faults.

She responded to Ell's request. "You'd like to stay here? Of course you can. For as long as you like."

It was the only decision that she could make. Ell had let her stay in her spare bedroom when she came up from London, and she had to reciprocate. And she did not mind, anyway, as she got on well with the other woman, and she had been wondering about taking a flatmate. Ness, whose flat it was, had explicitly told her she could take somebody in, and she did not expect rent. No, there was no reason why she should not positively welcome Ell. Except for . . . A reservation came to her, but she put it out of her mind, even without having to resort to thoughts of Portobello mushrooms—which were ready now, she noticed, as she glanced at the frying pan.

"You're terrific," Ell said.

"My breakfast is ready."

"Portobello mushrooms? Scrambled eggs? Smoked salmon?"

"Why change something you've always liked."

Ell agreed. "Can we talk about details over lunch? My treat—since you're being so obliging."

Katie laughed. "I'm sure it'll work out really well. And I'll be happy to have you—you know that, I hope."

But she thought: Men. There could be problems. Ell had many positive points, but her taste in men was idiosyncratic. There had been that rock musician who glowered out at the world from underneath heavy eyebrows—an expression of challenge, as if he were looking for provocation. There had been that Irishman who spoke with a fake American accent, and of whose Irishness several of Ell's friends had expressed more than passing doubts. "Real Irishmen," one had remarked, "do not go on about Guinness and misquote Yeats all the time—they just don't. He's Polish, I'm sure, pretending to be an Englishman who's posing as an Irishman."

These two, she thought, were just the tip of the iceberg. But perhaps Ell had grown up and realised that men like that were a bad proposition if one was interested in a stable relationship. And when they had last talked about this, Ell had said that she was looking for somebody artistic. "I'm fed up with men who don't *understand*," she had said.

Katie had wondered how one could tell whether a man understood.

"You sense it," Ell continued. "He doesn't need to say anything."

"Ah."

"It's expressed through manner, as much as anything," Ell explained. "You look at somebody, and you can tell more or less immediately whether he's simpatico." She paused. "There's no

English word that expresses it quite so well as *simpatico*—or *simpatica*, depending."

"Charm?" Katie suggested. "Is that the English word you're looking for."

Ell considered this. "Charm is different. It's superficial. It doesn't necessarily say anything about what's underneath. Somebody's manner might be charming although they don't mean a word of it. You can charm the birds out of the trees only to put them in a pie."

"True."

Ell sighed. "Your William is simpatico," she said.

The air between them was briefly silent. Then Katie said, "Not *my* William. He's a friend—that's all."

No sooner had she said this than she wondered whether she should have allowed Ell to imagine that she and William were together. Ell had shown a barely disguised interest in William when she had first met him—she had been convinced there had been a spark of—but it did not seem to have come to anything. In fact, Katie suspected that William did not like Ell very much—he had once said something about how he was wary of what he called pushy women—and Ell, bless her, thought Katie, was certainly pushy. But a determined pushy woman might be able to get past a man's natural reserve and nudge him into a relationship. She did not want Ell to get William; she did not want *anyone* to get William, now that she came to think of it. She brought the telephone conversation to an end. She looked forward to seeing Ell, she said, and they could sort out the details then.

"You're the kindest friend I have," said Ell. "I don't know what I'd do without you."

Katie said that she thought Ell would get on perfectly well.

"You know what I mean," said Ell.

"I suppose I do."

"You're my very best friend," Ell enthused.

Katie did not respond. Most of us, she thought, are happy to be a best friend, but may be wary of that description.

Ell rang off. Katie put her phone down on the table and stared at it. She wondered what it would be like living with Ell. They would develop ground rules about things like washing up or playing music or the use of things in the fridge, she thought: flatmates usually did that in the first few days of their sharing. And then, one by one, the ground rules tended to be breached . . .

CHAPTER NINE

He held her hand

Dr. Timmins wore half-moon spectacles and a blue linen jacket. From his breast pocket, the tops of two pens protruded, along with what looked like the cap of an old-fashioned mercury thermometer. Of course it could not be that, thought Ness, because no modern doctor would carry in his pocket an instrument that would be regularly inserted into the mouths of patients—and yet if any doctor were to flout the antiseptic ethos of the day, it would be a country doctor like this: endowed with experience, common sense, and indifference to all but the more ill-intentioned germs. Seeing him now for the first time, as he rose from his desk to welcome her into his office, she decided that he was exactly the sort of doctor she liked—reassuring, not given to alarmism, and a believer in the benefits of soup, bed-rest, and the power of the human body to heal itself, given a chance to do so.

Herb had ushered Ness into the doctor's waiting room, where he had a brief bantering conversation with the receptionist, who, as he explained to Ness, was the daughter of one of his cousins. Then they both waited for a few minutes before the doctor buzzed through that he was free.

"That's Herb la Fouche who brought you in," said Dr. Timmins. "A neighbour?"

Ness nodded. "He's been very kind."

The doctor considered this carefully. "Folks are," he said, adding, "except when they're being unkind—which they can be."

He invited her to sit down.

"Not feeling well?"

Ness nodded.

"I can see that," said the doctor.

He rose from his chair and asked Ness to lie on the couch on the other side of the room. A nurse now appeared, and was introduced.

"I'll need to examine you," said the doctor. "Have you been running a temperature?"

Ness said that she had not confirmed it as she did not have a thermometer. She glanced at the thermometer in his pocket. He followed her glance.

"I have one," he said, and smiled.

He carried out his examination. "You certainly have a fever," he said. "Any rashes? I don't see any, but sometimes one misses these things."

She shook her head.

"There's a bit of Lyme around here," he said. "Are you aware of having been bitten by any ticks?"

She was not.

"There's a telltale rash that follows on an infected bite," he said. "It's a bull's-eye—unmistakable. A ring with a clear centre to it. It's an indication of Lyme disease."

He took a blood sample. "There's another tick-borne disease it could be," he said. "It's called anaplasmosis, and it's spread by our little friend, the black-legged tick. They're out there as we speak." He nodded towards the window, through which she could see the edge of the forest. "You rarely see a rash with anaplasmosis, unlike Lyme. We can check for both with a blood sample."

Ness tried to suppress a shiver, but it asserted itself nonetheless.

"That shaking . . ." she said.

"I see that," said Dr. Timmins. "A rigor. Nasty. After I've taken the sample, you should get back to bed. I'll send that to the lab, but in the meantime, I'm going to start you on something that we use to treat both Lyme and anaplasmosis—it's the same medication."

Herb drove her home. On the way, she started to shiver uncontrollably. He looked at her with concern.

"I feel ridiculous," said Ness. "It's warm outside, and yet here I am shivering."

"You're really sick," said Herb. He shook his head, and emitted a long, regretful sigh. "Really sick."

They reached the house. Ness would have seen herself in, but Herb insisted on accompanying her into her living room. "I'll stay here until you're safely in your bed," he said. "I'll make a pot of tea while you get yourself sorted out. A fever doesn't like tea. The more tea you drink, the better—liquids, you see. I know a guy up north who had a bad attack of the rotten burps. He was real sick. Lay on his bed for three days without moving."

The nausea that Ness had been experiencing had momentarily lifted. She looked at Herb with a mixture of surprise and distaste. "Rotten burps?"

"Yes," he said. "Some folks get them. He did—real bad."

"But what . . ." She wondered whether this was a condition

that she should have known about—that she had somehow been remiss in not knowing the risk of coming here and falling victim to the rotten burps. "But what exactly are the rotten burps?" she asked.

Herb seemed surprised that she did not know. "You've never known somebody with rotten burps?"

She shook her head.

"You get the burps," he said. "You know what those are?"

"Burps? Yes, of course."

"Well, you get burps, and they have a bit of sulphur in them—in fact, a lot of sulphur. Rotten eggs. The rotten burps smell of sulphur—as if you've eaten a whole lot of rotten eggs. It's a stomach condition, but it can be connected with other things that have gone wrong. Sometimes it's serious—sometimes not so much." He paused. "Anyway, I made tea for this guy up north . . ."

"The one who had the rotten burps?"

"Yes, him. I made tea and made him drink it. Eight, nine cups—until he was full to the brim. But it did the trick."

In spite of her temperature and the slight dizziness she felt while standing, Ness could not help but smile. "A happy ending."

Herb looked disconsolate. "There are a whole lot of things that can get you—a whole lot."

In Herb's world, perhaps, people did not die in their beds: they froze in some distant snowdrift, they encountered an angry bear, they went down to Toronto and picked up rampaging food poisoning, as he had told her had happened to one of his friends . . . or were bitten by a microscopic tick and came down with a fever that made them shiver uncontrollably, as she herself was beginning to do once again.

"You're shivering," said Herb, his voice full of concern. "You need to get to bed."

She nodded, and left. She felt light-headed, and wanted now only to slip between the sheets and close her eyes. Somehow she managed to undress and put on her warmest nightie. Even then, she knew she would be cold—because she was too hot. Too cold from being too hot . . . Her feverish mind struggled with the apparent contradiction. And once she was in bed, and staring up at the ceiling, at the light that she switched on and now did not have the energy to get out of bed to switch off, she heard footsteps in the short corridor outside her bedroom. She suddenly thought: This is John. John is back from his parachute jump, the one that they said killed him—but he was not dead after all—that was a mistake. Somebody had made a mistake, and now he was back, coming into her room, having just landed by parachute on the patch of grass outside the kitchen. He was so accurate in his jumps; he could choose a handkerchief below him, a handkerchief of grass, and land on that. He was as good at doing that sort of thing as that man who got himself into the *Guinness World Records* by jumping out of an aeroplane without a parachute and landing in a great net that he had had rigged up down below. He actually did that—he made a descent without a parachute, and lived to see himself in the record books as a result. His name was there, alongside the names of all those others who did something exceptional that guaranteed their immortality—like Joseph Stalin, for murdering so many, or those disgusting types who gorged themselves on over eighty pizzas in less than an hour—that sort of thing. John was back, and they had been wrong all along—he was not dead. It was extraordinary, and she would have to let people back in Edinburgh know that he had survived after all and was with her here in Canada. She stopped. She had been dreaming. It was the fever. The fever made her think that John was here, which could not be true, because he had died on that final parachute jump—the one that he had attempted in a kilt, and the kilt had come up over his eyes, and he had been unable to find the cord. It was not John at all—it was Herb, and he was carrying a large mug of tea that he put down on her bedside table. She smelled it—the smell of tea. She looked at Herb, and smiled. He smiled back.

"Tea," he said.

She closed her eyes. "I'm feeling very hot."

He reached out and put his hand on her brow. "You're burning up," he said. "You must drink this tea—all of it. Try to sit up, so that it doesn't go down into your lungs. You don't want tea in your lungs."

She did as he suggested. Her head felt slightly clearer, and she was strong enough to hold the mug herself. She sipped at it.

"I'll come back to check on you later," said Herb. "Don't lock any doors. You'll hear me. I'll knock."

"You're very kind," she said.

"Well, you're real sick," said Herb. And then he gave his diagnosis. "As Doc Timmins said, it's most likely one of those tick diseases. I know two people who got them and died."

"I see."

"But you're not going to die," he said. "Doc Timmins won't let that happen."

"He's very kind."

"It's what he does," said Herb. "It's what all doctors used to do."

She asked drowsily, "But no longer?"

"Nobody cares any longer about anybody—more or less."

Had she not been ill, she would have disputed that. But she did not feel up to it. She wanted to sleep now, and she hoped that Herb would not stay more than a few minutes. He sensed that, and stood up to leave.

"I'll go now."

She held out a hand towards him. He took her hand in his, and gave it a squeeze. "Your hand's so hot," he said. "It's the fever, of course."

"Yes," she said. "It's the fever."

He looked down on her. She allowed her gaze to slide away. There was a strange intimacy about this encounter—an intimacy that suddenly makes its presence felt when an act of kindness is directed to one who is feeling weak or vulnerable, as she was. She held his hand briefly, but for a longer time than was strictly necessary in a farewell. Then he allowed her hand to fall back onto the bed.

"I'll come to see you later," he said. "I'll let myself in."

She nodded weakly.

"Unless you'd like me to stay," he said. "I can sit through there in the kitchen."

She shook her head. "You mustn't. I appreciate it, of course, but you can't."

He hesitated. "I can, you know. In fact, that's what I'll do."

She protested, but he seemed to have made up his mind. "You rest," he said. "I'll turn out the light."

She closed her eyes. It was reassuring to know that he was there—it made it easier for her to abandon herself to the fever that now came back over her in waves, making her shiver, causing her hands to tremble, her shoulders to shake. She wondered if she would be able to will these near convulsions to stop, or whether that would only make them return later, and probably worse. Perhaps they were the body's way of dealing with infection; perhaps the shivering itself was the main defence.

She drifted in and out of sleep. She was thirsty, and became aware of the fact that Herb had come back into the room and was helping her to drink from a glass of water. She spilled the water over her chin, and he gave her a tissue to dry herself. She dropped the tissue, and he picked it up and gave her another one. He held the glass carefully now, and let her take a few sips. He said something to her, but she was not quite sure what it was—something about how we needed water. She muttered, "Everyone needs water. Everyone." She was not sure why, but she felt that she had to tell him this. Herb had to know about water.

He said, "They sure do." Then he gave her another tissue. She said, "Tissues . . ." but did not finish what she was saying. She felt herself dozing off again.

She slept for several hours, but when she awoke, Herb was still there, sitting by her bed. She was conscious of his presence, of the fact that he went in and out of the room and was fetching things—a cup of tea, which she drank eagerly—a towel, that he tucked around her shoulders for some reason—a piece of bread and butter, that she refused, and left on the plate on her bedside table.

The following morning, when she awoke, Herb was still there, sitting in the chair, asleep now, his mouth open. The fog of confusion brought on by the fever had lifted now, and for a brief moment she felt the euphoria that comes with recovery. She sat up in her bed and then got up altogether, tiptoeing round the figure sleeping on the bedside chair.

She thought, *He has been here all night. He has watched over me all night.* Nobody had done that since she was a child. She turned and looked at him. She had not really looked at him before, not as intensely and with such curiosity as she brought to bear on him now. It occurred to her that this was because she had felt that he was so ordinary—not the sort of person to whom one tended to pay much attention. And yet he had watched over her.

CHAPTER TEN

He's very well-behaved

When Katie told William about Clea, he was silent for a short time before saying, "What a pity—oh, what a pity."

She agreed with him. "Yes, it's a real pity, isn't it?"

"I don't understand," he continued, "why she should have given him the brush-off like that—not if they seemed as well-suited as she thought they were." He paused. "Why?"

Katie thought for a moment. It was always simpler for men, she thought; men were less vulnerable than women were—they were less likely to get hurt in a relationship entered into casually or on the spur of the moment. Men might deny that, but she had seen that happen and felt that she was entitled to believe the evidence of her experience rather than the orthodoxies of the times. There were emotional differences between men and women that could not simply be wished out of existence because we thought it would be good were things otherwise. And one of these differences was that women invested far more in their relationships than men did, she thought, even if the official line, as she called it, was that no distinction should be made. She could understand how Clea might have felt that there was a risk involved in giving her number to a man she had just met in a supermarket. There were men who preyed on women precisely in such circumstances, who were quite capable of exercising charm to get them to lower their defences. Caution—even abundant caution—was better than misplaced trust.

"I can see why she might have been concerned," she said to William. "Women have to be careful."

Even as she said this, she told herself that it was hardly necessary to make this observation to William, who clearly understood these matters; who was sensitive to the nuances of feeling; who so obviously knew how women felt. There were men like that—probably more and more of them, as the old defences of masculinity were dropped, and it became possible for men to open themselves up to a broader emotional experience.

"Oh, I know that," he said. "But surely she could tell that he was all right. It was broad daylight; it was in a public place. And you have to trust *someone*, surely. You can't go round being suspicious of absolutely everybody."

"That's easier said than done," Katie replied. "The point is that she got cold feet, and once that happened, she had no real choice."

William shook his head. "I can't imagine what it must be like to be frightened. I suppose it's because I'm a man and I can look after myself." He paused. "I'm sorry. That doesn't sound good."

Katie reassured him that he need not worry. "I know that," she said. "And all that I'm saying is that I understand why Clea went cold on the idea of another meeting." She gave William a searching look. "What do you think she should do now?"

William thought for a moment. "Why ask me?" he asked.

"I'm just interested," said Katie. But that, she realised, was inadequate, and so she added, "I can't help but feel that she gave up too quickly. If she had tried harder to find him . . ."

William nodded. "But that's just what I was thinking," he said. "If I were in her position, I would have gone back to that supermarket every day until he returned."

"*If* he returned," said Katie. "He may not have been a regular customer."

William considered this. "I'm only guessing," he began, "but I suspect—and I really don't know if this is true—that most people you see in a supermarket go there pretty often. They live in the area, too—people don't travel long distances to do that sort of shopping."

Katie looked doubtful, but William warmed to his theme. "He'll be a local," he said.

"Possibly," said Katie. But then it still seemed unlikely that Clea would want to spend hours, if not days, loitering in the supermarket in the hope of seeing somebody who may go there only occasionally. "I don't think one could expect her to *stake out* the supermarket. It's just too tall an order."

"But look at it this way," said William. "Let's say that you've just met the person you've been waiting to meet all your life. Let's say you're convinced that this is the one—the person you fancy spending the rest of your life with. How can anything be more important than that? What are a few days spent hanging around a supermarket when weighed against years of potential happiness?"

William frowned, and continued, "I still think she could have done more. Perhaps he said something that might tell us a bit more about who he is. What he does, for example—his job. Did he say anything about that? Where he lives? A single fact—a snippet of information—may sometimes be enough to paint the big picture." He gave Katie an enquiring look. "Did she say anything about any of that?"

Katie shrugged. She did not recall everything about her meeting with Clea, but she did not think that she had gathered any such information. Now she explained this to William.

He did not seem discouraged. "What about a picture?"

Katie was puzzled. "A photograph?"

He shook his head. "No, I'm not suggesting that she reached for her phone and took a photograph." He smiled. "That sort of thing can be a big turn-off."

She waited.

"Have you heard of police artists?"

"The artists who draw pictures of people who are wanted by the police?"

William nodded. "They're sometimes called forensic artists. I knew one back in Melbourne. Her main job was in the fingerprint department, but they used her as a police artist when they wanted to get a likeness based on a witness's description. You've probably seen that sort of thing in the newspapers."

Katie had. *The Scotsman* newspaper had carried a sketch on its front page of a man who had robbed a jewellery store on Princes Street. She had remembered it because it had made the suspect look so like a former moderator of the Church of Scotland—a man whom her father had known for years.

"Yes," she said. "There was one in the paper the other day."

"Well, there you are."

"A man who had robbed a jewellery store on Princes Street."

William nodded.

"Who looked like somebody my father knew who . . ." She

did not finish. It would be too complicated: former moderators of the Church of Scotland were unlikely to rob jewellery stores, of course, but the likeness had been uncanny.

But William had the knowing air of one who was about to produce the answer to a difficult question that had, until then, eluded solution. "She should describe him to a police artist."

Katie smiled. "She may not remember him well enough; she only saw him once, remember."

"Once is enough," countered William. "Most witnesses see whoever it is who's committing the crime for only a few moments. Yet they remember enough to give a good description."

Katie shrugged. "I see two issues. One is where one gets a police artist. Does she go to a police station and ask to speak to their artist? I doubt if you can do that. And then, even if she gets a picture, what does she do with it? Keep it on her wall, like the picture of a . . . well, a lost lover?" She paused. "Do people keep pictures of their former lovers? Or is it all too painful—in most cases?"

Katie spoke without thinking—and immediately regretted the question. "Do you keep a picture of Alice?"

William looked away. *I've been as tactless as I possibly could be*, she thought. She blushed, and muttered, "I'm sorry. That was stupid . . ."

William turned to look at her. *He doesn't mind*, she thought. *He's really doesn't mind.*

"I do, actually. But I'm not sure whether I want to."

For a few moments, they were both silent. Then Katie began, "Maybe you should . . ." And stopped. Having said something tactless once, she did not want to compound her error.

"Maybe what?" asked William.

"Nothing. I was just thinking."

He was looking at her expectantly. "Thinking what?"

She sighed. You could not start off saying, *Maybe you should*, and then leave the suggestion hanging in the air. "I was going to say that you might want to get rid of reminders of her. You don't want to carry the past around forever—particularly when, well, it has painful associations."

She felt that she was making matters worse. He had never actually said to her that he regretted his engagement to Alice. Rather to the contrary, he had acted with remarkable forbearance—assuming, of course, that he knew what Alice had been doing, which, she reminded herself, he might not. Alice had persisted with the engagement even though she had a lover in Melbourne, and had then had the effrontery—no, sheer wickedness, Katie thought, to bring her lover with her to Edinburgh when she came to see William, and then to put him up in a hotel somewhere in Edinburgh. All of that had been at William's expense, and without his knowledge, and it had all been done in pursuit of the continued support she received—for her medical school fees and living expenses—from William's family. When William had brought the engagement to an end, it had been on the grounds that his feelings for Alice had changed—he had decided that the two of them were incompatible. Unless, of course, he had discovered what was going on and had decided to conceal it out of some, completely misplaced, feeling for his former fiancée. That was possible, Katie thought, because William was so generous in his attitudes—even to somebody as calculating and, once again Katie thought of the word *wicked*, somebody as *wicked* as Alice.

He seemed puzzled. "Painful associations?"

If she had spoken spontaneously before, now Katie was more guarded. "Well," she said, "when things come to an end, it can be a bit painful, can't it?" And then she added, hurriedly,

"I'm not saying that is always the case, but it can be. It's natural, of course."

William hesitated. Katie thought: *He doesn't know.* And, of course, if he did not know, there was the issue of whether she should say something to him. She wondered whether it was part of the duty that we owe to friends to pass on to them something that we may know that perhaps they might wish to know. Or should we leave our friends in blissful ignorance when we know something that might end that ignorance, but that they do not necessarily *need* to know?

Now William said, "I might, I suppose." He looked up at the ceiling—that place from which so many of the answers to life's problems seem to come. "Yes, perhaps it's best to forget."

Katie felt a surge of relief. *Oh yes*, she thought, *it's definitely best to forget. Because if you forget, then you can get involved with somebody else.*

"Perhaps," she said. And thought, how restrained. "Yes, possibly. For example . . ."

William brought his gaze down from the ceiling. "Yes? For example?"

"Well, I was thinking of myself. You remember that I was involved with somebody in London."

"Yes, you told me."

"We didn't actually share a flat," Katie said. "But we went out together for quite a long time."

"Sometimes that can be tough," said William. Then, as if he had just remembered something, he said, "I have a friend from back home coming to see me next week. Did I mention that?"

She shook her head. She did not remember his saying anything about it. "Perhaps you did. I don't recall."

"Yes, Andrew and I have been friends for ages."

"He's from Melbourne?"

"Yes. Sometimes it seems that everybody's from Melbourne—at least everybody in my life."

"That's true for all of us," said Katie. "For Melbourne read Edinburgh, in my case. Edinburgh or London. I suppose there are people from other places, but what do they call those close friends? Homeboys?"

"Yes. Friends from the neighbourhood, so to speak."

She waited for him to say something more about Andrew, but he did not. So she asked, "How long is he staying?"

"A couple of weeks. Maybe more. He's travelling."

"Working over here?"

William nodded. "Andrew's an engraver. They're in short supply, apparently. He engraves jewellery, watches, trophies and so on. But he also does glass engraving, which is the artistic end of it. His work is starting to be picked up by collectors, so he doesn't have to worry. There are always people keen to give him commissions—as long as he has access to the equipment—and a studio."

Katie asked whether they had been at school together, and William replied that they had. "We've known one another since we were fifteen. A bit like you and Ell. You knew her at school, didn't you?"

"Yes."

"And you've been friends all along?"

Katie explained that there had been periods during which they had lost touch. They also had their differences, she said. He then asked if Ell had moved in and whether they would get on as flatmates.

"We'll get by," said Katie. "As long as . . ." She did not complete the sentence. She was about to say that things would work provided that Ell did not bring the wrong sort of men into their communal life—and that was always a possibility.

But she did not say that. Instead, she said, "As long as she does her share of washing up."

Then she asked, "Is Andrew going to stay with you next door? In the studio?"

William nodded. "Yes." He frowned. "There isn't that much room, but I'll fit him in somehow. He could live in the kitchen, I suppose. There are some empty cupboards there for his stuff." He paused. "Unless I could find somewhere else for him."

Katie was unsure whether this observation was a request. Ness's flat was large: it had four bedrooms. There would be plenty of space for Andrew there, even now that Ell was moving in.

"I suppose I've got a couple of spare rooms."

William's face broke into a broad smile. "He's very well-behaved. He doesn't smoke. He's terrifically neat—he never leaves things lying about. He can cook. He loves doing the washing up—he *hates* seeing dirty dishes piling up."

They both laughed. Then William asked, "Are you serious?"

"Why not?" Katie replied.

William blew her one of his kisses, but returned almost immediately to their earlier discussion. "If Clea gets a picture, she could show it to the people at the supermarket and ask them if they knew him."

Katie was doubtful. "They probably wouldn't say. And I doubt if she would want to go about showing it to people. They'd think: What's going on here?"

He looked thoughtful. "Maybe. But at least she would be doing something—rather than just giving up."

"Perhaps," said Katie. But she had moved on to something else. She had offered to provide accommodation for Andrew, without really knowing anything about him, other than that he was William's friend. She asked herself now whether she should have discussed this with Ell, who was after all going to be living in the flat too. It would have been more courteous to find out whether she was happy about it, she told herself, as flatmates had to get on with one another. But it was too late: she had made the offer, and William had clearly been pleased. She could hardly turn round within minutes and say that she had changed her mind. Of course, ultimately it was up to her: she had every right to offer a room to Andrew, she told herself: she was Ness's tenant, and Ness had said that she could share the flat if she wished. So, rooms in the flat were within her gift. She had offered a room to Ell, and now, in the exercise of exactly the same prerogative, she was giving one to Andrew. She had no reason to reproach herself. And yet she wondered whether she would have made this offer had the request not been made by William. She had done so because she wanted to please him, and that told her something about how she felt about him—even if she had yet to acknowledge her feelings to herself, which she would have to do at some stage. But for the time being there was the St. Augustine exception: not just yet.

CHAPTER ELEVEN

Meeting Maddy Balquorn

"Horatio Maclean," William said. And then, repeating the name as one might do when exploring the sound of the words, he said, "Horatio Maclean."

"Yes," said Katie. "Horatio Maclean."

William, she thought, looked mischievous, and sounded mischievous, too, when he went on to say, "What sort of name is that?"

Katie shrugged. "A bit old-fashioned, perhaps. There aren't many Horatios around, I suppose."

"There are none in Australia," William said. "At least, none that I know of."

Katie asked if a boy called Horatio would be teased, and William nodded. "Kids are cruel," he said. "They tease you if you have an unusual name. Sirius Persimon was a boy I knew at school. He hated his name, and the bully in our class sensed that. He teased him mercilessly." He paused. "I did nothing, I'm afraid. I should have, but I didn't. I didn't join in the teasing, but I stood by."

Katie reassured him that he was not alone. "We all stood

by," she said. "I don't imagine that there's a single one of us who didn't stand by when we were young. We probably felt relieved that it was somebody else at the receiving end rather than us."

William took a sip of his coffee as Katie talked. She had discovered that he was a good listener, unlike her previous two boyfriends, both of whom had a tendency to talk at great length about themselves and their concerns, showing little interest in what anybody else had been doing. The ability to show an interest in what others had to say was a gift that she particularly appreciated, especially since it was comparatively rare. For most of us, she thought, the class of person in whom we were most interested was ourselves; indeed, for some, we ourselves were the only subject that could engage our attention for any length of time.

"It's about not standing out," said William. "Nobody wants to stand out from the crowd."

Katie considered this. It was easy to come up with a broad generalisation without ascertaining whether there were any real grounds for what one said. William had said that nobody wanted to stand out from the crowd, but she felt there were numerous people who wanted precisely that, and would often pay generously for the privilege.

"There was Horatio McCulloch," said Katie. "He painted Highland scenes in Victorian times. Dramatic mountains and so on."

"So there are precedents?"

"Yes. And Hector was a popular Scottish name. There used to be a lot of Hectors—not so many now, of course."

William winced. "Do we have to have him?" he asked.

"As a client?" asked Katie.

"Yes. Can't we tell him that we don't have anybody suitable for him and that he would be better to go elsewhere?"

Katie shook her head. "No," she said. "It's tempting, but we can't."

"Ethics?"

"Yes."

William sighed. "I suppose you're right. I suppose we'll have to match him up with . . ." He glanced at the filing cabinet behind Katie's desk. "Match him up with somebody from in there."

Katie followed his gaze. "No time like the present," she said, putting her coffee mug to one side. "I'll take a look."

She moved over to the filing cabinet and extracted a file. This was the list of clients that Ness had left behind—names of people who had been active clients of the Perfect Passion Company but who had not been successfully matched up with anybody. "These are the people who might still be interested," she said. "Ness said that they're a mixed bunch."

She had given the file a cursory examination when she had first taken over, and had a vague memory that there was somebody there who fitted the bill. She could not remember the client's name, but what she did remember was a note, in Ness's characteristic handwriting, *Landed gentry! Very good conceit of herself!* The exclamation marks had been significant: Ness believed in meritocracy and had no time for the hereditary principle. "Nobody is born any better than anybody else," she remarked. "We're all Jock Tamson's bairns." It was a powerful and popular expression of Scottish egalitarianism, and it lay behind the occasional note that Katie found in the records. *Jock Tamson*, was the man in the street, the ordinary, average man. *We're all Jock Tamson's bairns* meant that we were all his children—nothing more than that. And, from Ness's comments, Katie could tell that she subscribed to the ethos behind that phrase. *Dreadful snob!* had been written on the cover of one file, and *Name-dropper!* on another.

She opened the file and read out the name of the client: Maddy Balquorn, followed by her address: Balquorn House, near Peebles . . .

William smiled. "That's some address," he said.

And now, approaching the house along the driveway that led up from the winding local road, William pointed to a building just visible through the trees. "That's it over there?"

The house had been built in the early nineteenth century, early enough to embody Georgian proportions rather than those of the Victorian age. As they drew nearer, and the architectural detail of the building became discernible, Katie reverted to her earlier, art gallery self, and drew William's attention to the Palladian proportions to either side of the imposing front door. "Those," she said, "embody the golden ratio. The height-to-width ratio is phi."

She had not expected William to know about that, but he did. He had always been keen, he remarked to her, on the phi number, and its significance for architecture. "And for everything," he went on. "It's in nature, isn't it? The proportions you find in seashells and so on."

"And in paintings by Nicolas Poussin," Katie added. "It's there too. All those static characters in their landscape."

"I love Poussin," said William.

That pleased her, as it was another thing, she thought, that they had in common—an understanding of phi and a feeling for Poussin. Once again William had surprised her, but she reflected on the fact that he had told her he had done three art options at university—along with his main design and textile subjects.

"It's just so *right*," said Katie. "The Victorians became so much *heavier*. Their buildings are often simply the wrong shape."

William was wearing a navy blue blazer. He adjusted the cuffs of his shirt so that now a bare half inch of white protruded from the sleeves of the blazer.

"I'm trying to picture her," he said. "Maddy Balquorn . . ."

"Tell me how you see her," said Katie, as they drew to a halt at the edge of the lawn.

"Tall and forbidding," William began. "Piercing eyes. I think she probably looks down the length of her nose, and doesn't always like what she sees. A disapproving look, I think."

Katie reached forward to turn off the ignition. The sound of the engine died quickly, to be replaced by a sudden silence. This was soon interrupted by a buzz-saw cutting wood somewhere not far away.

"She's average height," said Katie, adding, "whatever that is these days. I don't think I would call her forbidding—at least not in appearance. It may be different when it comes to her behaviour, of course."

"I hope I'm going to like her," said William. "I don't like disliking people—if you see what I mean. I try to start off on the right foot, but you can't feel warmly about absolutely everybody."

Katie understood. William was easy-going, but nobody could be expected to be a saint. "You felt that about Horatio Maclean too, didn't you?"

William did not disagree. "I know. I know I shouldn't make these snap judgements, but I wasn't wild about him."

Katie admitted that she had not met Maddy, but was inclined to trust Ness's judgement. If Ness thought that she had a very good conceit of herself, which was another way of saying that she was pleased with herself—possibly even smug—then Katie felt that she would probably concur.

"But let's not go in having made up our minds in advance," she said. "Think positively, William. If she still wants our help, that is what we should give her."

William chuckled. "It's probably a good idea to hook her up with Horatio," he said. "Two snobs will have a lot in common."

Katie glanced at him. "You need to be serious," she said.

He grinned. "I am."

"Well, I'm not convinced that you are. This isn't a game, you know. This is an intervention in the lives of others—and that's not something to be taken lightly."

He composed his features in a look of suitable solemnity, but, after a few moments, allowed them to relax into a smile.

"Do you want to bet as to whether those two will get on—Horatio and Maddy Bal-whatever?"

"Balquorn."

"Yes, her. Five pounds—I say they'll get on like a house on fire."

Katie hesitated, but eventually accepted. "All right, five pounds that they don't."

"We'll see," said William, and opened the door of his side of the car. Looking at the house, he noticed a movement in a window. "She's watching us," he said to Katie.

Katie looked towards the house. There was a quiet grandeur about it. Not just anyone could live in a place like that, she said to herself: this was a house for landed gentry—and above—exactly the sort of people whom Horatio Maclean might be expected to appreciate and, she imagined, to marry.

They got out of the car and walked across a short expanse of lawn to the front door. A child's scooter lay abandoned on the grass, a spider-web extending from the handlebars to the front wheel, small flecks of airborne detritus caught in its silken guy-ropes.

William pointed to the scooter. "Perhaps we're a bit late," he said. "Perhaps things have moved on."

Katie shook her head. "No. I contacted her. She's expecting us. She knows why we're here."

"And she's still interested?"

"Sort of," replied Katie. "She was a bit guarded, but she said that she had been too busy over the last eighteen months to do much about anything. But she said that things were quietening down a bit. I had the impression that she would not mind another introduction."

William's gaze moved along the sweep of the house. "I've never been in a house like this," he said, his voice lowered.

"We haven't been invited in yet," Katie said, smiling.

He looked disbelieving. "She wouldn't. She wouldn't leave us standing on the doorstep, would she?"

Katie grinned. "Of course not. And, as I told you, she's expecting us."

William looked relieved. "It's just that I haven't lived long enough in this country to know about these things."

Katie looked up, towards the masonry along the edge of the roof. Ornamental stone thistles had been placed at regular intervals on the top of the façade. Above the front door was a carved stone egret, eroded by the effect of the weather on the sandstone. "Sometimes these places are badly eroded," she said.

"Granite is better," William replied.

"But isn't it radioactive?" asked Katie. She thought of the issue in Aberdeen, where granite was widely used as a building stone, and where the cellars of houses were found to be full of radon.

"Not much," said William. "You can run your Geiger counter over it and it hardly registers."

William looked thoughtful. "Everywhere has its risks," he said. "Back in Australia, it's the things that you can step on, or sit down on, or find under the house—spiders and brown snakes and so on. In this country, it's the people you have to watch out for."

Katie thought that people were dangerous wherever one went, but they were now at the front door, and that would be a discussion for another time. Her finger hovered above a large ceramic button with its brass circumference, set into the stone jamb: *Press*. She pressed, and, as she did so, gave William an encouraging glance.

If it had been Maddy Balquorn whom William had seen at the upstairs window, then the intervening time had given her the opportunity to make her way downstairs and open the door for them. Now, as the sound of the bell died away somewhere within, they heard a key engaging with a lock. Then the door opened, and they saw a woman in her mid-thirties, or thereabouts, standing before them. She had an open, friendly face, slightly freckled, and wide hazel eyes. She was dressed in what looked like gardening clothes—loose-fitting trousers and an olive-coloured fleece. She was not dressed for guests.

"I'm a complete mess," she said, adding, apologetically, "I was expecting you a bit later." Her voice was warm.

Katie was quick to apologise. "Oh, I'm so sorry. I thought..."

Maddy interrupted her. "No, I'm sure it's my fault. I didn't look at my diary this morning. I had a time in mind, but . . . well, you know how it is."

Her smile was transformative, and unforced, and it removed

any vestige of awkwardness. Katie now introduced both herself and William. They shook hands.

Maddy's eyes rested on William—just for a few moments, but it was enough for Katie to notice. That happened with William—she had observed it many times before: it was an inevitable human response to the strikingly good-looking. For the most part, those who brought about such a reaction in others were aware of it, of the power they had to attract those whom they met; rarely did they not know. In William's case, though, there was an innocence that seemed to preclude any awareness of the effect that he had on others. It was a characteristic that Katie found particularly appealing—an almost boyish modesty, with a hint of reticence, of shyness. It was almost as if the whole issue of physical attraction was a matter for others—something that he himself was somehow above and could not be bothered about.

Maddy said to William, "You're Australian?"

"William is a knitwear designer," Katie interjected.

Maddy's eyes widened. "Really?"

"Yes," said William. "That's what I do."

Maddy was looking at William with increased interest. "Like Kaffe Fassett?"

The effect on William was electric. "You like his work?" he asked eagerly.

Maddy put a hand against her heart. "Like it? I love it."

William grinned with pleasure. "I wouldn't compare myself with him," he said, adding, "not for one moment. But I try . . ."

Katie interrupted him. "William's work is really beautiful."

"You knit it yourself?" asked Maddy.

"Mostly," said William. "But I do designs for fashion houses. I'll do anything, really."

Maddy wanted to know more. "And you're working in Edinburgh?"

"Yes," replied William. "I have a studio next to Katie's office. You might like to drop in some time. I could show you some of my work."

Katie noticed how quickly Maddy responded to the invitation. With indecent haste, she thought.

"I'd love to."

This conversation had taken place just inside the entrance hall of Balquorn House. Now Maddy led them through the hall into a large drawing room, dominated at the far end by a high—almost too high—fireplace. The room was furnished comfortably, with the chintzy sofas and occasional chairs that are de rigueur for the lived-in country house. There was a large mahogany bookcase against one wall, a writing bureau, and a library table on which had been stacked various books and magazines. A baby grand piano occupied one corner of the room, and on this were ranged silver-framed family photographs, most of them revealing their age in black and white tones. A dog's bed, tucked in beside the bureau, added to the domesticity of what could have been a rather formal room.

"You have a dog?" William asked.

Katie glanced at him. Of course Maddy would have a dog, she thought, and it would be a black Labrador, of the sort that invariably occupied such houses in the country.

"That's Henry," Maddy said. "He's gone to stay with his uncle . . . By that, I mean my brother." She smiled. "He lives over in Ayrshire. His own dog died a couple of days ago, and he's feeling a bit bereft. Henry cheers him up."

"Pet therapy," said William.

Maddy approved of this. "I'd never pay to see somebody about my problems," she said. "An hour with a dog usually works far better than an hour on the therapist's couch."

"Cheaper too," said Katie.

Maddy now turned to William. "Do you like dogs?"

William said that he did. He had been brought up with Sydney Silkies.

Maddy seemed pleased with his answer. "Those are great dogs," she said.

Now she invited them to take a seat while she went off to fetch the coffee. While she was out of the room, William leaned across to say to Katie, "Very nice."

Katie was unsure whether he meant the room, or Maddy herself, or both. He made it clear. "She's very attractive, don't you think?"

Katie hesitated. Maddy *was* attractive, but she felt a pang. She did not want William to find other women attractive, even if his comment was no more than a casual observation.

"Yes, she is," she whispered back. "She's . . ."

She cut herself short. Maddy had reappeared, bearing a tray with a cafetière of coffee and three cups. She put the tray on a low table and started to pour out their coffee. After a few minutes of small talk—the statutory observations on the weather—Maddy launched into an account of a trip she had made to Australia two years before—"One of my favourite countries. The birdsong. The air seemed full of birdsong—all the time. And friendly people."

William basked in the approbation. "It's a great place. We have our little issues, of course."

"Who doesn't?" said Maddy.

Katie raised the reason for their visit. "As I said to you on the phone," she began, "we were going through our files, and I wondered whether you were still interested in meeting somebody."

Maddy did not hesitate. "Yes, I am. Yes, definitely."

It was a quick and unambiguous response, and it took Katie by surprise. Maddy had not been that enthusiastic over the telephone; her reply to the idea had been much more guarded.

"We thought at this stage we would just discuss it in general terms," Katie continued.

"Yes, of course," said Maddy. As she spoke, she glanced at William, even though the response was directed towards Katie.

Katie said, "I'm running the agency on behalf of my cousin while she's in Canada."

Maddy nodded. "So you said."

"And although we have a certain amount of detail in the file," Katie went on, "some of it will be out of date, I expect. I thought that we would start from scratch."

Maddy had no objection to that.

"And it might be a good idea to bring William up to date."

Maddy smiled at William, who returned her smile. "I'm all right with that," she said.

Katie took a sip of the coffee Maddy had handed her. She put down the cup. "Perhaps you could give me a short bio," she said. "Don't worry about the detail—just a summary."

William sat back in the sofa. Katie saw that he was looking intently at Maddy. Once again, she felt a pang of . . . what was it? Envy?

"I married when I was twenty-four," Maddy said. "I wasn't very mature. Nor was he. He was more or less exactly the same age

I was. Hugh. I met him at the Melrose Sevens—you know, the seven-a-side tournament down in Melrose. My father used to go to that every year. He loved it, and he started taking me to it when I was ten. He would have loved to have a son to take, but he didn't—I was his only child. They divorced when I was sixteen. They waited until then, which was considerate of them.

"My mother married a man who had an estate up near Inverness. I opted to stay with my father. I was at school in Edinburgh, and it was simpler. I also felt a bit responsible for him, I suppose. He was a very decent man—a bit vulnerable, I suppose. My mother was harder than he was. More ruthless, I think.

"Anyway, I stayed here with him, and gradually I took over the farm. We have two thousand acres—some of it hill, but quite a bit of arable. We've been here since the seventeenth century. It's a long story. I don't know if any of it would interest you."

Katie thought: This is perfect for Horatio.

"I'd love to hear about it," she said. "Family history is always interesting."

"Provided there's a bit of colour to it," Maddy said. "Sometimes it can be a bit dull—if nobody's done anything."

"Of course," said Katie. "Ours is a bit like that. We never really went anywhere."

"My family didn't go far," said Maddy. "I had an uncle who went to New Zealand, but that was about it. The rest stayed in Scotland. A link with the land, I suppose. A sense of belonging. My grandfather had the earldom—my father was a younger son, and so it went to his older brother, who married into one of those Northumberland families and never came back to Scotland."

Katie noticed the casual way in which Maddy referred to "the earldom." Had William noticed this? she wondered.

He had. "So, he was an earl?" he asked. "Your grandfather was?"

Maddy waved a hand carelessly. "Yes, he was. The eighth earl. There are more ancient titles around, but to reach eight isn't too bad." She pointed to a small portrait above the bureau. "That's him. He looks a bit thin in that picture. Hollow cheeks. I think he had an eating disorder. They're rare in men, I gather, but I think he did."

"I knew a guy who had one," offered William. "They cured him eventually, and he spoke about it a bit. He said that it was his mother's fault for putting pressure on him to do well all the time. He said he lived in a constant state of anxiety."

"It happens," said Maddy.

"You said you got married too young," Katie said.

"Yes. I met Hugh at the Melrose Sevens. He was sitting in front of me with a group of friends. He went out to get something to eat from one of the stands, and I met him when I did the same thing. We got talking. I was struck by his looks. What can one say? He was a helicopter pilot. He came from Melrose. His father was a mechanic who ran a small garage there.

"My father was tight-lipped to begin with. I suppose he hoped that it would blow over, but when it didn't, he came out with it one evening. He said that Hugh was perfectly decent, but that he wasn't what he called *the right sort*. I knew what he meant—of course I did—but I pretended that I didn't. I wasn't going to make it easy for him. He said that Hugh came from a very different background, and that the differences between us would eventually be a problem. I took the usual line that one would expect from somebody aged twenty-four. I said that

Hugh and I loved one another, and that was the important thing. He said that love was all very well, but in the long run it was never enough. There had to be similar interests—a similar outlook. And he kept coming back to the term *background*.

"He was right, of course: there *was* an issue of compatibility. It was staring me in the face, but I didn't see it. You don't when you're in love, do you? Hugh and I lasted eight years—just. He was away a lot, and of course that gave him the opportunity to conduct his affairs. And we just didn't see eye to eye on a whole range of things. He was rude to some of my friends. He didn't fit in with people I had been brought up with. He said that he despised most of them. He accused them of being privileged. He used the words *stuck up*. We were all stuck up, according to him."

Katie made a sympathetic gesture. William shook his head. "Bad," he said.

"Yes," said Maddy. "It was bad." She winced. "However, that's all in the past."

There was a brief silence, eventually broken by Katie, who asked, "Have you been in any relationships since you and Hugh split up?" And she quickly added, "You don't have to say anything about that if you don't want to."

Once again, Maddy's response was quick and open. "One or two," she said. "Nothing special, I suppose. With one, we got fairly close to making a commitment, but he was in the army, and, frankly, I couldn't face the peripatetic life that army officers lead. I sometimes regret that, as we got on very well, but . . ." She shrugged.

"So, you'd like to meet somebody who'd join you here?" asked Katie. "That is, if it got to that stage."

Maddy thought for a few moments. "I suppose so. I don't think I'd like to leave this place."

"Not after three hundred years, or whatever," said William.

Maddy turned to him and smiled. Katie thought that her expression was indulgent—the look of somebody who encourages a younger friend who has joined in a conversation that he or she is not quite ready for. "That's one way of looking at it," she said.

They continued their conversation for a few minutes more. Then Maddy suggested that they might like to look at the walled garden. There was a man in the nearby village who helped her with it—any credit for it should be his, she said. "I grow the most delicious garlic," she said. "This year's crop won't be ready for a few months," she said, "but I can show you a few bulbs from last season. They're superb. Garlic likes plenty of water. I also put seaweed on the beds. I have a friend who brings it over from North Berwick."

"I love garlic," William said. "I eat it with everything."

This seemed to please Maddy. "Good," she said. "That's great."

Katie wondered why it should make any difference to Maddy that William liked garlic.

They walked round the gardens. Maddy showed them the espaliered apple trees, some of which she said were over one hundred years old. There was an ancient fig too. "Nobody knows when that was planted," she said, "although my grandfather claimed that it had provided figs for Bonnie Prince Charlie before the Battle of Prestonpans. I doubt it. But it was possible—we were Jacobites in those days—in fact, my grandfather himself was that way inclined. He was very scornful of the Hanoverians. He called them boot-faced. He had particularly strong views on Queen Mary and George the Fifth. He said that George was completely uneducated and bullied his sons. He said the fact that they both stammered was a result of their abusive father. I doubt if the Stuarts would have been any better. They clung on to the idea of the divine right of kings in spite of everything. Dreadful."

William was interested in the fig. "I love the idea of old trees," he said. "Think of the things they've seen."

"Some trees are a thousand years old," Maddy said. "And more. I think there's a very ancient fig tree somewhere in the East that's said to have been around for two thousand years."

William said that he would like to take a photograph of the fig tree. "I'll just go and fetch my camera from the car."

Maddy waited until he disappeared through the high wooden gate in the garden wall before she turned to Katie. "Very nice," she said.

It took Katie a few moments to realise that she was talking about William. She took a deep breath. William *was* very nice, and she should not find any difficulty in acknowledging the fact. It was a harmless comment—that was all. "Yes," she said. "William's a sweetie."

Maddy laughed. "Delicious," she said. "He's delicious."

Katie felt a tinge of irritation. She did not want to discuss William's attractiveness with this woman who had only just met him.

"So," Maddy continued. "What now?"

"We'll look at our files and see . . ." Katie began, but trailed off as the realisation dawned that Maddy was under the misapprehension that William was there as a potential date. How could she have drawn that conclusion? It was ridiculous. Nobody would imagine that a potential suitor would be allowed to sit in on the taking of a personal history.

It took Katie a few moments to gather her thoughts. Then she said, "Oh . . . I'm sorry. Look, William is my assistant. I should have mentioned that."

Maddy's mouth fell open. "Of course he is. You didn't imagine that I thought . . . Oh heavens, no. All I thought is that he's the *type* I'd like to meet."

Katie smiled broadly. "It crossed my mind, but no more than that." Her smile faded. "William sets the bar rather high, I'm afraid. I'm not sure that we could produce anybody quite that appealing. We are where we are, so to speak."

As she said this, Katie thought: Did Maddy really imagine that she would be a suitable match for somebody like William? There was a difference of more than ten years between them, and although that wide of a gap might count for little later on, when the man is twenty-six and the woman is thirty-eight, it would be, for most people, a matter of remark. But quite apart from that, would somebody like William, with his artistic interests, want to bury himself in the country, in a house filled with chintzy sofas and dog beds? That was unlikely, and, looking now at Maddy, who was blushing, she thought that perhaps she understood that. For a few moments, then, Katie felt a surge of sympathy for this lonely woman with her large Georgian house and her surrounding acres. Wealth often meant so much to those who did not have it, and so little to those who did.

William returned, and went straight off to photograph the Jacobite fig. Katie saw that Maddy avoided looking at him, and William, for his part, seemed quite unaware of the stone that he had thrown into the quiet pond of this woman's existence.

When Katie spoke to Maddy, her tone was as gentle and reassuring as she could make it. "I think we may have somebody who might suit you," she said. "We have in mind somebody who shares your interests."

Maddy looked at her with a certain resignation. "Which interests?" she asked.

"History. Family. That sort of thing."

Maddy thought for a moment. "All right. When will you be able to set it up?"

"Soon," replied Katie.

"That doesn't mean he's desperate, does it?" asked Maddy, with a smile.

"No, he's not desperate . . . and . . ." Katie trailed off.

"Yes?"

"I'm not sure if he's right for you," said Katie. "But see what you feel."

She felt better to have made this qualification. She liked Maddy, whom she thought had probably been a victim of Ness's tendency to make snap judgements. She had not warmed to Horatio Maclean, though, even if she was not as hostile towards him as William seemed to be. She should be strictly professional, she reminded herself: the whole point of the work that she did was to foster happiness in others; it was not to make her feel better in any way. The only question here, then, was whether Maddy and Horatio would get on. She wanted that now—and not for reasons of professional pride.

CHAPTER TWELVE

Anaplasmosis and kindness

It was a real letter, written on paper, folded and tucked into an envelope. The postman had delivered it to the flat on his morning rounds, sandwiched between a circular from a Liberal Democrat councillor. *We have had enough of excuses: Where are the promised nurses?*—and an advertisement from a local Indian restaurant—*our chicken korma is unbelievably good*. Katie opened the envelope and extracted the letter, which was written in Ness's unmistakable handwriting. She sat down and read it, trying to picture the room in which it was penned; a room in Ness's house in that small Canadian town. Ness had said that on Saturdays she could sometimes pick up the smell of barbecues drifting up from the lakeside not far away, where local families picnicked in the summer months. Each hamburger, she had pointed out to Katie in a previous letter, requires six hundred and sixty gallons of water to produce, and each T-shirt, worn by the consumer of the hamburger, requires six hundred. "So, the group of teenagers I saw the other day," Ness had written, "barbecuing burgers by the edge of the lake, represented twelve thousand gallons, more or less, of precious water. How can our world support that burden? And yet, and yet . . . We were teenagers once, Katie—you more recently than I. And we thought of ourselves most of the time, I think. We were selfish, as young people often are. Not all of them, of course, but quite a number."

"Dearest Katie," she read. "You have not heard from me for over a week, and may have been wondering what was happening. Of course, that may not have been the case at all. You have your life to lead and have so much to do rather than wondering about what I am up to over here in Canada."

> I've been doing a bit of thinking. I suspect that many people don't ask themselves why they're taking a gap year. They go because they want to be somewhere else than where they are—and who, when they're nineteen or twenty, doesn't want to be somewhere else. I wanted to see India. I dreamed of being in some hill station, or in an ashram, or buying spices in a Goan market with palm trees in the background—all of that. I never made it. I had to make do with going off to lectures in George Square in the winter when it didn't get light until ten in the morning and the Edinburgh mist, the haar, insinuated itself like wraiths through the streets of the Old Town. Some of my contemporaries—quite a few of them, actually, went off on gap years—several of them actually going to India and coming back with the look in the eye that I call the *I've been to India* look. One went to teach as a volunteer in Morocco. She wrote to me and put her address at the top of her letter, *Rue de Vélodrome, Casablanca*. How I envied her that address! She married a Frenchman and became a commercial pilot. I felt so envious; so excluded from the far more exciting and fulfilling life that I thought everybody else was leading.

Of course, thinking like that is a mistake, because every life—even the most apparently humdrum one—has something of interest in it.

That desire to be somewhere else weakens as you get older. As you get on in life, I believe, you find that you don't want to go anywhere, and are content to stay where you are. I suppose I thought of that before I made the decision to go off earlier this year: it seemed to me that if I didn't do it now, I never would. So, I took the plunge. And it was largely thanks to you that I was able to do it—I would have been reluctant to leave the Perfect Passion Company in *any* hands, but leaving it with you, with family, was a different matter. And I think that choosing you to run the business in my absence was exactly the right thing to do: from what you tell me, everything has been going like clockwork, and you have been pulling off some conspicuous successes. Think of the happiness you've brought to those couples you have successfully brought together. I hope that you are allowing yourself to be proud of what you achieve. We Scottish people are far too reticent about ourselves. We don't like to boast, but you would have every reason to do so. Your work is making a *huge* difference to the lives of those whom you help. Pat yourself on the back for that, Katie—nobody else is going to do that for you. There's nothing wrong with the occasional piece of self-congratulation—as long as it's kept occasional and doesn't become a habit. Too much self-congratulation and you become smug, which is another department altogether. Nobody likes smugness—in fact, smugness is more likely to invite a violent response than any other observable state of mind. I find myself wanting to *pinch* smug people. Or I imagine what it would be like to take a pin and stick it into them, and watch the accompanying deflation. That is so tempting—probably the gravest temptation I have to face in my personal life.

This is an aside, of course, but bear in mind that now that I have told you about these secret desires of mine to deflate the smug, you will know that if you ever hear that I have been arrested for sticking a pin into somebody, you can safely assume that I am guilty and that I did it no matter what my defence lawyer says. But don't worry—so far, I have resisted temptation to do something like that, and the therapist I once consulted said that I never shall. He explained that it's something to do with superstition: you think of things that are quite out of character for you, as a way of reassuring yourself that you will not do them. By thinking of the thing in question, you prevent its occurrence. Clear? It wasn't really clear to me, but it *sounds* convincing.

That, by the way, is how I look at Freud. There's no *proof* for any of Freud's theories—it's all surmise. It's a gorgeous system built up, like an obscure theological theory, on certain givens that you can never really demonstrate. I love reading about it—about Little Hans and the Wolf Man and so on—it's a complete mythology, not unlike classical mythology when it comes down to it. Of course, he believed that classical mythology reflected what was going on in our unconscious, and that if we wanted to understand our deepest concerns and desires, then we should turn to myth to get an understanding of them.

But that is not what I wanted to write to you about. We can talk about Freud once I come back to Scotland . . . I have written *once* I come back. Perhaps I should have written *if* I come back. For something has happened that is making me reassess what my future plans might be; and I feel the last thing I would want to do is to mislead you as to my intentions. When I left, I really did think that it would only be for a year. Now I'm not so sure. The agent of this change is a small, almost invisible tick, that, without my knowledge, happened to bite me and pass on in this way an obscure illness—well, I had never heard of it—called anaplasmosis. If one is going to be ill, Katie, there is much to be said for having something obscure that will interest and entertain one's friends. There is a certain dignity in being on the receiving end of an unusual misfortune.

It all began with a raging fever. The local doctor, an old-fashioned GP straight from central casting, had an idea of what it might be, and his suspicions were in due course confirmed by a blood test. Fortunately, this condition—which hardly ever turns up in Europe—is treated by the same antibiotic they use for Lyme disease—something called doxycycline, bless it. It has done its noble work in my case and I am now restored to health. The memory of the fever is fading, but the same is not true for my recollection of what happened while I was laid low at home. That remains very clear.

Throughout my illness I was looked after by my neighbour. I think I have mentioned him to you before this—he's a man called Herb la Fouche. He's a trapper, believe it or not, which is an old Canadian occupation. I don't like the idea of it, frankly, and Herb himself is beginning to understand the objection that people have to fur. He tells me that he is looking for something else to do and is talking about starting a lawnmower repair business, which is what his father did and what he used to do himself. I have never met anybody who fixes lawnmowers, and I suspect that the same goes for you. One leads such a sheltered life . . .

During the four days I spent in bed, two days of which involved recurring fevers, Herb rarely left the room. At night, he either slept in an armchair in the bedroom or in my living room, from which he came through to check up on me every couple of hours. He insisted that I drink cup after cup of tea—Herb believes in the curative power of tea. He also made bowl after bowl of thick soup, which he laced with strong Tabasco sauce. For hours on end he sat at my bedside reading me *Anna Karenina*, which he says is one of his three favorite novels. The other two, apparently, are *Anne of Green Gables* and *Kidnapped*. He says that he is planning to read another novel when he has the time, and that this will be *To Kill a Mockingbird*.

I cannot begin to tell you how reassuring it was to have him there when I was feeling the full effect of the fever. In the realm of metaphor, people are said to have fevered brows that are mopped by those looking after them. Well, the metaphor, like most metaphors, is based on what actually happens. I had a fevered brow that was cooled by his mopping it with a cold face towel that he fished out of the fridge. He also put small pieces of ice in my mouth, which he said would make me feel more comfortable.

Being looked after by somebody is a moral experience. You may wonder what I mean by that, and I shall tell you. We need to see kindness in action to understand what kindness is. It's the same with love: you can pontificate about love at great length and still not understand what that great and elusive force is. Then you see what love does, and you suddenly realise what lies at the heart of it. And that understanding cannot be taught in the abstract: you have to see how love transforms people; how it comforts and uplifts them; how it heals the divisions and hatreds that we are so adept at creating as we go through life.

I looked at Herb, not just through the lens of the fever, but through the eyes of one who has recovered from a fitful spell of confusion. And what I saw was a very ordinary man—a man whose life was never going to add up to very much—and yet one who could rise to the great moral challenge that all of us face in this life—which is that of caring for another. I looked at him in the light, and I felt ashamed of how I had felt about him before this episode. I had seen him as a rather quaint backwoodsman—a man of little education and even less knowledge of the world. I thought it would be impossible for us to have a meaningful conversation—simply because our interests were so different, his world so much more limited than mine was. In my intellectual arrogance, I thought there would be a whole lot of subjects on which it was not worth our even beginning a discussion, so wide was the gulf between us. I regarded myself as being superior, and that he would never be able to converse with me beyond the level of anecdote. In other words, I assumed an air of intellectual condescension.

Then I happened to ask myself how many of my Edinburgh or London friends would nurse me for days on end, and I answered none. There was nobody like that in my life, try as I might to locate the names of at least one or two such people. How many of your friends, Katie, would come to your bedside and sit there for days on end—and not show any signs of impatience, of wanting to be somewhere else? Herb never gave me that impression—not once.

You will see where this is going. I'm getting to know Herb better. Yes, we do not have a great deal in common when it comes to the books we've read (or failed to read), or music (Herb likes country and western and Cajun music, which has, until now, not featured on my playlist), or art (Herb likes pictures of the Rockies, if possible, or lesser ranges if there are none of the Rockies). But does that matter? What counts, I think, is kindness, and Herb has that in unfathomable quantities. That's what makes him such an unusual man in a world of selfish, self-seeking people, most of whom are only too ready to sneer at others outside their self-satisfied circles. And there's another thing: Herb has started to read about Greek mythology. He's just beginning, but he seems to be enjoying it. So there is something there that we can share after all.

I think that Herb and I are going to see more of one another. Are you surprised? Isn't it interesting how many bourgeois people (sorry, Katie, that is what you and I are) feel uncomfortable about relationships that cross divides—in this case, an educational and cultural divide. Some of these people go on about equality and a class-free society, but do they stick to their own class in these matters? The answer is that they do. So even if you're not shocked you will probably be puzzled that I should take up with this uneducated backwoodsman (literally) who earns his living by setting traps for animals in the snowy wastes of Canada and who has never once read, or even seen, the *Guardian* or the *New York Times*, or even, for that matter, the Toronto *Globe and Mail*.

How can I do it? Good question; but some questions, although they seem to demand a response, are difficult to answer until you are actually there, *in* the question, so to speak, and you realise that what may seem obvious to others, is not always so clear to you yourself. That is why people make choices that, from the outside, may seem unwise, but that are unavoidable—something you just feel you have to do. We don't always ask for the person with whom we fall in love: the other person *happens* to us. Attraction to another person—even if it is short of love—is a bit like lightning. We cannot tell when it will strike and who will be its object.

All my professional life I have tried to match people to those who seem suited to them, given each person's character and interests. And here am I getting closer to a man whose background is completely different from my own. We speak the same language, English, but, even then, our versions of English are so different. He says, "You done good" if I do something well. I never thought I would be particularly close to somebody who was short of auxiliary verbs, appropriate past participles, and necessary adverbs. But that's the old me talking.

It never occurred to me that this was a form of intellectual snobbery. But if it isn't that, then what is it? And why should I not be ashamed of myself? Foolish Ness. (And I never dreamed I would refer to myself in the third person—such an irritating habit—so *arch*, I've always thought, although don't ask me to explain what exactly I mean by *arch*. There are some things, of course, you recognise without difficulty but can't necessarily define—like goodness itself. Have you read Iris Murdoch on the subject of the good? In one of her books she describes a small dog, smuggled into a Quaker meeting, as being composed of pure goodness. That has stayed with me ever since I read the book. I look for it in people, hoping to find it, but rarely do.) Which brings me back to the situation I described, where I lay in my bed of illness and Herb sat by my side, unasked. I had a glimpse of goodness then. I saw it and I knew what it was.

Your devoted cousin,
Ness

CHAPTER THIRTEEN

What people should feel

Over their regular morning cup of coffee Katie and William discussed what to do about Clea. Katie had identified somebody from the files who might be a suitable introduction—a lawyer named Edward Thomas who had consulted them a few weeks earlier and who had called by phone to find out when he might expect his first date. Katie had assured him that they had not forgotten about him, and that a meeting would be arranged sooner rather than later.

"We need to arrange somebody for Edward," said Katie. "He's been on my conscience for the last week or so. I think that he and Clea might click with one another. He's the right age. Right outlook. Solvent. I don't see why not."

William was silent. He was staring down into his mug of coffee.

"You have reservations?" asked Katie.

He shook his head. He had met Edward, and he liked him. He had, in addition to the qualities Katie mentioned, a good sense of humour.

"Of course, Edward has an artificial leg," Katie said.

William frowned. "I didn't know that. Are you sure?"

"You mean you didn't notice?"

William said that he had not.

"He lost it in a car accident," Katie explained. "I'm surprised you didn't notice that he limped. In Scotland we call it hirpling. If you hurt a foot, you hirple."

"Should it make a difference?" asked William. "Do people not want to go out with somebody who has . . . ?"

He hesitated.

"You can say it," she said.

He looked down at the floor. "It seems . . ."

"Insensitive?"

"Yes."

She sighed. "We have to be honest. Edward has an artificial leg. You can call it a prosthetic limb if you like, but the words don't change the situation."

"And it shouldn't make any difference," said William.

Katie hesitated. There was often a difference between what people *should* feel, and what they actually felt. There was no reason, for example, to dislike red hair, but there were some people who did. And the same might be said of any physical characteristic. You could not ignore the fact that people liked or disliked different things, unfair or unjustified though these individual preferences might be.

"Some people might not like it," she said. "They might want a partner with no disability—that might just be the sort of thing they want—in the same way as they might prefer blondes to brunettes, or the other way round. And who are we to tell them they can't think that way."

William shrugged. "No, they should be allowed their views on these things."

"And yet," began Katie.

She stopped. It was a big "and yet."

"And yet what?" asked William.

"And yet, when looked at from the point of the person who is at the receiving end of a preference . . ."

William waited.

Katie struggled. This was an important point, but it was not easy to find the right words to express it. "What I'm saying," she began, "is that if somebody dislikes you for something about you that you can't help, you feel that they're doing you a wrong—you just do. People should—"

William interrupted her. "People *should* . . . You're about to say what people should do—not what people are actually like—what they *feel*."

Katie hesitated. He was right—but was that not the way we all thought? We expected things of people because we had to. That was what held us together as a community, as a society: an expectation of certain behaviour.

She gave a general answer. "We all have ideas about what other people should do. We have to think like that. All I was saying is that people shouldn't put too much store by things that don't matter—and that means how they look."

She said that, but even as she spoke, she wondered whether she believed it. She glanced at William. Would her feelings for him change if he suddenly lost his looks? Why did beauty make a difference if what mattered was the inner person? And money . . . what difference did that make?

William persisted with his point. "Yes, okay. But let's say that I'm skinny and somebody says they don't like skinny people. Am I entitled to expect them to like me?"

"No. But you'll feel offended if they never give you a chance. You'll think it's unfair."

He thought about this. "I'd be entitled to expect them not to *treat* me badly—just on the basis of their dislike of skinny people?"

Katie said that she thought he would be entitled to think that.

"So, this guy with the artificial leg . . ."

"Edward Thomas," supplied Katie.

"Yes, him. He wouldn't be entitled to complain if Clea said to you, *I don't want to go out with a one-legged man*—is that so? Because it's so . . . so brutal? So tactless?"

"In practice," Katie said. "In fact, the way to deal with that would be for me to say to her in advance, *Look, we have this client who has a disability: How do you feel about that?*"

It occurred to William that Clea might be reluctant to say that she did not want to meet him. "She might not want to be thought to be discriminating," he said. "I think a lot of people would say, *That's fine*, because they think that's what they're supposed to say. Whereas in secret they might be saying to themselves, *The last thing I want is somebody with a disability.*"

Katie admitted that this was possible. "People have become very guarded," she said. "They don't want to say anything that will have them branded as insensitive." That was true, she thought: we live in times when there is very strong pressure to be accepting. And there was a reason for that, she thought. It was because we understood how dangerous our feelings about others could be; how easily we could slip into hatred and division.

"Maybe it's all about kindness," she said.

He stared at her. Then he smiled, as might one who had been given a glimpse of a solution to some knotty problem. "I think you're right. Kindness. Yes, kindness." He uttered the word with what almost amounted to awe—as if it were a shibboleth, capable of unlocking a future.

She returned his gaze. Of course, you're kind, she thought. And like all, or many, kind people you do not spend time contemplating your own kindness—you simply do it. You *do* kindness with all the naturalness of those who act out their nature.

She brought the conversation back to Clea. "I'll ask her about Edward," she said. "But I'll make sure that she won't be embarrassed if she would prefer somebody else." She paused. "You never know how people will react."

"And then?" asked William.

"And then we'll find somebody." She pointed towards the filing cabinets in which the details of the agency's clients were kept. "There are at least thirty men in there who might be suitable."

William looked thoughtful. "I think we should try to help her in another way altogether."

Katie waited for him to explain.

"Let's help her find the man she met."

Katie's immediate reaction was to shake her head. "That's not what we do. We're not private investigators, or anything like that. No, I don't see myself doing that at all."

William's response came quickly. "You don't have to do anything," he said. "I'll do it."

"But . . ."

He was ready for her objection. "I'll go to see her," he said. "I'll speak to her about it. I'll see what she feels."

"We already know what she feels," Katie pointed out. "She's made it clear enough. She wants to meet somebody else."

William hesitated—but only briefly. "Just let me have a go," he said. "I don't see what harm there could be in my trying to find him."

Katie struggled to reach a decision. There was, she thought, a strict limit to what the Perfect Passion Agency could offer its clients, and this, she thought, went well beyond that. But she did not have the heart to deny William the opportunity to help. She had encouraged him to become involved in the work of the agency, and now he was merely carrying that initial involvement to its conclusion. He was doing it out of kindness, she realised, and kindness should not be thwarted.

"All right," she conceded. "Have a word with her. But don't cajole her."

William put on an expression of injured innocence. "Me? Cajole anybody?"

Katie smiled. She thought: You don't need to cajole anybody—not you. You have only to look at them. You have only to stand there and let people become aware of you, of your presence, and they will instantly give in. Of course, they will. That was William, and the miracle of it was that he had walked into her life; that he had chosen to spend time with her; and yet he was not in any sense *hers*. Not yet, anyway.

Clea had not shown any surprise when William called her to introduce himself and ask if they could meet. She suggested that he come to her office, late the following afternoon. "I'm free at four," she said. "If that suits you." She paused, and before he could say anything else, she asked, "Just you?"

William replied that he worked closely with Katie, and that she had authorised him to deal with some matters connected with the approach she had made to the agency.

"You've found somebody?" she asked. There was eagerness in her voice.

"Not exactly," said William. "In fact, no. But we've been thinking about things."

He could tell that she was disappointed, and he reassured her that Katie was optimistic. "And she's quite successful," he added. "Nobody's guaranteed a match, but things often work out."

They rang off on that note.

William liked to be punctual and was outside Clea's office several minutes before the agreed time of four o'clock. It was in a quiet street in Newington, a South Side suburb that was mainly residential but was home to various small concerns: estate agencies, family firms of decorators, and antique dealers. A discreet notice beside a bell button announced Clea's reception, and when William pushed this, an outer door was buzzed open from within. A shared stone stairway led up to three landings, each bordered by ironwork railings. Clea's door was on the first floor, and was already open by the time William reached the landing.

He smiled at her, and she reached out to shake his hand. "I hadn't expected . . ." she began, and then stopped herself. She seemed embarrassed.

He quickly put her at her ease. "The messenger boy?" he asked, and laughed.

"I would never call you that," she said quickly.

"I help Katie out," he said. "I have a studio next to her office, and I find I spend a lot of time in her office." He shrugged. "I work by myself, you see, and it gets a bit lonely."

She asked him what he did, and he told her. Did she know the work of Kaffe Fassett?

"Of course I do," she said. "You do that sort of thing?"

He nodded.

"You're not Scottish?"

He was used to this: an Australian accent almost inevitably prompted that question.

"I'm Australian. But I'm a bit Scottish and a bit Irish from a long time ago—just like almost everybody else round here."

She led him through a small reception area into a room furnished with a desk, easy chairs, and a large bookcase. On one wall there were several paintings and a couple of framed certificates. He saw on one of these certificates the easily recognised crest of the University of Edinburgh.

She offered him coffee, which he declined.

"I can do you tea," she said.

He accepted, and she made her way to the side of the room to switch on a kettle. As she made the tea, she spoke to him over her shoulder. She had visited Queensland, she said—there had been a cognitive therapy conference in Brisbane that she had attended a few years ago. She wanted to go back to see other parts of the country.

She brought him a cup of tea, and settled herself in an armchair facing his.

"Usually, when I sit here," she began, "it's the person sitting opposite me who has the problem. This time, it's me."

He laughed. "Oh, I have plenty of issues," he said. "I think we all do." He paused. "I expect you'd blame my mother if I told you everything. Isn't that what you decide at the end of the day: mother's fault?"

"If I thought you were serious, I'd take offence," said Clea.

"But there must be some cases at least where it *is* mother's fault?"

"Some," she said. "But there are plenty of other reasons for unhappiness."

"I'm not unhappy," said William. "Or at least, not as far as I know."

"You're lucky," said Clea. "Less than half the population thinks it's happy. That's a lot of unhappy people."

For a few moments, they looked at one another appreciatively: William at her because he sensed her intelligence; she at William because he was a young man with a pleasing, sympathetic manner, and the appearance of Adonis.

William broke the silence. "Katie told me."

She waited.

"She told me," he continued, "how you'd met this man at the supermarket."

Clea looked embarrassed. "Oh, that was some time ago. Last year. I'm not really thinking about that any longer."

William fiddled with the cuffs of his jacket. Clea watched. She thought: He's nervous. She sought to reassure him. "I don't mind talking about it. I know I may come out of it seeming a bit . . . well, foolish, I suppose. But we all miss our chances, don't we? Some time or other we do things we regret."

William hurried to tell her that he understood. "I'd have done the same thing myself," he said. "You find yourself having to make a quick decision, and you do the wrong thing."

"Well, I did it, and that was that." She paused. "Of course, I shouldn't assume that it would all work out. We were only in one another's company for an hour."

William said that an hour was long enough. "Sometimes you just know," he said. "You meet somebody and you think: This is the person I want to spend the rest of my life with. You feel it; you just do. And sometimes, you'll be right. Not always, of course, but sometimes."

Clea smiled. "I think that's true. Of course, I spend a lot of my time sitting in this room listening to people telling me about their impulsive decisions and how those have affected their lives. And I help them to realise that they must be more cautious. And yet here I am doing exactly what I tell others not to do."

William remembered a story. "There was a German professor—I forget who he was, but I read about him somewhere. He had something to say in favour of hypocrisy . . ."

Clea laughed. "Hypocrisy gets a bad press, doesn't it?"

"Mostly," agreed William. "But this German professor pointed out that street signs don't travel themselves in the direction they point in."

It took Clea a moment or two, but then she claimed, "Of course!" She looked at him in admiration. "That's very funny."

"But true, don't you think?" said William. "A smoker may tell other people not to smoke—and mean it. He's being hypocritical, but there's no reason why he shouldn't give that advice, is there?"

Clea said that she was not sure that this was hypocrisy. "If he said, *I don't smoke, and so you shouldn't* . . . That's hypocrisy—because he isn't telling the truth. But he isn't saying that, is he?"

William started to fiddle with the cuffs of his jacket once more. "I was going to suggest something," he said. "I hope you don't mind, but I think you shouldn't rule out finding that man you met."

She frowned. "But it was a long time ago."

He countered this. "A year isn't all that long."

"I won't be able to," she said, in a tone of resignation. "I went back to the supermarket, you know. I felt so foolish—sitting there, pretending to read a magazine, but actually looking for him—in case he came in again, and we would be able to have coffee together. Can you picture it? It was a bit pathetic."

He glossed over her protestation of embarrassment. "No,

I don't think so. Not at all." He paused before continuing, "I wondered if you'd let us help you find him? You came to us to get us to find somebody after all—well, can't we try to find *him*? After all, you know that you like him. So why go off and meet somebody else when you already have someone."

She looked at him with amusement. If he had feared a negative reaction to his suggestion, this was not what happened. "Except the someone you refer to . . . well, I don't have him, do I?"

William was not to be deterred. "Could we get a picture of him?"

Clea looked at him with puzzlement. "I don't see how—"

He interrupted her. "You know those pictures that you see in the newspaper? The police are looking for this man—and then there's a drawing—all done on the basis of descriptions given by witnesses."

This brought laughter. "You're not serious."

He assured her that he was.

"But what's the point?" she asked. "Even if we had a picture, what would I do with it?"

He was ready for this. "I could take it to the supermarket. I could ask the staff there if they knew him." He watched to see her reaction; she was clearly unconvinced. He ploughed on. "Or nearby coffee bars. The baristas get to know their customers."

She shook her head. "They'd be suspicious. It wouldn't work."

He looked wistful. "I really think it's a good idea. I really do."

She softened. "Do you think so?"

"Yes."

She asked who would do the drawing. He hesitated slightly.

"I did art and design at uni—as well as my textile courses. I can draw. I'm not Leonardo da Vinci, but I think I can get a reasonable likeness."

She considered this. She felt that there was something irresistible about this young man, and he wanted to help her. Why not?

"All right." And then she added, "When?"

William shrugged. "Right now?"

They talked as William drew. She asked him about his work, and about how he had become involved with Katie's agency. He told her about how he had recently been approached to do an exhibition at a gallery in Edinburgh, with a promise that the show would be taken on to Milan and then Copenhagen. "Not that there's any pressure," he added, with a smile.

She looked at the sketch that was emerging on the pad of paper he had brought with him. "The head's the wrong shape," she said. "He had a higher forehead. No, not that high . . ." And, "The hair's not quite right. Make it shorter on that side." He worked quickly, and the sketch took shape. He held it up to her, and she looked at it thoughtfully. "Maybe," she said. "Yes, maybe that looks like him . . . a bit."

He sighed. "I could start over again."

She hesitated. "Perhaps the problem is that I've forgotten the details. You meet somebody and you forget what their ears looked like. Or their nose. You don't necessarily pay attention to these things when you're having a conversation."

"No, I suppose not."

She looked at the sketch again. "On the other hand, it's not really *unlike* him."

"No?"

"No. It could be him, I suppose."

William put the drawing into his bag. "I'll see what I can do with it," he said. "It's better than doing nothing." He paused. "Could we just go over what happened once more? Just in case?"

She made a gesture of acceptance. She did not think that there was anything that she could add to what she had already told Katie, but she did not mind talking about it again.

"What sort of day was it?" asked William.

She looked surprised. "What's that got to do with it?" she asked. "We were inside. It's not as if we were in a pavement café somewhere."

"It's just to help you get back to that particular day," explained William. "If you describe what was going on about you—what the weather was like, for instance—then that might help to bring it all back to you. That's all."

She looked up at the ceiling. "What sort of day was it?" she mused. "Let's think."

"Sunny?" he prompted. "Wet? One of those cold Edinburgh winds coming in from the North Sea?"

"Or a warm wind from the south-west, from the hills, smelling of gorse, and heather . . ."

He smiled. "Does heather smell?"

"It should do," she said. "It should smell of purple, don't you think?"

"Ah!" William said. "Synaesthesia."

She was about to respond to this when she suddenly frowned. "No, I remember now: it was quite a warm day. Yes, it was—because I was wearing a shirt that I often wear on warm days. It's made of particularly light linen, and it's the coolest thing I have. I was wearing that, and yes, I remember that it was sunny as I walked down Morningside Road. There were children eating ice creams. I remember that clearly. They had ice cream all over their faces."

William laughed. "That's what happens to me when I eat an ice cream. I get it all over everything." He paused. "Did you tell Katie this?"

"About the ice cream? No. Why should I?"

He said it did not matter too much. "Let's go on."

"I went shopping. I told her that."

"And then," said William. "After the shopping?"

"I got my token for the coffee machine at the check-out desk, and I sat down at the place they have for you to sit down and drink it. Then he came and sat down next to me."

"Did he introduce himself?"

She shook her head. "Nothing that formal."

"But he gave his name?" William paused. Katie had not told him what this man was called. That, he thought, was odd.

Clea looked sheepish. "No, he didn't. And so, I don't know what he's called. Katie didn't ask me."

William was disappointed. "It would have been helpful even to have just his first name."

"Well, we were talking so much," Clea said, "that I suppose we didn't have time. And we would have given it when we exchanged phone numbers—if we had done that."

William found himself marvelling at the thought: here was somebody who had been convinced that she had encountered her soul-mate and yet had not asked him his name. That seemed almost absurd—and yet, did a name matter all that much? You liked the person for what he or she was—not for the name or for . . . He stopped himself, remembering his English teacher at school, who had read Yeats to the class on those hot Wednesday afternoons when they had a longer than usual English period; and he had said that Yeats was absolutely right about how Anne Gregory would always be loved for her yellow hair and not for herself alone. The lines had stayed with him when the rest of Yeats had gone.

Now he asked, "What did you talk about?"

"I don't really remember many details," said Clea. "It was one of those conversations that drifts around so naturally. It was very easy."

"Did he tell you what he did? Did he tell you where he worked?"

Clea thought for a moment. "No, I don't think he did. He said that he had to go to France from time to time—to Lyons, I think. I assumed that was work, but I didn't ask him." She looked abashed. "I know that sounds odd, but it was such an unusual meeting. We had something special—you might say. It was . . ." She was struggling, and William felt the need to reassure her.

"I can imagine what it was like," he said. "I really can." He paused. "So, you talked for an hour?"

She nodded. "Thereabouts."

"And you say you can't remember the details. All right, but is there *anything* you can remember."

Clea did not reply immediately. Eventually, she said, "He said that he cooked. He said something about the cookery books he used." Her brow furrowed as she reached into the recesses of memory. "I think he said that he liked Ottolenghi. Yes, he did, actually. He said that he had been to Jerusalem and had discovered Palestinian cuisine. We talked about that a bit—about how Ottolenghi, who's Israeli, and his Palestinian friend, Sami Tamimi, had been an example of how people could overcome differences. They wrote those cookery books together. I remember that now."

"Anything else?" William encouraged her.

Clea shook her head. "Nothing comes back. There must have been more, but I'm afraid that . . ." She trailed off.

William sensed that something was coming back to Clea. "Yes?"

"He said that he had bought oranges," said Clea. "Yes, I remember now. He had a big bag of them at his feet. I noticed them and asked him about them. He said they were Seville oranges."

William asked if there was anything special about Seville oranges. "Are they any different from Florida oranges?"

"They're very different," replied Clea. "They're bitter. They have a very high pectin content."

"Is that the stuff—"

Clea interrupted. "Yes, pectin thickens. That's why Seville oranges are used for making marmalade. Anybody who wants to make good marmalade will use them."

It was the mention of marmalade that triggered the recollection. "Yes!" Clea exclaimed. "He said that he made marmalade. I'd forgotten about that."

"Well, that's something," he said. He did not think, though, that it helped in any respect. The person they were looking for made marmalade, but that hardly helped very much. Hundreds of people in Edinburgh made marmalade—perhaps thousands. Marmalade was a Scottish speciality—they were in the marmalade latitudes, so to speak.

William sighed. "Anything else?" he asked.

Clea looked apologetic. "I wish I could say that I remembered more, but I don't. Sorry."

Their conversation drew to a close. On the way back to his

studio, William thought about what his visit had achieved. It was not very much—he had a rough sketch which might, or might not, look a little like the object of their search; they knew that he enjoyed cooking; they knew that he made marmalade. Apart from that, they were still in the dark.

CHAPTER FOURTEEN

Katie drops in on William

Katie looked at her watch. The only occasions on which William was late in coming through from his studio to make morning coffee were when he had a client in. She knew that he had no clients that morning—he had told her he was free all day, and would be catching up on a piece he had to finish by the end of the week. "It's for a very demanding client," he said. "She thinks she should have priority in everything—and I mean *everything*. If the Grim Reaper were to turn up, complete with shroud and scythe, she'd elbow everyone out of the way and say, *Me first*. I'm sure of it—she's that sort."

But William was now fifteen minutes late, and Katie was beginning to feel uneasy. Whenever anybody failed to turn up when expected, she tended to think the worst. William sometimes rode a bike—he kept it in the hall downstairs, and it had not been there when she came in that morning. She knew, though, that he lent it to a neighbour who had a grandmother in Ratho and used it to ride out there along the canal path to see her. But what if he had gone for a ride himself that morning, as he often did, and had been hit by a car. There had been a report in *The Scotsman* newspaper of an incident a week or two ago of a cyclist's front wheel getting stuck in a tram line—they were recessed in the road surface. He had been thrown off his bicycle into the path of an oncoming vehicle. She had shown it to William and told him that he should be careful—but perhaps he had forgotten her warning. William was a bit dreamy—it was part of his appeal—but it made him vulnerable. And that was part of his appeal too, she thought, in a moment of frank self-understanding. Women like men they feel they have to look after—and I am no exception, she thought.

She went over in her mind the conversation she and William had just before he went off to see Clea. They had talked about his visit to her, of course, and about what he hoped to find out, and then he had gone on to say something about his clear day ahead and the client who thought the world revolved around her. Then he had told her that he had heard from his friend Andrew, who had been in touch to say that he would be arriving in two days' time. He was in France for a few days, William said; he was a climber, and there was a mountain in the Pyrenees that he and some fellow Australians had tackled. They were now spending a day or two in Pau before going their separate ways. Had he mentioned anything else that might explain why he had not come in to make coffee? She did not think so.

She stood up and began to make her way towards the office door. But then she stopped, turned round, went back to her chair, and sat down again. She recognised her behaviour for what it was: this was how you acted if you were in love with somebody. It was a form of complete obsession in which anxiety and longing combined to make you jumpy. You paced about. You looked out of the window and thought of the person you loved. You could not get him out of your mind. Time hung heavy when he was not there, and you did not know how to pass it. When he was there, it flashed past, the hours no more than minutes.

She was ready to admit to herself that she was in love with William. She would accept that, but she did not want to make herself miserable over it. She would try to keep some sort of distance between herself and her feelings for him—out of self-preservation, if for no other reason. It was only too easy to find that soon there was no room for anything in your life but thoughts of the other person. She would not allow that to happen to her with William; she would not. And, of course, he had said that he was not interested in another love affair just yet. She had no reason to believe that he did not mean it, and yet, and yet . . . The whole point about love was that you could not inoculate yourself against it. You could be grimly determined not to fall for anybody, and then it simply happened to you, however firm you thought your defences were. You fell in love . . . and the word *fall* was important there: you did not control whether or not you fell into anything—falls happened because of gravity. And perhaps there was gravity at work in love too: the gravitational force was something deep within us, some destiny encoded somewhere in our genes that made us fall in love with others in response to simple biological imperatives.

She stood up again. She could not bear it. She had to go to check up on William. She had to go round to his studio door and listen to see if she could hear if he was there. Perhaps he was on a long telephone call and had lost sight of the time. There was bound to be a simple explanation like that.

She went out onto their shared landing. She stood outside his door. She listened, without putting her ear to the keyhole or anything ridiculous like that. She just stood there and listened.

She thought she heard a noise within. A voice. And then laughter—or what sounded to her like laughter. Then there was silence for a few moments before a voice could be heard again—a voice that did not sound like William's.

She hesitated, and then stepped forward and rang the bell. When William came into her office to make coffee in the mornings, or indeed on other occasions too, he did not bother to knock—he simply came in. Now, without really thinking about it, she did the same—immediately after she had pressed the bell.

The door was not locked. She pushed it open.

William's studio, being so small, had no entrance hall. The outer door opened straight onto his main workroom, which also served as a general living room.

William was sitting on the sofa—an old piece of furniture that he had bought at an antique warehouse in Leith, covered with a throw that looked as if it was of his own design. Next to him was a young man of much the same age as him. They both looked at Katie with surprise—as if they had been interrupted in an exchange of confidences.

Katie saw that the young man had an arm resting on William's shoulder—not quite round it, but upon it. As her eyes went to his arm, the young man dropped it.

William quickly overcame his surprise. He smiled at Katie.

"Well, good morning," he said. He glanced at his watch. "Oh my God, look at the time. I'm sorry—I wasn't thinking."

William's friend was looking at her. His expression had

been impassive when she came in; now he smiled at her. She noticed the whiteness of his teeth. She noticed his tanned skin. He looked at her, and then looked back at William, as if to ask who she was.

William rose to his feet. After a moment's hesitation, his companion did the same.

"This is Andrew," William said. "Andrew, this is Katie."

Andrew stepped forward and offered his hand. Katie took it. She thought: This is the hand that has been on William's shoulder. It felt warm and dry. The skin was smooth.

"Katie's the person who offered to put you up," William said. "She's my lovely neighbour."

Andrew smiled at her again. Now she noticed his grey eyes. She thought: He looks just like William: they could be brothers. But Andrew had a dimple on each cheek, which William did not. She looked away, as if she had inadvertently stared at the sun.

"That's really kind of you," said Andrew.

William began an explanation. "Andrew wasn't going to arrive until the day after tomorrow," he said. "But he pitched up this morning. I was going to come round to tell you." He paused, and gave Katie an enquiring look. "If it's inconvenient, he could stay here for a day or two—before he goes to your place."

"It's not inconvenient," Katie said quickly. "It makes no difference to me."

She was thinking of what she had seen and wondering what it meant. It was not only the fact that Andrew had his hand on William's shoulder—it was the fact that he had moved it when she came in. It was as if he felt embarrassed, even guilty over being interrupted in a moment of intimacy.

Yet people put their hands on the shoulders of others, and it meant nothing—or at least nothing beyond some incident of friendship.

William brought Andrew round to Katie's flat late that afternoon. They told her after morning coffee that they would be going out to lunch, and she had watched them from her window, setting off down the street. William had looked up and had seen her before she had time to draw back. He had waved, and Andrew had turned round to look up and had raised a hand in a form of mock salute. Katie felt herself blushing, and wondered what Andrew would think of her. Not only had she burst in on them earlier on, but now she was apparently spying on them, as might an inveterate curtain-twitcher. It was hardly a good start.

She stayed where she was at the window, hoping to give the impression that she was not watching them, but was simply looking out on the world in a moment of pensiveness. People did that—they looked out over the street from time to time to break the routine of sitting at a desk. And when Andrew looked back again, as he did a few moments later, she managed to gaze out over the other side of the street without meeting the glance directed upwards.

She returned to the flat at three o'clock, intending to ensure that everything was ready for Andrew. When she arrived, Ell was in—she worked from home two days a week, or purported to, as Katie often found her either asleep on the sofa in the living room, papers on the floor beside her, or conducting a phone conversation that did not sound particularly work-oriented. "You may think I don't do very much when I work in the flat," Ell had said. "But you'd be wrong. My job involves a lot of intelligence gathering, and then moments of intense activity when I shift funds around. What you're seeing here is the entr'acte. Don't you love that word? *Entr'acte.*"

Ell worked for a firm of investment managers. She specialised in an obscure corner of the market that for the most part fluctuated very little. Every so often, though, a drought or a distant conflict changed the pattern of economic activity, and Ell would burn midnight oil in the preparation of reports for colleagues.

Katie had told Ell that Andrew would be staying for a while, and she had said that she was sure he would fit in. "It's a pity that William won't come too," she said, giving Katie a mischievous glance.

Katie had seen the effect that William had had on Ell on the occasion they first met. At that time, William was engaged to Alice, and Katie had warned Ell off. Now, of course, that was no longer the case—but she had not told Ell about the change in William's circumstances. Ell was a flirt, and Katie was convinced that William would not respond to any advances from her. Besides, William had told her that he wanted a period of non-involvement, and if she were to do anything to keep Ell from him, then that would clearly be out of consideration for William. Of course, it was . . . Unless, of course, she were to be completely honest and admit that it was for her own reasons—because she felt the way she did about him, and she did not want Ell, or anybody else, to get in her way. Aren't we all, ultimately, concerned about ourselves and *our* needs? That is what she asked herself as she now said to Ell, "No, I wouldn't want William to stay. He's not available."

"Of course not," said Ell. "He's engaged. I know that. I wasn't being serious."

Katie said nothing. Ell was looking at her as if she expected a response.

Katie corrected her. "*Was* engaged."

Ell raised an eyebrow. "Oh, I see." And then went on, "I'd really like to dream about him you know. I try to dream of attractive men I meet, but it doesn't seem to work. You drift off to sleep saying to yourself, *Dream of him, of him, of him* . . . and you end up having some dream about being at a party in your pyjamas or writing an examination in a subject you've never studied. Do you have dreams like that?"

Katie nodded. "Insecurity dreams. We all have them."

"Because at heart we're all anxious about being found out?" asked Ell.

"Possibly. I suppose we all have to do a bit of acting—just to get through life."

Ell considered this. "I don't think I do. I hope that what you see is what you get. And I think William's like that. I had the impression he was—how should I put it?—absolutely genuine. All there. Lovely." She paused. "So, you met Andrew this morning?"

"I did."

Ell looked at her expectantly. "And?"

"I liked him. He seemed . . ."

"Well?"

"He's nice."

Ell gave her a sideways look. "Nice is such a tiny word." She held up a thumb and forefinger separated by a fraction.

"All right, very nice then."

Ell laughed. "I'm in a mood to meet a very nice Australian."

Katie became purposive. "I'd better check on his room. I want him to feel at home."

"Don't worry," said Ell. "I'll make him feel welcome."

Katie looked at her. Ell was an old friend from school days, and such friends have particular claims on one. Would she have chosen her as a friend if she met her now? She was not sure. There was something in her manner that made Katie feel uncomfortable. It was not an attractive quality, she thought; to be constantly aware of other people as possible . . . what was the word? Targets. Possible *targets*.

CHAPTER FIFTEEN

Cheese empanadas

Over the next three days, Katie found herself busier than usual. There was a sudden influx of new clients—a result of an article that had appeared in *Scottish Field* featuring Katie and the work of the agency. The tone of the piece had been upbeat, implying that anybody who consulted the Perfect Passion Company was more or less assured of finding somebody. This was not because the writer of the article had any intention of misleading—it was more a concomitant of her natural optimism. The effect, though, was to trigger a deluge of telephone calls and emails, each asking for an early appointment. Katie was working her way through these and had, within days, accumulated thirty-two new clients. Each of these would need an introductory meeting that would last an hour, and would require a new file, with all its attendant paperwork. The balance of the sexes was another issue: twenty-four of these new clients were women, and only eight were men. This was good news for the men, even if depressing news for the women, but it did not surprise Katie. "It's demographic," Ness had said to her during one of their discussions. "We are subject to demographic factors—which means, in plain English, there are insufficient men. Men die, you see, Katie. It's most unfortunate, but men have a habit of dying rather earlier than women."

Ness had gone on to say that the male mortality rate was higher because men faced more risks. "That's an important factor. Employment patterns are different. It's changing, of course. In the past, men used to go down the pits, for example, or out to sea on fishing boats—both highly dangerous places to be."

Katie winced. "And children too," she said. "They put eight-year-olds down the pits, hauling coal. Can you believe it?"

"I certainly can," said Ness. "And child labour still exists in some places. Brick factories in India. They use bonded labourers—virtual slaves. You work for years to pay off your grandfather's debts." She looked down at Katie's trainers. "Are you sure you know who made those?"

Katie frowned. "No."

"Or that shirt you're wearing? Made where—and by whom?" Ness made a gesture of hopelessness. "The world is a sea of suffering and exploitation. It always has been, I suppose, but that doesn't make it any easier to bear." She sighed. "But back to men and women: the women survived them because their work was different. But even today, when the pits are closed and the trawlers are bigger and safer, men still put themselves in the way of harm more than women do. Men drive faster. They can't resist motorbikes—how many women do you see roaring around on motorbikes? We have so much more *sense*, Katie."

Katie had often thought that a motorbike would be fun— but did not say that now.

"And men get stressed for all sorts of reasons," Ness went

on. "They live faster, and shorter, lives. And I'm sorry to say they take their own lives much more often than women do. Three times more often, as it happens. Three-quarters of suicides are male."

Now, seated at her desk, with the morning sun, thick, like yellow butter, streaming in the window behind her, Katie looked at the list of appointments that would begin the following week. Each of these people, she reflected, would be hoping for something from her—wishing for some miracle to transform their lives. Behind each name on the list would be a hinterland of yearning and disappointment; of hopes unfulfilled or unrealised, only to be dashed by selfishness, or incompatibility, or sheer misfortune. All of these people would be hoping to find somebody to appreciate them, to keep them company, to satisfy the need that we all had, that grave, insistent need, to be loved by another. She hoped that she would be able to help at least some of them, but she knew that in some cases anything she might try would only pile disappointment upon disappointment—like Pelion upon Ossa, as Ness might say. She had learned what Ness had meant when she said, "This is a calling, Katie. It's not a job: it's a calling." She was right.

William had told her that he would not be in for coffee that day, just as he had not been in on the two days prior to that. She had tried hard not to react to this news, and had asked casually, as if she were not really interested in the answer, what he would be doing. It was not easy for her to pretend not to want what she wanted, at that moment, more than anything else: to have him *for herself*.

"I'm showing Andrew Edinburgh," he said. "It's the Portrait Gallery today. I thought we'd have lunch there or even go down the hill to Valvona & Crolla."

Andrew, she thought. Why *Andrew*?

She made a supreme effort. "Wonderful," she said.

"Andrew can cook," William went on. "Back in Melbourne, he used to make superb cheese and onion empanadas. We used to pig out on them sometimes."

She tried to smile. What else could one do but smile, when there was nothing really to say about cheese and onion empanadas?

But she could at least say they were nice—that word that Ell used, or overused, perhaps. "Nice," she said.

"Very nice," agreed William. "Do you like cheese empanadas?"

She assured him that she did.

"With onion, of course," added William.

"But naturally. Onion gives . . ."

"A kick?" he suggested. "Or sweetness. Onions are quite sweet, aren't they?"

She nodded. "They caramelise. So I suppose you could call them sweet."

William looked thoughtful. "French onion soup . . . I really love that. All that cheese, and how it becomes all . . . stringy, like streamers between your mouth and the soup. And you have to use your hands. You wouldn't think you had to use your hands when eating French onion soup, but, boy, you do."

"Oh, I think you do," she said. "There are some things you just have to use your hands for when you're eating them. Chicken, for example. I was told when I was a girl that you are allowed to pick up bits of chicken—drumsticks, and so on. My mother was very uptight about these things, but she always picked up her chicken bones."

William smiled. "It's sad that people get so hung up over what other people think about how they do. Who cares about how others lead their lives—as long as they aren't harming anybody?"

He looked at her intensely as he said this, and she wondered whether there was a subtext. She felt a momentary twinge—perhaps William was testing her attitude towards something he felt she might not like to hear.

But if he was, he let the moment pass. Now he said, "I'm really grateful to you for putting up Andrew. He is too, you know."

She said that she was delighted to be able to help.

"It would have been possible for him to be next door with me," he said, nodding towards his studio through the wall. "But there's all my work stuff through there, and we'd be a bit cramped." He paused. "Is Ell okay with the arrangement?"

"Ell's fine," she said. "Ell has her life . . ." She realised this was an odd thing to say. We all had our lives. "What I mean, is that Ell gets on with her things. She has her job, and she has quite a lot of friends. Ell's a social being, you might say."

He began to grin. "Yes, you could say that. She's friendly, isn't she?"

She remembered how Ell had reacted to William, and her angling at that first meeting for his telephone number. Ell was transparent, which perhaps was a good thing in an age of transparency: we were all being urged to be transparent. It had become a social expectation, rather like flossing your teeth, or signing up to a whole list of current orthodoxies.

"Ell likes Andrew," she said. "They've been talking a lot."

He looked at her. She waited. Then he said, "Andrew can talk about anything. He's one of those people. He likes to tell you the way he feels about things." He looked away briefly. "What do they talk about? Do you know?"

She shrugged. "This and that. They were talking about films

this morning. I was getting my breakfast. They were in the kitchen talking about some film that he'd seen."

William explained that Andrew belonged to a film club in Melbourne. "They show really obscure films. Iranian films, for instance. Iranian films aren't obscure if you're Iranian, but if you're not, they can be a bit hard to follow."

"Subtitles probably help."

He laughed. "I'd better go."

She wanted him to stay, but, more particularly, she wanted him to suggest that she should have lunch with them in Valvona & Crolla. She wouldn't mind even talking about Iranian films over lunch, if only he would ask her.

She said, "I love going to lunch at Valvona & Crolla. I love the deli part of it—it's like being, oh, in Florence, or somewhere, in one of those lovely food shops with hams hanging from the ceiling and all those trays of sun-dried tomatoes and olives and . . . everything. I just love all that."

He smiled. "Yes, it's great."

She waited, hardly daring to hope, and thinking, *Look at me. Just look at me sitting here, a grown woman, desperately hoping for an invitation to lunch that isn't going to come. Oh God.*

"We must have lunch there sometime," said William.

Yes, she thought. Now. Today.

"But I'd better go," said William, looking at his watch. "I'm going to be meeting Andrew at the gallery in fifteen minutes."

She thought: Can you invite yourself to lunch? Was there any reason why she couldn't say, *Can I come too?*

But it was too late. He moved towards the door. He smiled at her. "Bye," he said.

She suddenly felt angry. She could not have made it more obvious that she wanted to join their lunch, but she felt excluded. This friendship between William and Andrew was not something that she could ever be admitted to.

"Enjoy your lunch," she said. And then, almost, but not quite sotto voce, "I wish I were joining you."

It was a last roll of the dice, and, like so many last rolls of the dice, it had no effect.

As he reached the door, as an afterthought, he said over his shoulder, "Ell's meeting us there. She invited herself. I'd better not keep her waiting. You know what she's like."

He hesitated, and for a few moments she wondered whether he was about to ask her whether she would like to join them. But he did not, and once he had gone, and closed the door behind him, she closed her eyes and thought, *This can't go on.* She now had to choose: she could be open about her feelings for William—she could tell him; or she could distance herself from him, possibly curtailing their coffee sessions together, bringing to an end what had become a de facto working arrangement. A first step in getting over somebody was not to see him. That was simple enough, but it was also rude: you did not end friendships that way, with ice. So perhaps this *could* continue, after all, and she would simply carry on, making the most of what she had. There were plenty of people who did just that: they understood that there were limits to how far a relationship might go, and so they settled for the crumbs from the table.

She looked at the papers on her desk with a growing sense of helplessness. Who was she to advise these people on their emotional lives when it was her life that needed attention? She thought of Ness, who had entrusted her with the running of the agency. She had accepted the charge and Ness was relying on her, and so there was no going back on that.

She was unhappy because she had allowed herself to fall for a young man who was probably not going to reciprocate, even if she were to make it clear to him how she felt. Her unhappiness would affect the way in which she discharged her obligations. She would not, therefore, allow herself to be unhappy, although how one might dispel unhappiness was not immediately clear to her. By convincing oneself that one was happy, perhaps?

The day dragged. At lunchtime, she ate a roll that she bought from the sandwich bar round the corner—a dispenser of filled baguettes and focaccia toasties. Going out to pick this up at least got her out of the office for a short while, and improved her mood. Back at her desk, she wrote notes to several of her new clients, confirming the times of arranged meetings. As she finished off the last of these, the telephone rang.

It was Maddy Balquorn. "I know this is no notice at all," she said. "But I'm about one block away, and I wondered . . ."

She did not need to finish. "I'm free," she said. "And of course you can drop in."

She had a few minutes to clear her desk of the confusion of papers by the time Maddy arrived. Ushering her guest in, she waited for the report.

"You saw him?" she asked.

Maddy had sent her a message a couple of days earlier to tell her that Horatio Maclean had been in touch and that they were meeting for dinner in Prestonfield House.

"Yes," said Maddy. "We met."

Katie could tell by her expression and her tone that it had not gone well.

"It doesn't sound very promising," she said. "These things don't always work out."

She sounded lame, but she was not sure what else she could say. Maddy Balquorn was an intelligent woman; she would know the odds against the success of any introduction.

"We went out to dinner," Maddy said. "Prestonfield House."

"You mentioned that," Katie said. "I hope it lived up to expectations . . . the hotel, that is." It was the company, she thought, that would have been the problem.

"It did," said Maddy. "However . . ."

Katie waited.

"You don't need to spell it out," said Katie. "You were bored. I understand."

Maddy shook her head. "No, I wouldn't say I was bored. He did talk rather a lot, but that wasn't really the issue."

"Incompatibility?" asked Katie.

Maddy looked away. "This is a bit awkward," she said.

Katie held her breath. It was always possible that an introduction could go wrong because somebody misread the signals. Or there was the possibility that a man might make premature and unwelcome moves—that was unusual with this sort of client, but it could happen. "You don't need to reveal anything private," she said hurriedly.

"He didn't overstep the mark," Maddy said. "It wasn't that."

Katie's relief showed.

"And yet," Maddy went on, "I can't say that I thought he was my type."

"No," said Katie. "I fully understand."

"Yet he doesn't seem to get it," Maddy went on. "After our dinner, he asked me when we might meet up again. I gave the sort of response that most people would understand perfectly well. I told him that I was a bit tied up for the next little while.

I said that we might be able to do something at some stage in the future, but that it was difficult for me to make any commitment at this point."

Katie agreed that this should have been enough. But then she added, "Sometimes they don't pick up the signals first time."

Maddy smiled. "No, they don't, do they? He telephoned the following day and asked me whether things were getting any quieter and whether we could set something up for next week. I tried to be tactful, but I also wanted to come across as being a bit firmer. I said that he shouldn't worry about contacting me—I would get in touch in due course, but it wouldn't be for some time."

Katie winced. "He's being persistent, isn't he?"

"Thick-skinned, more likely," said Maddy. She fixed Katie with an intense look. "I wondered whether you could possibly have a word with him. I don't want to hurt his feelings, and so I'm not keen to be brutal. But he needs to know there's no possibility here."

Katie said that she would be prepared to tell Horatio that continued efforts to see Maddy would not be welcome. "I can certainly do that," she said. "And I'm sure he'll get the message."

"I hope so."

Katie hesitated. "It might be helpful if I were to know the reason why you and he didn't hit it off. Was it simple incompatibility, or was it something specific?"

Maddy seemed to be weighing up whether or not to reveal why the encounter had not been a success. At last, she responded. "It's not something I would normally talk about," she said. "I suppose, though, you're so involved in this that I should let you know. It's . . ." She faltered, but then, taking a deep breath, continued, "It's a matter of background, I'm afraid."

Maddy looked at Katie, waiting to see whether it would be necessary to say more, or whether the point—this rather embarrassing point—would be taken up by her without the need for further explanation. But Katie did not give her that comfort. Katie held her stare, and waited.

"It's just that he's, well, not quite the sort who my family would be comfortable with," she said at last. "I wouldn't want to run him down, but he hasn't got much *behind* him, so to speak." She gave Katie a look that seemed to say, *Don't make me spell this out.*

Katie understood, but at that moment was experiencing a feeling of renversement. She had taken to Maddy on their first encounter; she had found her warm, and had responded well to what she felt was a certain self-effacement. But this . . . She looked at her now, as the conclusion dawned that behind the friendly façade was a profound moral failing. And that was a failing for which there really was no other word than the simple, familiar term: *snobbery*. Maddy was a *snob*. But then so was Horatio. He had been open about it, and had spelled out that he was looking for somebody with a certain set of family credentials. She had been surprised—such attitudes were unusual and old-fashioned—but she had tried to meet his needs by finding somebody from what he would consider the right social drawer. She had not anticipated, though, that she would find somebody who had the same handicap as he did—for snobbery was surely a handicap, more than anything else. Unusually, it was a handicap that the afflicted person could do something about, but it was still a trait that could distort the way one looked on the world and, most importantly, could harm others. Snobs had *victims*. The snobs themselves may not think that their attitudes were anything but their own business, but they were wrong. Snobbery, when experienced at the receiving end, made people feel bad about themselves. Snobbery was cruel; snobbery was unkind. It was like racism in some respects: it proclaimed that I don't like you because of what you *are*—not for what you do or say or think, but for something that has always been outside your control: for what you *are*. And that could be intensely wounding.

Katie found that she was staring at Maddy, who, in turn, was meeting her stare with what had become puzzlement.

"You do see what I mean?" said Maddy, sounding rather uncertain.

Katie nodded. "I think I do. He's not quite good enough."

"You could put it that way," said Maddy. "I'm not one of those people who bother about what bed people are born in, of course."

Katie tried not to look surprised. "But of course you aren't," she said, thinking, *And I'm not the kind of person to say the opposite of what I mean.*

"It's just that there are ways of doing things," Maddy went on. "There are ways of saying things too. You don't say, *Pleased to meet you*, when you meet somebody, for instance."

"Oh, really?"

Maddy smiled. "I think you know that," she said.

Katie shrugged. "I don't see what's wrong with saying, *Pleased to meet you*. It's a pretty meaningless expression anyway. We all say meaningless things—all the time. *Have a nice day*. Who means that when they say it? It's no different from *Good morning*."

Maddy pursed her lips. "I wasn't saying there was anything fundamentally wrong with it. I'm just saying, I suppose, that the people . . . well, the people I feel comfortable with, don't say it."

"And they don't say *toilet* for toilet?"

Maddy laughed. "That's an old one. Nobody cares about that any longer. And I can't really be bothered about any of this stuff."

Katie thought that this was quite untrue. Maddy bothered very much about this. She looked at Maddy, and, as she did so, she reminded herself: this woman is my client too. And that meant that the feeling of distaste that had suddenly come upon her should be put aside. She owed Maddy exactly the same duty that she owed to Horatio. It was not for her to judge them; her role was to try to help them to discover the happiness that would only come if they found what they were looking for—or something reasonably approximate to that.

She took a deep breath. "Look," she said, "I know what you mean. You don't have to explain any further. He won't do."

"No," said Maddy. "I'm afraid he won't. But I don't seem to be able to get that message across. Could you do it for me?"

Katie said that she would. "It'll be easier for me," she said. "I'll tell him it's one of these chemistry things. I'll stress that it's no reflection on him."

"Good," said Maddy. "As I said, I don't want to hurt anybody." She paused. "Poor Horatio—he went on and on about his forebears—obscure Highlanders of some sort. Mac-this and Mac-that, all perching on top of some piece of windswept rock. But you know something? People who go on and on about their ancestors usually don't have any."

Katie stared down at her desk, unable to meet Maddy's gaze. We all had ancestors, and we all ultimately came from the same tiny band of wandering early humans. Those were our people, whether we liked it or not. They would definitely not be pleased to meet us, those hairy predecessors; their instinct would probably be to hit us over the head with the jawbone of a bison.

Maddy said, "Amused by something?"

"Just thinking," said Katie. "Nothing much." Then she added, "You have to laugh, you know."

Maddy agreed. "Life can be very amusing, can't it?"

CHAPTER SIXTEEN

All I want to do is cry

That evening she found herself alone in the flat. Ell was out on a team-building event organised by her office—"A complete waste of time," she had confided in Katie. "We end up disliking people we previously liked, or at least could get along with. But human resources has it in its mind that if we learn to salsa together, or abseil down the Forth Bridge, we end up working together more effectively. The people from human resources, of course, don't take part. No salsa, no rapid descents at the end of a rope . . ."

Nor was Andrew in, which did not surprise her, as he seemed to spend very little time in the flat, and had only been in for dinner on one occasion since he had moved in. Although his manner towards her was civil, she still felt that she had not got to know him very well. They had had one or two conversations, but these had mostly been about inconsequential things, and he had certainly not ventured much about his life back in Melbourne or about what his plans were. He had asked her if it would be all right for him to stay for a month, and she had agreed, saying that he was welcome to stay longer if he so desired. And she had no compunction in offering a longer stay, as he was a considerate flatmate, scrupulous in his attention to washing up after he cooked his breakfast—the only real use he made of the kitchen—and careful about cleaning the bathroom basin and vacuuming the living room and hall. There was not a single respect in which he could be faulted, other, perhaps, than when it came to his apparent distancing from Katie herself. Flatmates should be friends, Katie thought, and she felt that she could not yet call Andrew a friend—and nor, she suspected, could Ell.

Katie made herself what she considered the easiest of meals—a salad of tomatoes and mozzarella. This was accompanied by a glass of the Western Australian wine that Andrew had left in the fridge and to which he had invited Katie and Ell to help themselves. She read the label and then studied the map on the back of the bottle that showed the estate's location. She had been to Margaret River a long time ago, before her life had become complicated. She had stayed in a youth hostel, indifferent to the noisy parties and the uncomfortable bunks. There had been jarrah forests. She remembered those. She remembered the light in that part of Australia—the attenuated blue light; she remembered the smell of the forests; she remembered the sinking of the great, burning sun.

She thought of Ness, and her late gap year. Youth hostels let anybody stay in them, but Ness, she imagined, would hesitate to avail herself of their rough hospitality.

She reached for her laptop, and began a letter.

Dear Ness,

I am sitting here in the kitchen—your kitchen, of course—drinking a glass of Western Australian wine. I have just finished a caprese salad. It is just after eight at night and I am the only one in the flat. I am thinking of you. I hope you don't mind that. Some people don't like to be thought about, but I don't imagine you are one of those. And anyway, my thoughts are pretty positive—at least when you pop up in my mind. I see you in that little town with its lakes and forests and everything, which I hope you are enjoying again, now that you're better. Those ticks! The important thing, though, is that you're better. Don't go down to the woods today . . . Remember that song? I used to love it when I was small. "The Teddy Bears' Picnic." It has a really sinister ring to it, I thought. If you went down to the woods you were sure of a big surprise. Children love being frightened, of course—and that stays with us for life, I suspect. We all love a fright.

I don't want to burden you with news of the agency. There is nothing to report, really—which is a healthy situation, I suppose. Everything seems to be going well enough. We have a whole tranche of new clients as a result of a piece that was published in *Scottish Field*. I am working my way through their initial interviews, which is a slow business; you, I think, would be much quicker at that than I am. But I'm being very careful with the paperwork. (I was listening to you, you see, when you told me what to do.)

William has a friend visiting him from Australia. He's called Andrew and he is staying in the flat with Ella and me—just for a month or so. He's an ideal flatmate—unobtrusive and very tidy. What more could one want? However . . . well, I didn't want to say anything to you about this, but I can't help myself. I have been thinking a lot about William—does that surprise you? You know about his fiancée, Alice (shudder), and you know that's all over. So William and I could get together if he wanted it—but he doesn't, I'm afraid. It's not that he doesn't want to get involved with me—it's just that he said he doesn't want *any* involvement at the moment. That's what he said to me—explicitly.

And yet he and Andrew are spending all their time together and I feel . . . well, I feel excluded. William doesn't seem to want me around while Andrew is here and I'm beginning to ask myself whether I've misunderstood the situation. To be blunt, I'm beginning to think that William wants a boyfriend and that I've failed to read some very obvious signals.

If it's true—and I think it probably is—then I'm just going to get over it. It's not an uncommon situation, I suppose: people fall for people and don't see the obvious signs. Then they have to accept that it's not going to be, and that can be hard for them. I think that's what's happened here.

I'm not sure whether you will be surprised, or whether you will say that you knew all along. Should I have known too? Was William just too good to be true?

Ness, I may as well admit it: this is making me really unhappy. I don't know how to describe how I feel, but I suppose I could start by saying that I feel sad and empty. I was in love with him. You know—I didn't admit it to myself and I certainly didn't say anything about it to him, but I was in love with him. And now all I want to do is cry—because it's never going to be possible.

Please forgive me, Ness, for writing to you about this. I'm not some love-struck seventeen-year-old. I should be able to look after myself emotionally. But it's happened to me, and I suppose I'm just going to have to sit it out until it stops hurting. I know, of course, I should think of what's best for William. If he finds happiness elsewhere, then I should be pleased for him. I shall try that. I shall tell myself to stop wallowing in misery. I have to do that, I think. I have to. I'm not the first person to feel this way—it's the oldest story in the book, isn't it? I know all that. And I know the answer is always the same: *You can't have what you can't have.* It's that simple. Lesson number one about life—a lesson you learn when you're what . . . seven, say the psychologists. (I read my Piaget when I was at uni.)

Please forgive me for bringing this up. I had to talk to somebody about it, and I'm afraid you're it. I'll be all right.

She read her letter through, considered it, and then pressed a key on her laptop that deleted the whole text. Ness would not want to be burdened with any of this. And she should not indulge herself in self-pity. She had never liked self-pity when she had seen it in others. When people were self-pitying, she wanted to shake them. What did they want? Did they want you to say, *Oh, poor you, poor you* . . . And then? Self-pity led nowhere because the person invited to share the pain could do nothing to alleviate it.

She would do what she had to do, which was to put William out of her mind and try to think of something else. The difficulty with that, though, was that trying to think of something else was the most effective way of making one think of the thing one was trying not to think of. So, she closed her eyes and allowed herself to think of William. She would speak to him, she decided. She would tell him that she knew how he felt about Andrew, and she was sorry that she had not realised it well before this. She had assumed too much, and she needed to apologise.

In her mind's eye, William listened to her, smiled, and then said, "But Katie, surely you could tell?"

She imagined herself saying, "But what about Alice? Why did you get engaged if you weren't interested?" And she might add, she thought, "Why didn't you tell me?"

At first, she had no idea as to how he would answer that. But then she imagined him smiling again and saying, "These things are different now. They're much more fluid—and it shouldn't be necessary to tell anybody." And he would look at her with the pity—the tolerant pity—that is given to those who just don't understand something about the way things are.

Ell came in from her team-building evening rather earlier than Katie expected. She looked flushed, as if she had been asked to overexert herself. "A complete waste of time," she said. "I ended up being paired in a ridiculous competition with a really dim guy from the accounts department. He was a complete geek, I'm afraid, and he broke his glasses halfway through. They fell off his nose, and he trod on them by mistake. I shouldn't laugh. But, oh, my goodness. And he said that his wife was going to give him a really tough time because it was the second pair of glasses that he had broken this year. And that set him off on a long thing about contact lenses. He said that he had a cousin who had developed dry eyes as a result of wearing the wrong sort of contact lenses, and he was not sure whether he should make the change. And so it went on."

Ell sat down on the sofa. "I know you shouldn't drink when you come in. I know it's too easy to come in, sit down, and pour yourself a glass of wine. On the other hand, if you were to say to me, 'What about a glass of wine, Ell . . .' Well, that would be different, I think . . ." She stopped, and fixed Katie with a questioning look. "Are you okay?"

Katie looked away. "Yes," she said quickly.

"When people say yes like that," Ell said, "it means no."

"No, I'm all right."

Ell persisted. "If you ask me, you've been crying. Sorry to mention it, but that's what I think."

Katie continued to look away. Instinctively, a hand went up to her eyes. "Just a bit," she said.

Ell rose up from the sofa. Katie had been standing just a few feet away. She went up to her and put her arm around her friend's shoulder.

"William?" she whispered.

Katie nodded.

"I knew all along that you felt that way," said Ell. "I could tell. We women give ourselves away, don't we?"

Katie struggled not to cry. Tears were not far away. And now Ell led her to the sofa, and they sat down together.

"So where are we?" Ell began. "You've fallen for William. Of course, you have. Who wouldn't? But he was engaged to this little gold-digger from back home—correct? You accept that. You say to yourself—and to me, on one occasion—William's out of bounds. Unavailable. Meanwhile, the fiancée turns up, and, surprise, surprise, she's been two-timing him all along. Outrage. She heads back to Australia—via Paris, *naturellement*—and so you think, well, now there's a chance for William and me. But—and here I'm guessing—William says that he and you are going to carry on being just good friends, and that's all there is to it. And that's where we are—right?" She paused. "I'm really sorry, Katie. I can imagine how you feel. It's bad luck."

Katie said, "It wasn't quite like that."

"No?"

"He said that he didn't want to get involved just yet—with anyone."

Ell brightened. "Well, that's not an outright no, is it?"

Katie shook her head. "Except that . . ." She sighed.

"Except what?"

"Except there's Andrew. He turns up."

Ell frowned. "Andrew? What's he got to do with it?"

Katie did not reply, and Ell answered her own question. "Oh, I see. You haven't fallen for Andrew, have you? Is that it? On the rebound?" She smiled. "Talk about complications!"

"No," Katie blurted out.

"Then?"

"William and Andrew seem to be spending all their time together . . ."

It took a few moments for Ell to understand. Then her face broke into a broad smile. "No," she said. "I don't think so." She paused. Now she shook her head. "No, definitely not."

"But they do," Katie insisted. "I feel completely cut out. For instance, they went to lunch at Valvona & Crolla. I really wanted . . ."

"I went too," Ell interjected. "It was the three of us."

"I knew you were going," said Katie. "I wanted him to invite me."

"But it was just lunch," Ell retorted. "It wasn't a date, for God's sake. They didn't sit there looking into one another's eyes." She shook her head again. "You've got it all wrong. Listen, Katie—those two aren't an item. Andrew's straight. You can tell right away."

"But William's changed since he turned up. I'm not imagining it. They spend *all* their time together."

"But they're old friends," Ell said. "They go back a long time. They haven't seen one another for ages. Andrew turns up. What do you expect? William's far from home. He wants to catch up. So? I don't see anything unusual in that."

Katie said that she was not convinced. She did not think she was imagining things: William was different when Andrew was around. She could hardly help but notice.

Ell looked thoughtful. "It was William who asked you to let Andrew stay in the flat? It was his idea?"

Katie nodded. "I suggested it. But I could tell that he was hoping I would. He was pretty pleased when I made the offer."

"If what you think is true actually *is* true, wouldn't he have wanted Andrew to stay with him?"

Katie pointed out that William's place was a studio flat. "He works there. He's got all his work things. There isn't a proper bedroom. It's not big."

"If you're romantically involved with someone," Ell said, "you don't need a lot of space. In fact, not having much room may be ideal. You want things to be nice and close."

When Katie did not respond to this, Ell went on, "But more to the point: I think you're wrong about Andrew. He doesn't *seem* gay. There's nothing about the way he behaves that suggests that."

"Not that you're stereotyping," said Katie.

Ell reacted sharply. "I don't stereotype. I'm not talking about any of the usual tropes. I'm not talking about camp. That's pretty crude—and hostile. But there can be something in the way in which a gay man interacts with women. Sometimes you can sense it. It's a non-threatening sort of feeling."

Katie laughed. "And heterosexual men? Not every man has a sexual agenda when it comes to women. It's not always there, you know."

Ell agreed. "I'm not saying it is. But . . ."

"There are plenty of men," Katie continued, "who treat women as people first and foremost, with nothing else on the table. Not all relations between people are sexualised." She paused. "They're not all Seth Starkadders."

"Seth who?"

Katie explained about *Cold Comfort Farm*. Ell was not a great reader, and Katie assumed—rightly—that she would not have heard of Stella Gibbons. "There's a very funny novel about a young woman who goes to stay with farming relatives. Seth is one of her cousins, and he *seethes*. His shirt is always unbuttoned at the top, and he frequently undoes another button. He has a tremendously seductive voice. You see Seth Starkadder types about the place."

Ell smiled. "I've met him," she said.

"Well, Andrew's not that."

Ell agreed. "But I can tell he's interested in women. You can sense these things—just as you can sense it when a man isn't."

Katie thought about this. Ell was more experienced than she was—she had been the first of their group at school to have a boyfriend—in fact, she had had several boyfriends by the time she went to university. If Ell thought that of Andrew, then she could be right. But, on the other hand, it was perfectly possible that Andrew liked both men and women. That was an option—and an increasingly common one, she thought, now that boundaries had become less important. These matters were less binary than they had been before; choices were less exclusive of other possibilities.

Ell was looking bemused. "I could ask him," she said. "I don't mind talking about these things openly."

Katie shook her head. "No, please don't."

Ell shrugged. "As you wish. But bear in mind what I've said. I think you're wrong."

"Oh, well," said Katie. "It doesn't matter anyway—does it? Whatever is going on between William and Andrew, the point is that William at the moment doesn't seem to want to get involved."

"If I were you, I'd cool it. Wait and see. Maybe it'll be different in the future."

Katie said that Ell was probably right, and that she would take her advice. "I do have other things to think about," she said. "We're inundated with work at the moment. There was an article about us, and it's led to a lot of enquiries."

"There's a lot of loneliness," mused Ell.

"Yes," Katie said.

Ell said, "I wasn't going to have a glass of wine, but in the circumstances, why don't we? Look at us: two women sitting in their flat, talking about men. That's a perfect setting for a glass of wine."

Katie smiled. "Western Australian white? Margaret River, courtesy of Andrew?"

"Just right," said Ell. She looked fondly at Katie. "I'm glad that you and I have each other. It makes a difference, I think."

"To have a friend?"

"Yes," said Ell. "To have a friend you go back a long way with. You can have this sort of conversation with a friend like that. You can say things that you might not feel you can say to others."

Katie agreed. "That helps, doesn't it."

"And sometimes I think it would be simpler if we didn't let men come along and spoil it. I'm not entirely serious about that, of course, but the thought crosses my mind from time to time."

Katie laughed. "We'd eventually get on one another's nerves. Men are like salt. Food needs salt to season it. A world of women would be like . . . like unsalted bread—all right, in some respects, but lacking something."

Ell gazed up at the ceiling in a dreamy way. "I might try to get Andrew."

"Get?" exclaimed Katie. "That's an odd way of putting it."

"You know what I mean. Catch him . . . in a net."

"That's a strange metaphor . . . I assume it's a metaphor." She played with it. "Nets," she said. "Nets. There's a piece of music I rather like. It's called 'In Nets of Golden Wires.' It's by Thomas Morley." She almost added, "Have you heard of him?" but stopped herself. Ell would not.

"He wrote it in the sixteenth century," Katie went on. "The music is beautiful, but so are the words. *In nets of golden wires; with pearl and ruby spangled; my heart entangled . . .*"

"Just what I was thinking," said Ell.

Katie stared at her. Was Ell serious? "Would you be playing with him?" she asked. "Or do you like him?"

Ell hesitated. "I find that I like him a little bit more each day. He's growing on me."

"And what do you think he feels?" asked Katie. "Has he noticed? Do you think he knows you're interested in him?"

"We'll see," said Ell. "But let's stop talking about William and Andrew. They won't be talking about us, you know."

"What do you think they talk about? What did you discuss at that lunch the other day?"

Ell took a moment to remember. "This and that. They spent some time talking about films they'd seen. They had both been watching an Irish series about drug gangs in Dublin. They talked about that."

"Watching it together?" asked Katie.

"I think so," said Ell. "I think they watch quite a lot together. Or at least, that's the impression I had."

Ell said this almost apologetically. She realised that it would be no comfort to Katie.

CHAPTER SEVENTEEN

Bromance explained

The following morning, William reappeared at coffee time, resuming the routine he and Katie had enjoyed before Andrew's arrival. Katie was pleased, almost blurting out, *Where's Andrew?* The unposed question, though, was answered by William; Andrew, he told her, had gone to see the Burrell Collection in Glasgow, where there was an exhibition of glass engraving. Now he asked her whether she might be free for lunch. "Just the two of us. Valvona & Crolla—you wanted to go there the other day, but I was going with Andrew and Ell—who invited herself."

Katie looked disapproving, forgetting for the moment that she, too, had wanted to invite herself but had lacked the courage. She made a show of looking at her diary. "Let me see . . ."

William gave her a reproachful look. "You won't have anything," he said. "You never have anything on at lunchtime," and added, hurriedly, reproach being replaced with a winsome smile, "I'm the same. I'm always free at lunchtime—except when I'm having lunch with you, that is."

She returned the smile. She wanted to ask whether she

was being invited only because Andrew was away for the day, but she decided against it. Reproaching others for not paying enough attention to oneself was the surest way of putting people off.

They left the office at noon, walking together to the street off Leith Walk where a modest, olive-green façade concealed the premises of the deli. The café part of the business was at the back, in a long, narrow room lined with photographs from the long history of the business. Katie was known to the staff, and was quickly given a table. She saw, as they entered, several heads turn in William's direction—not an uncommon reaction, she had noted, to his entry to any room. That William seemed unaware of the effect he had on others was one of the reasons why she liked him so much.

They discussed the menu, both opting for a mozzarella and prosciutto *panatella*. That should be preceded, Katie said, by a plate of crisp focaccia and a bottle of Italian mineral water.

William glanced about him. "I'm sorry we haven't seen very much of one another over the last few days," he said.

She waited for an explanation, or even an apology, but neither was forthcoming.

"You've been busy," she said, and added, "with Andrew."

He nodded. "It's his first time in Edinburgh. There's a lot for him to see."

"Of course."

He gave her a look that lingered, or so it seemed to her, and she wondered whether he had detected a note of reproach in what she had said.

"I hope you're not feeling neglected," he said.

"Of course not." She was quick to deny this; the very idea . . .

"Andrew's really enjoying staying at your place," William said. "He's really grateful—as am I."

Katie assured him that Andrew was a very easy guest. She had not intended to talk about Andrew, but he seemed to be an unseen presence at the table.

"Most of the time, he's pretty laid-back," continued William.

Katie fingered the paper napkin beside her plate. "You two obviously get on very well."

William smiled. "Of course, we do. We go back ages." He paused. "Don't you have a friend like that? Don't you have somebody you feel really close to?"

Katie had plenty of friends, and some of them were close friends with whom she had been at school. There was Ell, for instance, although Ell was, perhaps, a special case; sometimes she felt she did not have quite as much in common with Ell as she might wish. "I have friends. But I'm not sure that I have a particular friend I'm that close to. I'm not sure that I have a soul-mate." Ell was definitely not that.

William took a sip of mineral water. "I'm lucky, I suppose."

She held his gaze. "You have a David and Jonathan friendship?"

He looked thoughtful. "You could call it that. Some people might use the word *bromance*." He raised his eyes to meet hers. "Do you know what that means?"

"Of course. A close friendship between men."

"Really close," he said.

She waited. Snatches of conversation drifted over from another table. "She's insensitive to criticism . . ." and "Things picked up after he went to live in Glasgow . . ." For him, Katie found herself wondering, or those who stayed behind? The dramas of the lives of others were familiar enough.

"A bromance is a sort of romance, you see—hence the name."

She had not expected this, and was embarrassed. If only

William had told her right at the beginning, they would not be having this potentially awkward conversation. "A romantic affair?"

He took a few moments to reply. "I wouldn't use the word *affair*. An affair implies that there's a sexual side to it. A bromance is non-sexual. It's romantic, in that it's intense—every bit as intense as a conventional affair between lovers, but in the case of a bromance there's strictly no . . ."

"Touching?" she suggested. She felt light-headed. Her assumptions had been wrong, and the implications of that were dawning on her. William was not lost to her. It was possible . . .

He shook his head vigorously. "No, that's not the point. It can be very tactile. Not all physical intimacy is sexual. Guys in a bromance can be quite physical."

"Are you sure?" she asked.

He did not let her finish. "Yes, but all that can be completely platonic. If guys hug one another, so what?"

Katie thought this might be a long-delayed response to her having seen Andrew's arm about him. William had been casual about that, as if it were nothing to remark about, but he must have been concerned that she would misinterpret the situation. And she had, she decided; she *had* misinterpreted it, as anyone would—unless, of course, they knew all about bromances, which she obviously did not.

"You don't expect it," said Katie. "I'm not saying that they shouldn't—all I'm saying is that there are still some taboos. I'm not defending these taboos, but they're there."

"*Were* there," said William. "*Were*, not *are*. Men used not to be able to express themselves physically, except in a very narrow range of ways. That's not so now. And why shouldn't men express their affection for a male friend by hugging him? Don't you hug your girlfriends from time to time?"

"I do. But it's different with women."

"Why?" he pressed.

"Because . . ." She found herself floundering. Was it simply a case of social expectation? Was it something to do with a general understanding of the nurturing instincts of women?

William struggled to provide an answer. "Perhaps it depends on the way we're trained to read behaviour subconsciously. So, if we see a woman hug another woman, we think, She's comforting her friend—that's all. Whereas, if we see two men hugging, we reach a different conclusion. We think they're an item." He looked at her enquiringly. "Do you think it's to do with the way we see male sexuality? We see it as aggressive, more insistent. So, we're immediately suspicious."

"Perhaps. But then—"

Once more he interrupted her. He seemed animated—as if the issue was one on which he had strong views. Perhaps he does, she thought.

"Or it could just be an historical hangover," he said. "For whatever reason, social disapproval of displays of affection between men has been drummed into us—and it will take some time to remove. That's happening, of course, but you can't change attitudes overnight." He sighed. "So, there we are."

For a few moments she said nothing, and wondered whether she could steer the conversation off the subject. But then she told herself that it was ridiculous not to have the frank discussion that the situation required. She would be direct.

"So, between you and Andrew . . ." Their eyes met. She had to continue now. "Is it a bromance?"

The question hung in the air between them, and it occurred

to her that she had gone too far. But William barely reacted. His eyes widened a bit, she thought, as if he had been surprised, but only moderately. But then he said, quite evenly, "Yes, you could say that. I don't mind, you know. It's a very important friendship for us both."

"But that's all it is?"

She asked the question, and then looked away. This was going too far. This was effectively implying the relationship might be sexual. She regretted it; she sounded like a prosecutor, an interrogator.

He frowned. "Yes, that's all there is." He hesitated. "Neither of us is gay, Katie. Did you think we were?" He was beginning to smile. "I can see why you might, of course. I'm not criticising you or anything, but you might have been thinking . . ."

She felt that she had to explain. "That time I came into your studio . . ."

"Unannounced," he interjected.

She felt she had to defend herself. "You don't knock either when you come into the office."

"Offices are different," he said.

"But that's your studio too. That's your office."

He spread his hands. "Fair enough. But yes, that time . . ."

"I came in," she went on, "and Andrew had his arm on your shoulder. I thought that perhaps I'd interrupted something."

William seemed unperturbed. "You had."

"Oh."

"But not what you thought you'd interrupted. It wasn't that. We were just talking, and yes, he will occasionally put an arm around me—and I'll do the same to him. We've always done that. It doesn't mean anything—other than that we go back a long way, and we love one another."

He stopped, and then added, "Love one another as friends,

you see. Is there anything wrong in loving your friends? Can't you say that?"

She was quick to reassure him. "Of course you can."

"Yet, you must have wondered about it—seeing us there. I can understand how you might have thought that there was something else."

She felt a sudden rush of emotion, and she stuttered as she sought to assure him that she had not given the matter much thought. "It hasn't been a big thing for me . . . Not at all."

She saw that this had an unexpected effect on him. His face, it seemed to her, showed disappointment. And why would that be? Was it because if he had secretly hoped that she might be interested in him, then she would, of course, have been much exercised by any evidence that *he* might not be interested in *her*. But it was all becoming unduly complicated, and now she wanted this particular conversation to come to an end.

"Let's talk about something else," she said.

He shrugged. "If you like. But one final thing on the subject of Andrew."

"Yes?"

"He says . . ." He hesitated for a few moments. "He says . . ."

"Yes?"

"I'm not sure that I should tell you this."

She urged him to continue. "You can't start to say something like that and then just stop. Come on, William."

He reached for a piece of focaccia. "I can't resist this stuff."

"No."

"And, okay, I'll tell you. Andrew told me that Ell has a thing for him."

Katie was impassive. Even if William was prepared to share Andrew's confidences with her, she was not going to reveal what Ell had said to her. So she simply said, "Really?"

"Yes, really. He says that Ell suggested that they shower together."

Katie stared at William. She was not sure whether to laugh or gasp. She wondered, too, whether this could be heard at the neighbouring table—just as they had heard what was being said there. What would they make of this? *Ell suggested that they shower together . . .*

She lowered her voice. "Did they?"

William was grinning. "Apparently, they did."

Katie found that William's grin took the tension out of the situation. She said, "Saving hot water. That's very thoughtful of them. Very green."

William's grin became a broad smile. "My thoughts entirely."

"I assume that I wasn't there at the time," said Katie.

"You were out at the gym," William said. "Or so Andrew said."

Katie asked what Andrew felt about Ell.

"He likes her," he replied. "He feels a bit pursued, though. He's not sure about that. He says that he'd prefer to cool it a bit."

"Cool the water?" asked Katie, and added, "It's very difficult to get the temperature right with that shower—it's either too hot or too cold."

They both laughed. Then Katie said, "Let's just leave this subject. It's none of our business, really."

"No," said William. "It isn't."

Katie thought: That settles that. If William had been involved with Andrew, then he would have shown some resentment towards Ell, but he had simply been amused, which was a relief. At the same time, though, she found herself angry with Ell, who had discussed Andrew with her without confiding that she was already on intimate terms with him—sharing a shower, irrespective of what happened in the shower, was surely an intimate event. She tried to remember exactly what Ell had said. She had commented on the fact that she could tell that Andrew was interested in women—well, he must be, if he willingly showered with Ell. Ell was just too much. She was man-mad. Who else was she showering with?

"You're smiling at something," William said. "What are you thinking about?"

She decided to be frank. "The thought of those two sharing a shower."

"I know," said William. He broke off a piece of focaccia and dipped it in a small bowl of olive oil. "Why would people want to shower together? To save water?" He paused, and gave her a mischievous look. "Only joking, of course."

Their mozzarella and prosciutto *panatella* arrived. William surveyed it with delighted anticipation. "Delicious," he murmured.

There was now no further mention of Andrew and Ell, and the conversation moved on to work. William had not spoken to Katie about his visit to Clea, and she was anxious to hear what, if anything, he had learned.

"She didn't mind talking to me about it," he began. "And I drew a picture for her."

Katie laughed. "And what are you going to do with it?"

"I'm going to have a word with a couple of people who run shops near the supermarket. There's a cheese place up there, apparently. And a bookshop. Somebody might recognise him."

Katie shrugged. "I wouldn't hold my breath." She took a sip of her sparkling water. "And you talked?"

"Yes. She told me a bit more about their conversation. Not much, but there was something."

Katie waited. William seemed reticent for some reason, and she had to encourage him.

"You won't laugh?" he asked. "If I tell you about an idea I have, you won't laugh, will you?"

She assured him that she would not. "Unless you say something completely ridiculous, of course."

"This idea I have isn't ridiculous."

"Then tell me."

He began with an unexpected question. "Do you think that people are creatures of habit?"

Katie shrugged. "Some are; some aren't. I am, I think and you . . . well, you always turn up for morning coffee at the same time each day. You may be a creature of habit, then—I think you probably are."

He nodded. "Yes, you're right. So, if somebody makes marmalade, they probably make it regularly?"

Katie was amused by the example. "Probably," she said. "People tend to stick to their enthusiasms. We all do, I think." She looked at him with puzzlement. "But why marmalade?"

"Because he—that is, the man Clea met—made marmalade. She told me that he mentioned it. I don't think she told you that when she first spoke to you."

Katie listened. She did not see the relevance of this minor detail of Clea's conversation in the supermarket. But then, quite unexpectedly, she guessed what William had deduced. "Seville oranges," she said. She half-whispered: it was a moment of sudden dawning, and for a while she struggled to find the words. "You need Seville oranges to make marmalade—or at least to make what I'd call *proper* marmalade. Seville oranges are bitter." She collected her thoughts, all the while looking at him with the brightening look of one who has realised something important. "And they come into the shops only for a couple of weeks each year."

William nodded his agreement—and encouragement.

"And all the marmalade makers," she said, "rush to the shops to get their supplies."

"So I've read," said William. "I looked it up online, you see." He waited for a few moments before continuing, "The oranges are in and will be around for ten or fifteen days. This weekend is mid-season, so to speak."

They looked at one another. Then Katie said, "She met him a year ago, didn't she?"

William smiled. "He'll be back for more Seville oranges. People make enough marmalade for a year, and then start again."

Katie gave him an admiring look. "You're brilliant, William."

He made a self-deprecating gesture. "It may not work. It's just an idea."

Katie frowned. "She may not want to go. I think she may feel a bit awkward about it."

William agreed that this was likely. "She seems to have more or less given up on him. But I'll go. Saturday is the most likely day for him to want to get his oranges. He could be making the marmalade on Sunday."

"Unless he's already bought them," Katie pointed out.

"That's a risk we should take. There's a good chance he'll buy them this weekend."

"You'll spend all Saturday," Katie said, "hanging about the supermarket—just in case?"

William explained that Clea had told him that the original meeting took place in the late morning. "I know it's a long shot—a really long shot, but I'm going to assume that this guy repeats himself. I'll go there at ten-thirty, and stay until lunchtime. If he hasn't come by then, I'll give up."

Katie looked doubtful. "And if he comes—a big if, of course—you'll know him from the drawing you did?"

"I hope so."

Katie reached out over the table and gripped his hand, to give it a squeeze. She did this automatically, and withdrew after a second or two, but not before he had responded to her gesture with a conspiratorial squeeze of his own. She wanted to hold hands with him, there at the table, in full view of everybody in the restaurant. When we are in the company of the charming and the beautiful, we want others to see—it is as if some of their qualities will rub off on us. But the moment passed; perhaps one day she would be able to proclaim that she and William were together, but that day was yet to come.

After lunch, they walked back together along the quiet streets of the eastern New Town. The Georgian buildings were more modest in their proportions than those in the more expensive centre, but still had the charm of regularity. The sun had been obscured that morning by cloud; now in early March it was beginning to have some warmth in it, and was daubing the rooftops with a soft gold. The sky above them was an attenuated blue, barely disturbed by high wisps of cirrus, falling crystals of ice, translucent white strands. This was north. Scotland was north.

Neither spoke for a few minutes. A cat crossed the cobbled street and darted down steps leading to a basement. A gull glided past, mewing, intent on scavenging.

She broke the silence between them. "This city is so beautiful, isn't it?"

He said, "Yes, it is. Sometimes I think I'm living on an opera set."

"And could burst into song?"

"Yes," he said. "For the sheer joy of being here."

He looked at her. She wanted the outside world to go away, leaving only this place, this city, this small part of Scotland that was about them. She wanted to forget what was happening in that broader world: the conflicts, the uncertainty, the loss—all those things that hung dark over the future. Love was what counted—not all that.

"*Che gelida manina*," he said, half-singing the words. He looked at her. "Puccini. *Your tiny hand is frozen* . . . Bohème."

He reached for her hand, to brush against it lightly, but he did not take it. Now he smiled. "Do you think we're in an opera, Katie? Do you ever think that?"

"Right now," she said, "yes, I do."

CHAPTER EIGHTEEN

Our work is love

Katie was to say of the following day, "Hardly anything happens on a Saturday, but then you get a Saturday like that, and you can't generalise about Saturdays."

Katie did not usually come into the office on Saturday mornings, but had done so on this occasion because of the sheer volume of paperwork untouched on her desk. It was the day after her lunch with William, and she was still experiencing the glow of relief at the resolution of her doubts. She could now allow herself to hope that there was a future with him, even if they were still in the strange state of uncertainty created by his discouraging comments about new relationships. People said things like that, of course, and often did not really mean what they said. But even if William did, even if he was entirely serious about leading a monastic life, she would be patient; at some point William would recover from the disappointment of his broken engagement, and at that stage she hoped he would turn to her. She found the thought a calming one. She was in no hurry—as long as nobody else snatched him from her in the meantime. That was a danger, of course. Every woman who met William, if she were single, and, in some cases, even if she were not, would be bound to make a play for him. And one of these could conceivably appeal to him.

She had told William that she would be in the office that morning, and had hoped that he would come in to make coffee as he did on weekdays. This was the morning that he was due to go to the supermarket in Morningside on his errand of mercy, as she had decided to call it. He would have time, though, to drop into the office before he went off, and she was pleased when that was what he did.

He seemed slightly downbeat when he came in; his enthusiasm for his own idea seemed to have collapsed. "This isn't going to work," he said. "I'm wasting my time. It's absurd to think that just because somebody bought Seville oranges last year they will do so again. It's clutching at straws."

Katie tried to encourage him. "Many of the best ideas seem absurd at first," she said. "But then they work, and everybody remarks on how brilliant they were."

"But this isn't brilliant," he said. "This is a straightforward waste of time."

"Listen," she said. "I'd tell you if I thought it was a waste of time. I haven't said that, have I?"

He answered reluctantly. "No, you haven't said that. But you may be thinking it."

"I'm not. I told you what I think: this is worth trying. It's a long shot, as I think I said to you before, but give it a go." She looked at her watch. "Are you going to go? I've made a few appointments for this morning, in spite of all this." She gestured to the papers on her desk. "Somebody you don't particularly approve of is coming in. He wanted to see me, and I was unable to put him off."

William looked interested. "Somebody I don't like?" He hesitated for a moment before saying, "That Horatio character?"

"Yes. He'll be here soon. I think you should scarper."

"I shall," he said. "I don't normally avoid people, but I'm always ready to make an exception, particularly when it's as deserving a case as his."

Katie laughed. "I don't think I told you what happened," she said. "That woman we matched him up with . . ."

"Maddy Balquorn?"

"Yes. She got in touch with me and told me that she did not consider him to be . . . well, her equal socially."

William's eyes widened. "So, he's met a bigger snob than he is himself? Oh, that's delicious. What a perfect match."

Katie could not suppress a smile. "I shouldn't be pleased when an introduction fails, but I must admit . . ." She hesitated. "I don't think we should write them off as snobs. They may have social ambitions, but . . ."

She did not finish, as the doorbell rang. She looked at William.

"I'll show him in," he said.

"Don't say anything," said Katie. "No Schadenfreude, please."

"Schadenfreude isn't part of my Weltanschauung," William snapped back.

Katie blushed. "I didn't know you spoke German."

"Just a few words," William said, rising to his feet. "Just a few everyday phrases. *Wo ist der Bahnhof?* That sort of thing."

He left the room. Katie heard him greet Horatio Maclean at the door. Then the two of them came back into the office. William, she saw, was smiling with what looked like anticipation. She gave him a warning look.

"You met my colleague last time," Katie said to Horatio. "He's just leaving."

"Not just yet," said William quickly. "Not for another half hour."

It was clear to Katie that William was looking forward to seeing how Horatio would receive the news of his rejection. It was going to be embarrassing enough as it was, even without unhelpful interventions by William.

"Thank you for seeing me," Horatio began. "I know you're busy."

Katie gestured to her desktop. "Very busy—at the moment."

Horatio went straight to the point. "That person you arranged . . ."

"Maddy Balquorn?"

"Yes. As you know, we went out to dinner."

William suddenly intervened. "Where did you go?"

Horatio half-turned to look at him. His reply was curt. "Prestonfield House."

"I went there for a drink once," said William. "I had a look at the dining room. It looked good."

"It was all right," said Horatio.

Katie waited, but Horatio did not seem to want to add anything. Eventually she asked, "How did it go?"

"Very well," said Horatio. "She's a very interesting woman."

"That's what I thought," said Katie. "Broad interests."

"And a very distinguished family," Horatio continued, becoming more enthusiastic. "The Balquorns are connected to *everybody*—right back to the sixteenth century. It's an old connection."

"Wow!" exclaimed William.

Horatio smiled. If there was irony in William's reaction, it was lost on him. "Yes. And then more recently a Balquorn married a member of the Forbes family, who were direct descendants of Henry Benedict Stuart, who was, of course, the younger brother of Bonnie Prince Charlie. He was a cardinal, as I imagine you know: everybody seems to be interested in the Jacobites these days."

William raised an eyebrow. "Well," he said, "that's something. But if this Henry Stuart was a cardinal, would he have had any descendants? I thought that cardinals weren't meant to."

"What they were meant to do is neither here nor there," said Horatio. "The fact is that they often had families—discreetly, of course."

"Hypocrisy," muttered William.

Katie gave him a discouraging look. "These things happened," she said mildly. She hesitated before continuing, "I've heard from Maddy. She enjoyed her dinner with you, but . . ."

"She's being a bit elusive," Horatio interjected. "I can't understand why. We got on perfectly well, and she implied that we would meet up again. But she's been a bit difficult to pin down." He fixed Katie with an intense look. "I was wondering, in fact, if you might be able to have a word with her. I feel that she and I would be a good match, but we need to see a bit more of each other."

Katie and William exchanged glances.

"Yes," Katie said hesitantly. "I was going to speak to you about this."

Horatio shook his head. "No, I wanted you to speak to *her*."

"I have spoken to her," said Katie. "We've discussed the situation."

Horatio frowned. "And?"

Katie took a deep breath. "I'm afraid that she feels that this isn't going to work. That happens, you know—it's not uncommon. Sometimes the chemistry just isn't there."

Horatio was silent. Katie glanced at William, who raised an eyebrow.

Then Horatio said, "That's not the impression I had. It seemed to me that she thought we were pretty well-suited." He looked up at the ceiling, as if to find help in remembering precisely what had been said. "No, I'm not imagining it—we hit it off. We share a lot of interests—family history, and so on. We have a great deal in common."

Katie sighed. "I don't think that's the way she felt. I'm not saying that she disliked you. She was complimentary enough."

Horatio was staring at her. Katie noticed that he had clenched his fists. She felt quite uncomfortable.

"I think you're trying to put me off for some reason," Horatio blurted out. "You can spell it out, you know."

Katie's expression registered her surprise. "But I'd never try to put you off," she protested. She looked at William for support, and he made his decision. Katie felt threatened by this man; she was being bullied.

William shifted in his seat. "Actually, the truth of the matter, Mr. Maclean," he interjected, "is that Ms. Balquorn thinks you aren't . . . sorry to use this term, but I can't see how else we can put it—she thinks you aren't quite socially right for her. My colleague doesn't want to hurt your feelings, but that's the truth of the matter. She comes from a very old and distinguished family—as you yourself have just explained. She feels—and it's not us who are saying this—she feels that you haven't got quite the same background. I think that sort of attitude is ridiculous—snobbish, even—but you know what people are like. There really are people who judge others on such ridiculous grounds."

Horatio's jaw dropped. For a moment it looked as if he was

going to say something, but then he closed his mouth without uttering a word. His fists unclenched, and then clenched again.

"I'm so sorry," said Katie in a gentle voice. "I agree with William. Of course, people shouldn't judge people by things that have nothing at all to do with their individual worth—as people, simply as people. We're all the same under the skin, aren't we?" She paused, to allow this to sink in. "I am not at all pleased by the way this has worked out."

Horatio Maclean sat quite still for a couple of minutes—and said nothing. Then, with a mumbled excuse about having to be somewhere else for another appointment, he left the office. Katie and William looked at one another impassively.

"Do you think we saw a lesson being learned there?" Katie asked.

William considered this. "We saw a lesson being taught, yes. Whether or not it's been learned, I don't know. Possibly."

"I wish you hadn't felt it necessary to be so explicit," said Katie. She was trying not to sound too critical, but she felt that she was not succeeding. She tried again. "I'm sorry that it developed as it did, but I can see why you may have felt that you had no alternative."

"I didn't," said William. "He needed to know. So, I told him. And now, I suspect he'll be doing some thinking. It's an old story, isn't it? People who hand it out sometimes have to take it. And at least some of them learn." He paused. "I think we might have helped our stuck-up friend, even if it might take him a while to realise it."

"I felt a bit sorry for him at the end," said Katie. "I feel I should try again—with somebody different."

"If he wants it," said William. He looked at Katie. "What

about Maddy. She'll remain an unreconstructed snob, don't you think?"

"I'm not sure that's fair. Anyway, we might be able to help her somehow."

William smiled. "Life's too short. We can't go round making our clients into better people. We just won't have the time." He looked thoughtful. There was something he wanted to clarify. "What is it that's so wrong about snobbery," he asked. "What is it that makes it so unpleasant?"

It was a little while before Katie responded. But she was sure of the answer she gave. "It's unkind," she said. "It's that simple. And it's also a sort of vanity, don't you think? It amounts to saying, *I'm better than others.*"

She looked at her watch. "You're going to have to go, William. Tempus fugit."

He said, "I didn't know you spoke Latin."

"You don't *speak* Latin," she admonished him. "You *read* it."

"I don't," he said, and then added, playfully, "Will you teach me one day?"

She said that she would. "The first thing you learn in Latin is the verb *amare*. You learn *amo, amas, amat*."

"Which means?"

"I love, you love, he loves."

He smiled at her. "Useful. *Amo.*"

"And then there's *amamus*, which means *we* love."

He walked towards the door. She heard him on the stairs, trying out the newly discovered words, *Amo, amas, amat*. It could be a refrain, she thought, like the chants of those people who used to go through the streets singing *Hare Krishna*. Love could be a religion, she thought, practised with the same care and attention given to religion. Love was the thing—the only thing, she thought—that could bring redemption, and yes, she did not mind being considered a priestess in the temple of love. It was a calling that she would proudly profess. And if it meant finding people for somebody even as difficult as Horatio Maclean, then she would do that with the same application as she gave to the affairs of any other client.

"I'll try again with him," she said to herself. There had to be somebody, somewhere who would see something in him. There was a category labelled *desperate* in the filing system set up by Ness. She had hardly dared look through the few files it contained, but perhaps this was the time to do so. She was not sure, though, whether Horatio had learned anything through today's salutary lesson. She was not sure whether people ever really changed. Some did, perhaps—a little. But then she stopped herself. If one didn't believe in the ability of people to change for the better, then was there much point in going on? Without a belief in the possibilities of change for the better, what was the point of schools, universities, churches, scouts, therapists, introduction agencies . . . ? She thought of Ness. Was that the response that Ness would give to that question. She thought it probably was. Ness had said to her, Do what you can. It may not be much, but do it anyway. She was absolutely right, of course.

And she thought of Ness and her unlikely friend, Herb la Fouche, and of how he had looked after her when she was ill. It was a little thing to sit by a neighbour's bedside, but it meant a lot. And did one really need more than that in life? Somebody to sit by one's side? Was that ultimately why people came to this place and asked to meet others? Was that all that they were after, and was the rest illusion? No, it was not, she decided.

She got up and went to stand by the window behind her

desk. She looked out. What a strange, frustrating, mysterious thing was love. In a world in which there would never be enough of everything, in which not all desires could be met, love was rationed, just as happiness was. Some were perfectly happy with the share they were allocated; others felt they got too little. And then there were some who failed to grasp a fundamental truth about the way love worked, which was that you got back roughly the amount you put in. That was so basic that you would think that everybody would understand it. But they did not, for some reason, and had to learn the lesson—if they ever learned it—the hard way.

She closed her eyes. She thought of William. She realised that she cherished him. She opened her eyes. Cherished? What a warm, gentle, lovely word. She looked down onto the street, with its cobblestones, or setts, and its black-painted railings marking the curtilage of each small mews building. She cherished this too, the place in which she lived and worked, and the land beyond its bounds, because love spilled over from one person, one object, to embrace so much else. Love spread.

In a moment, Katie knew what she had to do. She had to tell William what she felt. It would not be difficult. All she had to do was to take his hand in hers and tell him. She should have done it well before this, she thought, but it is never too late to do the things we know we should do.

William walked down Morningside Road. The road dipped sharply, and at the end, beyond the city limits, the first of the Pentland Hills rose up against a sky of scudding white cloud. He had brought work with him, a hand-knitted top that had been commissioned by the wife of an Italian industrialist. She had seen a picture of one of his pieces in a glossy magazine and had asked for something similar, but different, if he saw what she meant. He did, and he was pleased with the way the garment was taking shape. "I would like Scottish colours," the client had said to him, but had not been more specific. William had interpreted these as being russets and greens, with a suggestion of purple, the colour that heather gave to the hillsides of Scotland in the fullness of summer. He would make a few purchases in the supermarket—he had run out of cheese and olives, two staples of his kitchen—and then he would sit in the coffee bar for a few hours, watching customers come in and go out. Now, as he approached the supermarket, he felt the full absurdity of what he was doing. His mission would prove futile—he was sure of it—and he thought that he would spend no more than two hours there; no, an hour and a half would be more than enough to prove that the whole idea, even if he had conceived of it himself, was a waste of time.

He went straight to the cheese section, where he selected a triangular wedge of parmesan. Then he searched for Gouda and a strong Scottish cheddar. Olives were easy: he always bought the same brand—Italian olives bottled in their oil and still with their stones. Then he made his way towards the fruit aisles. He liked kiwi fruit, and he needed avocados. That would be that, he decided; he would have to carry his purchases home, and he did not want to do a big shop.

"Sorry."

William turned his head. The heel of his right shoe had been bumped, barely noticeably, by a shopping trolley. It was a small nudge, and William said, "No problem." Then he looked at the man pushing the trolley, and he knew immediately that this was him.

William froze. He had been ready to encounter this man,

but not in these circumstances. He had imagined if it occurred at all that it would happen at the coffee bar, when he would have the time to prepare himself before he made his approach. This was direct and unexpected, and he struggled to collect himself.

He noticed that the man's shopping trolley was empty.

"These things can have a mind of their own," the man said. "You push one way, and they go the other."

William was unsure what to say. But then he said, "Yes, you're right." And he added, without thinking, "The Seville oranges are over there."

William pointed to the far end of the fruit section. The man frowned. "I beg your pardon?" he said.

"The Seville oranges," said William.

The man was staring at him in his puzzlement, and William was able to see that his drawing had achieved a remarkable likeness. There was no question but that this was the man whom Clea had met. This was him, and he was standing before him.

He thought: *The Seville oranges . . .* why on earth did I say that?

"How did you know . . ." The man trailed off. He looked at William with incredulity, and went, "I'm sorry—do I know you?"

William shook his head. "No. I mean, not exactly. But I know something about you."

The man frowned uneasily. "Have we met?"

"No," said William. "But I know that you make marmalade."

The man's frown became a smile. "This is really weird," he said. "Who are you—and how do you know about me?" And then he added, "Were you at that marmalade-making course three years ago?"

"No," said William. "I wasn't, but . . ." He felt foolish. How was he going to tell this man what he had to tell him? They had started out on the wrong foot—that was clear enough, and now he was unsure how to go about explaining himself.

He decided to introduce himself. "I'm William, by the way."

The man seemed to struggle with competing inclinations. One was to bring this unexpected encounter to an end; the other was to observe the ordinary social niceties.

"I'm Ranald," he said.

The introductions made the difference. William relaxed. "It's an odd story," he said. "Could we go over there and talk about it over a cup of coffee."

Ranald hesitated. Eventually, he said, "What's it about?"

"I'll tell you," answered William.

There was a moment of awkward silence, and William wondered whether he should have handled things differently. But Ranald shrugged, and said, "Okay. If it's that important."

"It is," said William, and added, "Thank you."

As they crossed to the other side of the supermarket, Ranald asked, "Are you Australian?"

"I am," William replied. "I'm from Melbourne."

"I've been there," said Ranald. "I worked there for six months on my gap year. I was just out of school. I worked for a window-cleaning firm. A long time ago, I'm afraid."

There was something in his manner that had changed. Suspicion had been replaced with an emerging easy, warm manner. William was reminded that Clea had commented on his charm, and he felt that he could see what she meant. Now, for the first time since the surprise of their meeting, he allowed himself to feel satisfaction. His plan had worked after all, and he was looking forward to announcing his success to Katie.

They sat down at a couple of free seats at the coffee bar. Ranald looked at William expectantly. "Well?" he said.

"I work with a woman called Katie," William began. "She runs an introductions agency. It's over in the New Town. I have a studio next door."

Ranald frowned. "Introductions?" he asked.

William decided that he needed to get to the point quickly.

"About a year ago, a woman called Clea was shopping here, in this supermarket. She met you. You talked right here—in the coffee bar."

William noticed the effect this had on Ranald, who sat quite still, his hands folded on his lap, listening intently.

"Do you remember?" asked William.

Ranald's voice was not much above a whisper when he replied. "I do," he said. "Yes, I remember."

"She came to see us," William continued. "She wanted us to arrange an introduction—to somebody else. But she did tell us about how she had met you, and how well the two of you had got along."

"We did," said Ranald, his voice still low.

"She tried to find you again," William went on. "She came here. She asked one or two people if they knew who you were, but she drew a blank. She had given up."

"But she didn't want to meet again," protested Ranald. "I wanted to give her my number, but she . . ."

"Took fright," William suggested.

"Yes," said Ranald. "That's exactly what she did."

William held Ranald's gaze. "I know, but the point is this. She told us that not a day has gone past since then but that she regrets it."

Ranald was silent. Then, speaking slowly, he said, "But I feel that way too. Not a day goes past but that I think of that, and of what a chance I lost."

William stood up. He held his arms out before him, as

might a magician or a ringmaster at a moment of proud denouement. "Well, there we are," he said. "Nothing more needs to be said." He paused, and reached into his pocket to extract his phone. "I can give you her number right now."

They both laughed. "What a story," Ranald said. "But how did you . . ."

William interrupted him. "Marmalade," he said.

As he walked back up Morningside Road, William smiled at the people he met walking in the opposite direction. Each got a smile, tailor-made just for him or her—a smile fuelled by the sheer elation that William felt after what had just happened in the supermarket. And most of his smiles were reciprocated— sometimes in surprise, sometimes in puzzlement, and sometimes with pleasure at the occurrence of an act of human courtesy, supererogatory certainly, but still welcome.

He had made a single telephone call on leaving the supermarket, and that was to Clea. He was proposing to drop in on her flat, he said, and would she be in? She replied that she would.

"Expect me," he said.

He could sense her excitement down the line. "The picture?" she asked.

"Hardly necessary," he said. "But let me explain when I see you."

She began to say something, but it was too late. William had ended the call and was on his way. Half an hour later he was at Clea's door. Her flat was on India Street, a handsome Georgian street that ran sharply down from Heriot Row to the sweep of Circus Place below. Her doorbell was polished brass, and surmounted above it the ancient nameplate of an earlier owner.

Clea admitted him to a circular hall, the floor of which was paved with broad flagstones. An elaborate cornice ran round the edge of the ceiling, and on the walls were discreetly framed prints of old Edinburgh scenes.

She saw him glancing at the prints. "Those were my father's," she said. "This used to be his place. My taste runs more to Bellany and company. I have a lovely big painting by him in the kitchen. I'll show you. I like a bit of colour. That's why I like your work."

William blushed. "I sometimes think I'm a sucker for excessively bright colours—a bit of a magpie, even. They go for bright things, don't they?"

"Your colour sense is great," Clea assured him.

William smiled. "Thanks." He took a deep breath. "I found him," he blurted out. "I talked to him less than an hour ago."

Clea stood quite still. "Him?" she said. "You sure it was him?"

"Absolutely." He paused. He was relishing this, and he sensed that she could see that. Her eyes were bright with anticipation.

William reached into his pocket and took out the piece of paper on which he had written Ranald's number. "He's called Ranald, by the way," he said, handing her the paper. "And you know what he said? He said that not a day has gone past but that he's regretted what happened."

Clea opened her mouth to say something, but no sound came.

"And I gave him your number," William continued. "Just as we agreed."

"Oh," said Clea.

"You wanted me to do that, didn't you?" said William.

She nodded mutely, and it was at that moment that her phone rang. It was in the pocket of her jacket, and she fumbled as she took it out.

"Answer that," said William.

She pressed a button, and William heard the voice from the phone's small speaker. "This is Ranald."

He smiled at Clea. He would have liked to stay a bit longer. He would have liked to see the Bellany in the kitchen. He imagined that it would be a riot of red and yellow. But there were times when you should leave people to have a private conversation, and this, he thought was such a time.

He retreated to the front door. He raised a hand in a gesture of farewell. She was holding the phone to her ear. She raised a hand in a gesture that was part farewell, part thanks. He acknowledged this with a small wave of his own, and then slipped out onto India Street. The afternoon sun was on the cobblestones of the street. There had been a light shower of rain, and the stones were wet and glistening, as if touched with quicksilver. This is an achingly beautiful city, he thought, and I fall more in love with it every single day. I still love Melbourne, of course, but the heart is large enough, has enough chambers, to allow for more than one love. Not everybody knew that, he said to himself, but he did.

Katie was still in the office when William returned to his flat after lunchtime. She had made less progress than she had hoped with her paperwork, and was on the point of giving up for the weekend. She was prepared to work on a Saturday morning, in exceptional circumstances, but not a Saturday afternoon.

He said, "I hoped you'd still be here when I came back."

She looked up from her desk. "I'm about to give up. This stuff can wait until Monday."

He smirked. "I'm not going to wait until then to give you my news."

She hardly dared hope. "You didn't, did you?"

"I did. In the fruit and vegetables section. First go."

She waited.

"And you know what he said?"

Katie shook her head.

"He said more or less exactly what Clea said. He said that not a day went past without his regretting what happened."

She sat back in her chair. All she managed to say was a long drawn-out "No."

To which he replied with a shorter "Yes."

"You know what Ness would say? You know how she goes on about Greek mythology? She'd say that the gods are still capable of intervening. She might say that this is grey-eyed Athena working her magic."

"Why grey-eyed?"

"She just is. That's how Homer describes her."

William nodded. "I suppose he knows."

Katie glanced at her watch. She had a hair appointment at four. It was with Estelle, who was a good stylist, but who had nothing much to say about anything. "Are you doing anything this evening, William?"

He looked thoughtful. "Nothing I can't rearrange. I was going to go to the pub with Andrew, but he won't mind if I call off."

"Are you sure?"

He smiled. "Andrew and I aren't joined at the hip. I told you. And the rules of any bromance include the right to call off if something better turns up." He looked at her, and continued, "Which it just has—assuming you were going to ask me to have dinner with you—somewhere nice."

"There's an Italian restaurant I know. At least, I've walked past it and looked in the window. I've never had a meal there."

"It sounds ideal."

Katie sat at her desk. Dinner with William. *Dinner with William!* She smiled to herself. She felt light-headed, as if she were a schoolgirl who has been asked to dance by the most popular boy in the school. The day was turning out to be as perfect as it possibly could be. A remarkable outcome had been arranged for Clea, and yet . . . Katie sighed: she had not achieved resolution for two of her clients, Horatio Maclean and Maddy Balquorn. They were both flawed in a similar way, and if that particular flaw had resulted in a standoff, then that was no fault of hers. That is what she had told herself, and for a while she had managed to convince herself that she had done what she could, and it was beyond her to do much to change matters. Except . . . except that one of them—Horatio Maclean—had walked out of her office feeling unhappy, and it was that unhappiness that was bothering her. We all had our individual failings, and Horatio's failings were manifest. He was a snob. It was a rather horrible little word, laden with disapprobation, and even contempt. Yet that was what he was. Now, he was being taught a lesson, and yet Katie felt regret at what had amounted on her part to Schadenfreude. She had taken pleasure in his humbling—for that was what it was—and she felt that she should not have done that. *Horatio was her client.*

It kept coming back to that: she owed him not only a duty of care, but a duty of sympathy as well. She did not want him to be unhappy—of course she did not. And the same applied to Maddy. Could it be, Katie asked herself, that underneath Maddy's cold dismissal of Horatio there lay at least a measure of regret? It was, she decided, something that she might try to ascertain—and to do something about.

She looked at her watch. She could drive out to Balquorn House and still be back in time for her hair appointment at four. It would be tight, but it was doable, and she made her decision. She called Maddy to check up that she was in, and was told that yes, she would be happy to see her, although she had to go out shortly after three that afternoon. That would work, said Katie.

"May I ask," said Maddy, "what this is about?"

Katie hesitated. She had to be truthful. "I'm going to ask you to reconsider something," she replied.

There was a silence at the end of the line. Then Maddy said, "I take it that you're referring to Horatio Maclean."

"Yes, I am."

There was a further silence. Then Maddy said, "I thought I explained. I don't want to take that any further."

"You did. But . . ." Katie paused. "Sometimes people deserve a second look."

"But I told you . . ."

"I know you did. But there's something I need to say, and it's easier to do that face to face."

Rather to her surprise, Maddy's tone, which had become defensive, became softer. "It could be a good idea to talk," she said.

It was, Katie decided, a chink of an invitation. Most invitations are express, and in some cases voluble. Others are timid, indirect, and barely perceptible. This was one of those, but it was still an invitation.

Maddy took her into the kitchen, a large, lived-in room dominated by an immense pine table placed in its centre. The table was almost entirely covered by the artefacts of daily household life—jars of jam, mugs, papers, magazines, mail.

"Mess HQ," Maddy said apologetically. "Every so often I have a blitz and clear the table, but then it somehow fills up again." She sighed. "Like life, itself, really."

Katie said there was no need to apologise. She herself had a problem with clutter. "I have a monthly throw-out," she said. "It's very therapeutic."

Maddy invited her to sit at the table while she made tea with boiling water from a large, old-fashioned range kettle. Returning to the table, she fixed Katie with an enquiring stare. "Ever since you called, I've been sitting here thinking about what you said. You were somewhat enigmatic, if you don't mind my saying."

"I'm sorry," said Katie. "I didn't mean to be. Well, actually, I suppose I did. I didn't want you to simply decline to see me—that's why."

Maddy did not flinch. "Well?"

"We talked to Horatio Maclean," Katie began. "He came to see us. I think he got the message."

Maddy looked down at her hands. "I see. Well, thank you for that."

"However," Katie went on, "I have to admit that we ended up telling him why it wasn't going to work. I didn't intend to, but William jumped the gun, so to speak... Not that I'm trying to blame him."

Maddy drew in her breath. "You told him..."

"He knows that you think he's not quite your sort."

"Well, that's nothing out of the ordinary. Chemistry, you know..."

Katie decided to be more specific. "Socially, that is."

Maddy was silent.

"He was taken aback," Katie said. "I think he was quite hurt."

Maddy looked away. "I wish that you hadn't put it that way."

"I'm sorry," said Katie. "That was the way it developed. I wouldn't have chosen to do it that way, but sometimes situations develop along lines one can't anticipate." She paused. "I think he was shocked to discover that anybody would regard *him* as being not quite up to scratch."

Katie had not expected her words to have quite the effect they did. Maddy gasped, and then buried her head in her hands. "He must think me a terrible snob," she said.

Katie bit her lip. "He might..." she began.

"Well, I'm not," said Maddy defiantly. "You don't think I am, do you?"

"Not really," said Katie. Strictly speaking, she thought, this was true. Maddy might be a bit of a snob rather than a terrible snob. But then she thought: That was a slight and dishonest distinction. So she then said, "We can all be a bit like that at times. Who amongst us doesn't occasionally look askance at people because we think they're too loud or too vulgar, or deck themselves in flashy jewellery, or behave inconsiderately in public?" There were few saints when it came to tolerating others.

"I feel awful," Maddy said. "I didn't dislike him, you know."

"No?"

Maddy hesitated. "In fact, I rather took to him."

Katie raised an eyebrow. She had not expected this.

"Actually," Maddy continued, "if I were to be honest, I'd have to admit that it was not so much a case of what *I* thought of him—it's what one or two others in the family might think." She paused. "We're a tight-knit family. I have a couple of uncles who . . ." She shrugged. "Uncles and cousins who take a dim view of anybody who doesn't quite fit in with their circle. And there are various old family friends who are just as bad." She gave Katie a piercing look. "You know how it is in the country. If you live in a place like this . . ." She gestured—a small, sweeping movement of her right hand, but large enough to embrace the house, the land, the history. "I can hardly ignore all this."

Katie said that she understood. "I can imagine that," she said. She sensed that Maddy had something else to say. She waited.

"To tell the truth," Maddy said, "I was also thinking of what my father would have thought. He was a big influence, you know. He was very important to me."

"Of course."

Maddy lowered her eyes. "He would not have approved of Horatio, I'm afraid."

Katie took a deep breath. Maddy had been frank, and so should she. "Your father's no longer here, Maddy. You're here. This is *your* life you're talking about. It doesn't matter what your father would think. I know that sounds brutal, but it's true."

Maddy was silent. Katie reached out to touch her arm. "I'm sorry if I sound cruel, but it's true, you know. Our parents can't run our lives from the grave."

Maddy said nothing.

"And things change," Katie continued. "It's possible that if he were alive today, your father would look at things differently."

Maddy gave her a sideways look. "Posthumous modernisation?"

Katie allowed herself to smile. "Better late than never," she said.

Katie's smile was suddenly reciprocated. "You're probably right. I need to say goodbye to all that."

"Yes," said Katie. "I think that might be the right thing to do."

Maddy sighed. "I wouldn't blame you if you thought me weak. But it's hard for me to detach myself."

Katie nodded. She could imagine. Cages might be gilded, but they were still cages. What was significant, though, was the fact that Maddy had said that she had taken to Horatio Maclean.

"You said that you took to him. I think that he took to you, you know. That's the impression that I got when I broke the news to him that it wasn't to be possible." She paused. "I wouldn't want to suggest that you turn your back on your own people, but . . ."

Maddy interrupted her. "But that's what you think, isn't it?"

Katie nodded. "Yes, I suppose it is. When it comes to relationship issues, you have to do what *you* want to do. This is about *you*, not *them*. Follow your heart. I know it's easy to say that, and I know it sounds a bit sentimental, but it's true, you know. If you like him, if you would like to see more of him, then do so."

Maddy had been staring down at the floor. Now she raised her eyes. "You think he likes me?"

"Yes, I think he does."

"And you don't think he'll have taken offence because I cold-shouldered him?"

Katie shook her head. "I suspect he won't. And there's something else—I think that he may have learned something from all this—just as you may have."

"And what do you think I've learned?"

"To obey your instinct," replied Katie. "I don't think it's your instinct to look down on anybody. I don't think you're snobbish in your attitudes."

"I'm not," Maddy protested. "I'm not like that."

Nobody, thought Katie—not even the most crashing snob, ever admits to the vice of snobbery. But she was now satisfied that Maddy was not like that. Her problem was timidity in the face of social pressure, and that was a weakness, not a vice. "Good," she said. "In that case, why bother about what anybody else feels. This is nothing to do with them. This is about you and him."

For a short while, Maddy said nothing. Then she smiled. "I think I know what to do."

Katie waited for her to explain.

"I've been invited to dinner by some neighbours. I'm going to ask if I can take him with me."

Katie wondered whether this was venturing into the lion's den. "Sympathetic neighbours?" she asked. They might have been amongst the ranks of the disapproving.

Maddy nodded. "Yes."

"Then that's a start. See how it goes."

"I shall," said Maddy. She gave Katie a look of gratitude. "Thank you," she said, and then with a grin, "Does the therapy come with the service? Is it all-inclusive?"

"Absolutely," said Katie. "There's nothing else to pay."

William and Katie walked together to the restaurant. The proprietor, a man with a small, neat moustache, produced the menus with a flourish. They caught a glimpse of the chef when the kitchen door swung open. He turned to look back out at them, and smiled. He had few teeth, but that did not matter.

There were only one or two other couples there—it was a quiet evening.

There was music, played softly and discreetly. Katie said, "That's 'The Lament of Tristan.' Do you know it? It's early music."

"A nice change from 'Return to Sorrento,'" said William.

They examined the menu. William smiled, and pointed to an item he liked. "I'm going to have that," he said.

She glanced at his choice. "Oh yes," she said. "And I'll have the same."

He chided her playfully. "You must learn to think for yourself."

"Oh, I don't know. Menus always throw me into confusion. Do we really want too much choice in this life?"

He said that was a profound question. Did she want to talk about it now, or should they keep it as a topic in reserve, should their conversation ever dry up? "Not that I think there's any danger of that," he said. "We can talk, can't we?"

"I think we can." She paused. "And I have something I need to tell you about Maddy Balquorn."

"Oh?"

"She's going to give him a second chance."

William frowned, and it was a little while before he responded. Then he said, "You know something? I've been feeling a bit bad about him. Perhaps I was a bit too quick to write him off."

"We can all feel guilty about other people," said Katie. "Don't beat yourself up over it. The important thing is that *you* also seem prepared to give him a second chance."

He nodded. Then he said, "Good. Happy ending."

"Yes, it is," said Katie. "And there's nothing to be ashamed about in wanting a happy ending."

She wondered whether what she said was true—and she decided it was. Of course, it was. What was the point of carrying on with life unless there was the prospect of a happy ending—at least sometimes, and for some people?

He ordered a bottle of white wine. "This comes from the Veneto," he said.

She took an initial sip from her glass.

"Would you like to go to Italy some day?" Katie asked.

He said that he would. Then he said, "Would you come with me? We could go together."

"I'd love to."

She wanted to cry. It was strange, she thought, that at moments of great happiness one should feel the need to shed tears. She had to speak now; she had to. But it seemed to her that to speak now would be to imperil everything. There would be a time in the future when it would be different—she was sure of that. She would wait after all. William was one of those people who did not like to be rushed. That was what she had decided.

She said, "Our work is love, isn't it? Doesn't that make you feel proud?"

"It does," he said.

"Because there's no better work than that, don't you think?"

"I do," he said.

A NOTE ON THE AUTHOR

SIR ALEXANDER MCCALL SMITH is one of the world's favourite authors, with more than a hundred books to his name. These include novels in the award-winning and highly successful series *The No. 1 Ladies' Detective Agency*, which has sold over twenty million copies, and *44 Scotland Street* – the world's longest-running serial novel. He lives in Edinburgh, devotes his time to the writing of fiction, poetry and libretti, and has seen his books translated into over forty-six languages.

PRAISE FOR
ALEXANDER McCALL SMITH'S WRITING

'There is something about McCall Smith's writing that allows you to feel that his characters really exist'
Guardian

'A slice of life served up so perfectly'
Scotsman

'McCall Smith's writing is ... blissful. He doesn't shy away from the darker realities of life with his poignant exposures of human frailty, yet, somehow, he makes the world a better place'
Country Life

'McCall Smith is an engaging and a witty guide to the goings on (and comings off) at fictional 44 Scotland Street'
The Sunday Express

'A light-hearted, genial soap opera'
Financial Times

'A lovely read with a gentle pace that will transport you to a whole other world'
Independent

'The author's prose has the merits of simplicity, euphony and precision. This is art that conceals art'
The Sunday Telegraph

'Infinitely touching, beautiful novels, each of which is a miracle of gentle wit and perception'
James Naughtie

'A treasure of a writer whose books deserve immediate devouring'
Guardian

'Perfect escapist fiction'
The Times

'One of the most entrancing treats of many a year'
The Wall Street Journal

'It's hard to find fault with such good-natured and pleasurable optimism'
Observer

'I can think of no author writing today so deserving of an enormous audience'
New Statesman

'A joyous, charming portrait of city life and human foibles, which moves beyond its setting to deal with deep moral issues and love, desire and friendship'
Sunday Express

'A new adventure in a series that shows no signs of dropping in popularity or standard'
Daily Telegraph

'A charming, entertaining and uplifting book'
Daily Express

'Irresistible'
The Times

'Mma Ramotswe is a glorious creation'
Mail on Sunday

'Hugely enjoyable'
The Sunday Times

'Equally as brilliant as the previous novels ... McCall Smith writes with deceptive simplicity, yet his work is laced with worthy insight, and dry, yet charming, humour'
Scottish Field

'McCall Smith is an author who sees his characters and their world, fully and tenderly. And that makes for a book that is as comforting to sink into as a well-worn armchair'
New York Journal of Books

'McCall Smith can encapsulate the human condition in a plate of stewed pumpkin. His talent is to see the good in small things'
The Sunday Times

'Written with grace and charm'
Independent

'A funny, thoughtful book with a lot of heart'
Scottish Field

'Effortlessly charming ...[with] a grain of grit: an implicit acknowledgement that being a good person isn't all sweetness and light, and that hard choices are an inevitable consequence of striving to do the right thing'
Herald

'Reading the novel feels like a form of meditation ... There is much to enjoy'
Scotsman

'McCall Smith's detective series set in Sweden, which he calls Scandi Blanc, is a brighter version of the unrelenting bleakness and violence of the Scandi Noir genre ... in the cheerful setting of bright and sunny Swedish summers'
Herald

'Brilliantly pitched and packed with humour ... with witty, intelligent writing, sophisticated characterisation, as well as McCall Smith's effortless storytelling ability, it makes you think and makes you laugh'
Scottish Field

'Highly enjoyable ... [Alexander McCall Smith] has a supreme talent for sketching truly likeable characters. His novels are full of human quirks and the bizarre minutiae of everyday life'
Independent

'Wonderfully soothing and relaxing'
Daily Telegraph

'Tucking into a brand-new mystery series by Alexander McCall Smith is a lazy-dazy pleasure'
New York Times Book Review

'Will tickle your funny bone and resonate in your heart'
New York Journal of Books

'A charming, humorous journey of the heart'
Woman and Home

'His writing is as warm as cocoa, as cosy as thermal underwear, and just what the doctor ordered for cold winter evenings. Exceedingly good'
The Times

'McCall Smith's generous writing and dry humour, his gentleness and humanity, and his ability to evoke a place and a set of characters without caricature or condescension have endeared his books to readers'
The New York Times

'Warm, funny, poignant and touching'
The Good Book Guide

'All you can eat platter of humour . . . once again McCall Smith doles out an appropriately extra-large helping of fun'
Scotland on Sunday

'A scrumptious, joyous read, stuffed full of sharp wit, laugh-out-loud frolics and gentle soothing compassion – completely charming'
Lovereading

'If McCall Smith didn't exist, we should have had to invent him. He is that rare creature known as a storyteller'
The Washington Post